The Last Resort

"An impossible-to-put-down thrill ride of a read. . . . It will fascinate you, enlighten you, break your heart and mend it again. Read this book!"

JENNIFER ROBSON, internationally bestselling author of *Somewhere in France* and *The Gown*

"An exciting addition to the psych thriller world—with an emotionally complex twist."

ROZ NAY, bestselling author of *Our Little Secret*

"Fans of Agatha Christie will surely love this modern whodunit from the first to the very last page. One to add to your 'to read' list now."

HANNAH MARY MCKINNON, author of *The Neighbors* and *Her Secret Son*

"Stapley's writing is fast-paced while still cutting deep. I burned through the book, but it will stay with me. *The Last Resort* is all of these things: a nail-biter, a page-turner, a thoughtful, powerful exploration into who we are in relationships and on our own."

LAURIE PETROU, author of *Sister of Mine*

"Deeply addictive and simmering with tension, *The Last Resort* had me breathlessly turning the pages all the way through to its explosive conclusion."

LUCY CLARKE, author of *The Blue*

"Stapley delivers a twisty, expertly written mystery you can sink your teeth into."

KAREN KATCHUR, author of *River Bodies*

The Last Resort

Marissa Stapley

HODDER

First published in Great Britain in 2021 by Hodder & Stoughton
An Hachette UK company

This paperback edition published in 2022

1

A CIP catalogue record for this title is available from the British Library

Paperback ISBN 978 1 399 70384 0
eBook ISBN 978 1 399 70386 4

Printed and bound in Great Britain by Clays Ltd, Elcograf S.p.A.

Hodder & Stoughton policy is to use papers that are natural, renewable
and recyclable products and made from wood grown in sustainable
forests. The logging and manufacturing processes are expected to
conform to the environmental regulations of the country of origin.

Hodder & Stoughton Ltd
Carmelite House
50 Victoria Embankment
London EC4Y 0DZ

www.hodder.co.uk

This book is for my children.

May the world become a place that is worthy of you.

How do you know, wife, whether you will save your husband? Or, how do you know, husband, whether you will save your wife?

—Corinthians 7:16

He struggles to breathe. There's blood trickling into one of his eyes. His glasses are gone. He can hear the ocean rising to meet him. It wasn't supposed to be like this.

"Jezebel," he says through broken teeth, through the wheezing battle for air, through the anger that has cracked open inside him. He crawls across the rocky surface, struggles with his aching hands to find purchase. "Come here, you Jezebel." A wave hits him in the mouth. But he reaches the stone staircase, finally, and drags himself upward. He'll find her. And when he does, she'll be sorry.

CELEBRITY MARRIAGE COUNSELOR MILES MARKELL MISSING, PRESUMED DEAD, AFTER HURRICANE CHRISTINE PUMMELS MAYAN RIVIERA—*and foul play suspected!*

Hurricane Christine charged ashore late Sunday night, delivering a surprise direct hit to coastal communities in Mexico's Mayan Riviera—but as the local authorities sift through the debris, mostly concentrated around Zihua, they're also focusing on finding clues pertaining to the whereabouts of Dr. Miles Markell, who was already embroiled in a controversy (click here for details on the current accusations against Markell; two more were added today).

Miles, 52, and his wife, Grace, 35, were running one of their famed two-week intensive couples' therapy retreats at the luxurious Harmony Resort, La Hacienda, near Zihua—basically a tropical summer camp for rich, unhappy people—when the storm hit. Little information is available, but it has been confirmed that while damage to the property was extensive, Miles is the only one not accounted for and there have been no injuries—likely because the guests barricaded themselves in the immense main villa of the resort, which has survived decades of hurricanes and tropical storms and could have sheltered hundreds of the local people unable to evacuate the area.

It gets worse. News broke this morning that an anonymous Texas-based group—who will only say that they are "friends" of the celebrity therapist and some are suggesting are members of a local cult—have offered up a 500,000 USD reward for his recovery. This may be leading local divers to execute dangerous dives in an ocean still in turmoil from the storm. And social media has erupted, with many asking why that money couldn't be donated to rescue efforts directed at assisting Zihua residents (the ones the Markells didn't bother to help), whose homes have been destroyed and who are still searching for missing family members, instead.

Here's one thing we know for sure. The #MilesMarkell hashtag is a very strange place right now. Stay tuned for updates.

Her: Did you ever hear of that clinical study about
secrets?

Him: It sounds familiar.

Her: I read about it in a psychology journal. We talked
about it at the resort, in a strategy meeting once.
Because it wasn't always like that—like everyone
says, now. There were some good, calm times. There
were moments I was sure we were making a difference.
Moments I thought my life was perfect. [Extended
pause.]

Him: Do you need a tissue?

Her: I'm not crying. I just need a minute. I miss it
a lot, you know. I loved what I did. And I loved
that place. Then *they* came. Those women, and their
husbands—I just need a minute.

Him. Take all the time you need.

Her: You sound impatient.

Him: I just said, "take all the time you need."

Her: Yes, but this has been going on for a while. We've
been meeting in this same room for how long now?

Him: Just about a year.

Her: You must be getting bored.

Him: Not at all. On the contrary. You're a former
psychologist and we share that. It deepens our
conversations. And you're my patient. I'm here to
help you, not—

Her: Not extract my secrets, right? But we both know
that's not true. We both know it's all about the
secrets. Except I haven't really told you anything. I
haven't told you what really happened.

Him: [A shuffling sound.] You mean about Miles? Who killed
him? You want to talk about that today?

Her: [Long pause.] That study I mentioned, it concluded

that the average person has thirteen secrets that they live with—five of which they've never told a soul. That was our focus, at the resort: secrets. Pulling secrets into the light. Helping people unearth them. But thirteen? I still think about that.

Him: Yes, that is the point of therapy. We've talked about this before, the idea of digging deep and finding the issue the patient is avoiding, the thing that they're hoping will escape notice. It's often hiding in plain sight. And yet—

Her: Thirteen secrets. Only five that we've never told another soul. Does that seem like a lot to you?

Him: Thirteen secrets, or the idea that five remain buried?

Her: Both.

Him: I'd have to give it some thought.

Her: I've given it a lot of thought. I've had the time. And I think that number seems high. I think about them, about the people at the resort during those final weeks. I've used them as my test subjects—and while, yes, Doctor, I can admit this is an informal and unreliable mode of study and testing, I still think that study is wrong. All those people, they only had one secret. One secret each. Me, too. I only had the one. But it was a big one. And I have to tell it. It's time. I can't live with it anymore. Miles Markell was not what he seemed. But neither was I.

Day One

From: Miles and Grace Markell
To: Undisclosed recipients
CC:
Subject: Welcome email!

Welcome, friends! Barring any unforeseen circumstances, you should all have arrived by 4:00 p.m. and we'll meet on the Oceanside Terrace shortly afterward for Opening Night. We understand you may be tired from a day of travel, but the inaugural exercise isn't optional (in fact, none of the scheduled activities are). Don't worry, you'll have plenty of time to relax and settle in tomorrow. But please do use some of the time in your "settle in" day to catch up on your reading. The books you'll need are on your bedside tables.

After Opening Night, you are invited to retire to your luxury bungalow, where a personalized multicourse room service meal will be delivered. Our staff is at your service with just the press of a button; use them when and as needed. You won't need an orientation. Everything about Harmony at La Hacienda is intuitive. We promise.

We can't wait to meet you!

In solidarity,
Drs. Miles and Grace Markell

PS: ***No cell phones/laptops/devices!*** The lockboxes are in the lobby. Ruth Abrams, our clinician, will help you schedule approved check-ins with your families. From now on, all communication will happen on resort property only. ***There is also a strict no-alcohol policy***, so ditch the duty-free. See you soon!

*T*he plane circled the coast of an ocean the color of a bowl of blueberries or the heart of a turquoise ring, depending on where you looked. For a moment, the frothy white waves shone with an otherworldly aura and everything she looked at rose to meet her. She thought the plane was crashing. But it wasn't. It was just her.

Once they landed, the passengers were funneled into a van, where everyone avoided eye contact. Johanna's head felt heavy against the headrest. The vehicle glided smoothly out of the airport parking lot, but when it hit a pitted highway she raised a hand to her temple. She tried to focus on a flock of birds diving and swooping in unison, tried not to picture her finger as a drill that could relieve pressure. "How do they do that, do you think?" she asked.

"How does who do what?"

"The birds. Fly together like that. How do they know?"

Her husband's phone pinged. Ignoring her, he reached into his pocket and looked at it. He chuckled and held it up to her. "Look at this," he said, but she didn't want to look at it. She wanted to talk to someone about how birds communicate with one another using a method older than radio frequency. She squinted at the screen of his phone and saw the words *in solidarity* and a lot of bold underlines. She looked away from the amplified glare.

The van was slowing down and moving through a town that crowded against the side of the road. Shop fronts painted teal, yellow, pink and blue; taco stands; thatch-roofed stores; colorful dresses and hats hanging on poles; dogs and goats and people. Johanna locked eyes with a girl in a magenta top waiting at a bus stop and wondered who the girl was and where she lived and if she was happy or sad. She wouldn't find out. Once, she and Ben had agreed that it was wrong to hide away from a country on a resort that had sanitized the truth out of the land it stood on, the way they were about to for the next two weeks. But the things they had once agreed upon were as foreign now as Johanna's own face must have been to that girl, appearing in the bus window to stare, mute, at a village she would never know.

Her ears popped as the van ascended a cliff-side road. Wheels dipped into a pothole. The van rattled out and Ben reached over and squeezed her hand as if they'd narrowly escaped something—and maybe they had. The drop to the ocean was dizzying. His hand was cool and dry, but there was a nervous pulse beneath his skin, an unbalanced cadence to his breathing, like an orchestra out of synch. Her own hand was sweaty. "The bold and the underlines are a bit much," she said. He laughed.

"It's going to be intense." He squeezed her hand again as she clenched her body against a wave of nausea. "But we can do this." She looked left, breaching the unspoken code of conduct in the vehicle. The woman on the other side of the aisle who looked away, fast, had a curtain of seal-brown hair as shiny as glass. How did you get such gleaming hair? Was it something you were born with or something you paid for? The husband had silver hair that glinted, too. He was tapping the screen of a smartphone. "Next time," Ben said, "we'll do something you like. That bike trip in Vietnam? Something different. I promise. Not like this."

It wasn't long before a structure came into view: a garnet at the top of a hill lit by a sun that had without warning begun to descend and deepen above the ocean, orange-highlighted paper gliding down.

"There it is," said Ben, and for a moment she thought he meant the sun.

Johanna saw the high windows of the villa lit up. It was as if the structure, which scalloped down a cliffside and was ringed at midlevel by steaming mineral pools, was a giant sundial now signaling the end of the day or the lack of time they had, to be themselves, to remain

11

unobserved. The driveway wove in and out of trees so that the villa, cliffs and beach popped in out of view, tantalizing, disappearing, teasing, gone. One moment, Johanna could see it all: whitewashed walls, waves pounding rock faces, white sand nestled against boulders, jagged mineral jutting into ocean; the next, she couldn't see anything except trees and vines and playful birds.

"Wow," Ben said.

"Yeah, I know. Gorgeous."

But he wasn't looking out the window. He was inclining his head sideways, toward the woman with the burnished hair and her husband with his premature silvers. "The entire ride."

Johanna pressed her fingertips against her eyelids. "What are you talking about?"

"He's on his *phone*. We're supposed to put them away."

Johanna heard the man say something about a safety check. "We're responsible for these people," he said in an urgent voice. "Shortcuts aren't an option here. Redo it. Yes, the entire thing. I'll wait."

"Well, we're not inside the resort yet," Johanna said. "You had yours out."

"Workaholic," Ben whispered. She understood. He needed to feel they were somehow ahead of the class. To believe that, in comparison to all the others, their marital problems were minor. "We always knew he was going to work in law," his mother liked to say. "He knows the rules to *everything*." He also liked to argue—but that was another matter.

The van was at the edge of a circular driveway beside the sprawling white jewel of a building. The engine shut off. Towers, turrets, balconies, white railings, a steep terra-cotta roof and the individual villas scattered like diamonds leading to the beach. There were so many villas. More than necessary, it seemed, for only twelve couples. "*Recharge your marriage in a stunning and intimate fairy-tale setting*," said the pamphlets Ben had brought home the morning he had gone to church with his parents and come back with a desperate plea in his eyes. *Please, let's do this. Don't leave. Let's fix us*. The place really was like a fairy tale—but Johanna was remembering the dusty collection of stories she had discovered as a child on her grandmother's shelf, tales she had read in childish horror—a horror that is always tempered by delight at finding something not really meant for impressionable minds—about pecked-out eyes and a dead beast, or a love-struck mermaid turning herself into sea foam to save her lover. True love, Johanna had learned at a very young age, had consequences. Happy endings always cost you something.

"Come on, let's go," Ben said.

Outside the van, workers in white linen were unloading the luggage. She smelled sea salt on the breeze, sunbaked kelp, the sizzle-scent of garlic and chilies from some distant kitchen. Someone put a champagne flute of mango juice in her hand. She pressed the cool of it against her forehead and thought of their wedding reception at the MacArthur, only two years before. The bubbles in the champagne that day went straight to her head. Johanna had walked in on her mother-in-law crying into a friend's shoulder in the bathroom. "I'm just so happy," she lied when she saw Johanna. "She could have chosen a dress that covered those tattoos," the friend whispered as Johanna left. Johanna had her first migraine that night. Not a great start to their honeymoon.

She sipped the juice. She could hear the ocean far away and lounge music closer up, flowing from speakers set into the rocks. Ben walked ahead, glass in hand, and Johanna hurried to catch up. A woman was stepping forward to greet him, a woman Johanna knew—though it was disconcerting to know someone you'd never met. This was the woman pictured on the books Ben had brought home, the woman from the TED Talks he had played for her on his laptop, the voice from the podcasts they had listened to while cooking dinner. This was the gleaming smile she had seen on the clips from *Dr. Oz* and *The View*.

"You must be Johanna," Grace Markell said.

Johanna forgot about her headache as Grace reached for her hand. Grace didn't shake it, though. She held it in hers. She held it long enough for the connection to have meaning but not so long that it felt awkward. She looked into Johanna's eyes as she did this. Her eyes were gray, like storm clouds. "Welcome to Harmony," she said. "Thank you for coming."

"Thank you for having us," Johanna murmured as Grace released her hand. A younger, shorter woman with ash-blond hair swept into a tight bun and heavy makeup on her face was standing beside Grace. She looked as if she were about to go on television.

"I'm Ruth," she said, pumping Johanna's hand up and down. It was endless.

"Nice to meet you," Johanna said, letting her hand go limp.

"Ruth is our assistant." Grace checked her clipboard. "I don't think you're on her roster—" She shook her head. "No, you're on mine and Ben is on Miles's. But you'll see Ruth around. She runs a few of the group sessions."

Ruth smiled brightly. There was fuchsia lipstick on her tooth. Then she held up a clipboard bearing a white piece of paper covered in black type. "You both need to sign this, please," she said. "It's the couples' contract." Johanna signed without looking at it; Ben gave it a cursory glance, then scribbled his name.

"The porters are taking care of your luggage," Grace said. "You'll find a table upstairs on the terrace with your names, your check-in package and everything else you need. We're gathering there now."

"Our bags . . . are where?" Johanna's nervous elation turned to sudden panic. She'd put her carry-on bag on top of her luggage, and now it had vanished. She needed that bag: her pills were in there.

"In your villas by now," said Grace with a final smile, one that was likely meant to be reassuring.

"I just need to go to our villa and—" Johanna began.

But Grace was gone, moving along to greet another couple with Ruth slightly behind her, a gosling following a goose. Johanna felt bereft as Grace reached for someone else's hand.

Ben pulled her along. "Come on. Let's go."

Ruth had tucked their contracts into an envelope and was now looking back at Johanna, wide-eyed, too interested.

I am not a subject, Johanna wanted to shout. *I am a person*. But she didn't. She let her husband guide her; she let him lead.

*A*s Shell followed the small crowd through the lobby, she found herself behind a young couple who were holding hands. Through a veil of irritation at being stuck, unmoving, behind them, she read the woman's tattoos:

"*You are not your thoughts*" written in barely decipherable script on her left shoulder blade and another on her forearm: "*And meanwhile the world goes on.*"

Or it doesn't, she could say to this very young woman. *You don't know*, she could hiss. No wonder her husband despised her so much he looked past her instead of looking at her. No wonder he was still in the van. He was married to a bitter crone. Shell stayed silent.

But still, she imagined a parallel universe where instead of ironing her clothes until they had sharp creases, she wore tank tops with no bra and was as sexy as a pinup girl, and her husband was holding her hand instead of back in the van obsessing over safety checks for the northern Ontario gold mine that was his new lover, his new best friend, his new family, his new everything to replace all they had lost. Vacations had done this, once: stirred up fantasy.

The woman with the tattoos smelled liked neroli and musk. Her hair curled at the ends and reminded Shell of her young daughter's, when it dried while she was sleeping.

These thoughts, they were dangerous ones.

But her thoughts were interrupted by a voice behind her. "Hello, there." Shell turned and found herself looking up at Miles Markell. He was larger than he appeared on TV. Most people were smaller. "Is everything all right?"

"No," she found herself saying in the horrible woman's voice she could never quite believe was now her own. "I wouldn't be here if everything was all right, would I?"

His teeth were white against the tan of his skin. He smiled, then laughed, then took off his glasses and rubbed at his eyes before looking at her for a long, thoughtful moment. "Excellent," he said as he replaced the dark-rimmed spectacles. "A woman after my own heart. A woman who tells the *truth*." He had deep smile lines on either side of his mouth. His eyes danced, like he was suppressing some secret joke that he wanted to share. She felt like they were alone when he looked at her, and this embarrassed her. "Shell Williams, right?"

"Yes, how did you—"

"I like to guess at the identity of our couples," he said. "Grace and I keep score, actually." He winked. "But you're not supposed to be here alone. Where's your other half?" His mild Texas drawl was like butter melting, nothing like the voices she heard back home this time of year, when everyone's teeth involuntarily gritted against the winter's cold.

"Work call," she said. "Still in the van." Miles looked toward the driveway. "Ah. I see he's taking advantage of our unwritten rule— you're allowed to have phones until you set foot on resort grounds. Does he have a flask of whiskey with him, too?"

"No," Shell said, and now she didn't smile. She supposed there was such a thing as too much truth.

Miles lifted a manicured hand, snapped a finger and called out, "Ruth!" The young woman Shell had seen in the background of some of the Markells' online videos, their assistant, appeared. Her voice was firm, her manner capable. Her foundation was caked in her eyebrows.

"What can I do?" she asked.

"Could you please help Mr. Williams out of the van?"

"Got it," she said, and trotted off. Shell stood behind Miles and wondered what, if anything, she should say. But before long, Ruth reappeared with Colin at her side.

"Got him," she said, triumphant.

"Mr. Williams. You've arrived." Miles shook hands with Colin.

"I'll just put this in the lockbox," Ruth said, holding up the phone like a prize. But Shell knew Colin had another phone in his luggage. She could tell on him—but at her own peril. So she said nothing.

"All right, get going," Miles said. "Everyone else is already upstairs." He placed his hand on the small of her back and urged her toward a set of stairs at the far end of the lobby.

"I should see to our luggage," Colin said, frowning.

"I need to check in at home," Shell said at the same time and Colin looked at her sidelong, but just for a second.

"We have valets for your luggage," Miles said. "Do you see your bags anywhere? And there's no time to go to your villa now—but trust me, you'll feel refreshed after the ceremony." He put his hand on Colin's shoulder now and pulled him forward. "Come on, let's go."

Shell hung back. "I really do need to call home," she said to Ruth, although this wasn't true. "My daughter . . ." It was like a knife in her heart.

"We try to keep all contact with home minimal. Who's taking care of your children?"

"My mother," Shell found herself saying, and marveled at the fact that her heart was still beating, that she could still breathe.

"Would email be sufficient?"

"Oh. Ah . . ." *No. Not at fucking all.*

"Do you think that contact with your mother and daughter every other day would be enough?"

She had no choice but to fake a smile. It was either that or grab Ruth by the shoulders and shake her until her hair came loose from her bun—and then ruin her young life by telling her absolutely everything. God, she needed a drink. "Perfect," she said. "You're so helpful."

Ruth consulted her clipboard. "Every other morning, then, just after breakfast, in the twenty-minute window you have between the meal and your first appointment. All right?"

"Thank you," Shell said, and felt relief as she moved away from Ruth, but not the right kind of relief.

"Fuck," Colin said when she reached his side at the base of the staircase. "I really need to get back on that call."

"Of course you do," she said. "What could be more important than the people who work at the mine?"

He either didn't feel the bite in her words or he ignored it, and he headed up the stairs. The rooftop terrace was terra-cotta, like the one in the lobby. There were small, white-clothed tables dotting it, each with two teak chairs turned to face a small podium. White gossamer fabric twisted in the gentle breeze. The fabric was tied to pillars, crisscrossed above. There were little centerpieces on all the tables: caper berry and dust-colored air plants inside glass orbs. An infinity pool began where the tiles ended, ringing the terrace and dropping off into nothing. All the tables were occupied but one, close to the front. As she walked toward it, she saw a place card that said Mr. and Mrs. Colin Williams. It seemed so old-fashioned, to write their names out that way. And so strange, to look down and see herself entwined with her husband. She felt something like a remembering, something like a softening. But then Miles's amplified voice invaded her thoughts and she found herself wondering how he had gotten up there so fast.

"Spectacular, isn't it? The village you see at the base of the mountain is Zihua. Right now, to the villagers, because of the design of the building and the way the sun illuminates the windows, we look like we're engulfed in flames. Ironic, no? Since you've all come here in an attempt to save your marriages from hell." He laughed and there were a few guffaws in return. "Puerto Morelos is farther along the coast there, then Akumal. But we might as well be in another world." Was that a self-satisfied smirk? For a moment, she wondered if he saw himself as above all the little fishing villages, both literally and figuratively. Then the smirk was gone and maybe she'd imagined it. "Now, have we all found our tables? Please do not turn on your microphones until it's your turn to speak or we'll have an issue with feedback."

Miles moved between the tables now, holding a clipboard and a microphone, juggling both as he stopped at each table, nodding his head, writing on the paper.

"Forgive me," he said into the microphone. "I'm terrible at multitasking." Shell wondered where Ruth, the capable assistant, had gotten off to. She didn't see her anywhere on the terrace.

"Let me help you." Grace approached her husband and took the clipboard from his hand.

"Thank you, darling," Miles said. For a moment, it was just the two of them standing there in the center of the terrace, smiling, adoring, oblivious to the crowd in front of them. Miles covered the microphone and said something to Grace, then pointed to the clipboard. She examined it for a moment before walking the perimeter of the terrace, making marks on it as she walked. Eventually, she made her way to the front, where she sat on a stool and crossed her legs. Her shoes slid off and landed on the floor.

"All *right*," Miles said like an excited boy. "Are you ready for our icebreaker exercise?" No one moved. The few couples who had been talking stopped abruptly. "We want to know what you know about your partners. We want to know what you *don't* know. We want to know where we're starting."

Grace had her own microphone now. "Why don't you just explain to them what you need them to do, honey?" she said. "Look how scared they all are."

"Why don't *you*?" Miles said, rolling his eyes in mock annoyance. "You're so much nicer than I am. People always like things better when *you* say them."

"Okay," Grace said. "So, we're partnering y'all up. Everyone in the first row must move one row back and join the couple directly behind them. Those in the back row move one row up, and join the couple directly in front of you. Let's start there."

There was a flurry of movement. Shell and Colin were joined by the woman with the tattoos whom Shell had seen earlier in the lobby and her husband. He reminded Shell of a handsome puppy, all floppy hair and easy smile.

"Now, here's how it goes," Grace continued. Her Texan drawl was present, but not as strong as Miles's. They both sounded self-assured and velvety. "You're going to introduce yourselves to each other—and then, when time's up, you're going to introduce *each other* to the group. Very simple."

"Well, actually, it's not *that* simple," Miles said. "This exercise requires careful listening. If you don't listen, if all you do is sit there worrying about what you're going to say—and let's face it, we're all guilty of that, a lot of the time—you'll be in trouble. Seems like a lot of pressure, right? And that's the point." A grin spread across his face, and Shell began to recognize it as his trademark. "We have only two weeks, and in therapy terms, that's not long. In *any* terms, that's not long. The odds are stacked against us all, but we will succeed." A bit of nervous chatter. He waited a moment while the couples at the tables settled. Then a hand shot up close to the front: a woman with a lank blond bob and a T-shirt that slid down her small, bony shoulders.

"Do we have to do this introduction thing? My husband isn't great with public speaking . . ."

"Then you keep on doing the talking," Miles volleyed back. "This isn't optional, so put aside your stage fright and your fears and your excuses. You'll be washing dishes at Treehouse for the rest of the week if you don't do this. You think I'm kidding, but I'm not. You know the saying—Texans don't lie."

"That's not a saying, honey," Grace said.

"Well, it is here."

There was a server by their table now with a tray of rolled-up towels in his hand. He handed them out with a pair of golden tongs. They were silky and cool to the touch. Shell watched as the auburn-haired woman now seated across from her unfolded her towel and pressed it against her forehead, closing her eyes.

Next, a female server put a jug filled with cucumber and lime water on their table with four long-stemmed glasses. The floppy-haired husband lifted the jug and poured a glass for everyone at the table. Shell couldn't define why this irritated her so much.

"Our water, by the way, is the best in the world," Miles was saying. "Triple filtered, remineralized and alkaline. Y'all are going to feel better than you ever have by the end of this week."

"All right, we should get on with things," Grace said. "Any other questions?"

Another hand rose at the table beside them, that of a small man with short dark hair going gray in a line at the roots. Shell pictured him in his bathroom, using Grecian Formula. He had glasses and a goatee and was wearing a V-neck sweater that looked too hot for the weather. "How long do we have to speak?" he said.

"Two or three minutes, but we don't formally time you," Grace said. She had patience, Shell thought, to deal with these people, their questions and needs, day after day, week after week.

"Well, sometimes *Ruth* does use a timer," Miles interjected, and Shell saw that Ruth was back on the terrace off to the side, her cheeks turning pink in the high beam of Miles's grin.

"Put the stopwatch away," Grace said, and now Ruth was frowning. "This really isn't a big deal. Just a fun way for all of us to get to know one another. It'll be fun. And learning how to better react to the mistakes we and others make is part of what you'll learn here over the next two weeks, so don't sweat any of it." This sounded familiar. Shell was sure she'd heard it on a podcast.

A brown-haired woman sitting closer to the middle raised her hand and Grace nodded at her, but Miles shook his head. "No more questions," he said. "You have twenty minutes to chat, starting now." He tapped his Rolex.

Grace padded back to her stool, but he stayed where he was, a sentry among them. Birdsong and silence, until voices began to rise. "Hi, I'm . . ."

"We're from . . ."

"It's nice to meet you . . ."

"We were in the van together, right?" the husband across from Shell said. "I'm Ben." He turned to Colin. "Heard you on your phone. Tough to leave the office behind, I guess?"

Colin just stared at him. "Yes," he finally said.

"What sort of work do you do?"

"I'm in the mining industry."

Dead air. Ben said, "Come on, that's all? We're meant to be getting to know each other here." He smiled, but it was a fake smile, too big, belying irritation. *That's my department*, Shell thought. *I'm the one who hates all of you.*

She turned to the wife. "I'm Shell," she said.

"Johanna," the woman said faintly.

Forget all of this, Shell longed to say. *Let's run off and find a beach bar. Let's get a cocktail.* These two were young; they'd probably have interesting things to say, outside of the confines of this painful exercise. She sighed. "My husband is the director of operations at a mining company."

"What kind of mine?"

"A gold mine."

"Fascinating."

"Is it?" Shell said, and she saw the hurt look on Colin's face. For once, she wasn't angry at him, though. Her anger was rooted in the fact that she hadn't been able to think of a single interesting thing to say about herself by way of introduction. *I was working, too. We were working together. But then I had a child, and I took some time off. And now—*

Johanna brought the cool cloth over her eyes.

"And what do you do?" Ben asked Shell.

"I'm a stay-at-home—"

She couldn't finish the sentence.

"How many kids?" he asked.

Silence.

"One daughter," Colin said, and Shell released the breath she'd been holding and thought of the word in the email they had received on the way to the resort. *Solidarity.* It slipped away, fast.

"You?" Shell managed to ask.

"No, we don't have kids," Ben said. "Not yet. But we hope to."

The voices at the other tables were growing louder. Shell heard laughter, heard a man shout, "No *way*, I went to college there, too! Bobcats forever!" She gripped her water glass and thought about the crystal tumbler she had thrown at her husband several weeks before, the nasty bruise on his forehead, his bitter words: *You could have killed me! Was that what you were trying to do? Look at yourself!* There was still glass on the floor when she came to in the morning to find Colin gone. Later, he'd told her he'd left because he felt unsafe and she laughed at him, cruel and harsh.

"How did you two meet?" Shell asked, chasing away the ugly memories with words.

Ben smiled and visibly relaxed. Shell realized he was one of those people most comfortable when talking about himself. "I'm a district attorney and Jo is a social worker. We met in court. She was there with one of her clients, and I was trying to put her client in jail for driving the getaway car during her boyfriend's burglary attempt. For a second time." He turned to his wife, as if hoping she would pick up the thread of the story, but Johanna didn't speak. He continued. "Jo got up and spoke about this woman with such passion and faith, when I hadn't been able to see her as anything but a screwup. She believed in her so fully that it reminded me of why people do the kind of jobs we do—because we believe in something. In *people.* Plus, I thought she was totally gorgeous. I mean, look at my beautiful wife, right?"

Johanna lowered the cloth from her eyes and smiled weakly. Shell felt sorry for her and disliked her at the same time.

"Four minutes left," Miles's voice boomed over the microphone.

"Anyway," Ben said. "I ended up asking for community service for her client, but a lot of it. Afterward, Johanna came up to me on the courthouse stairs and she was *mad*." He turned to his wife again. "What was it you said to me? Come on, honey."

Johanna closed her eyes again. "I believe I said, 'You're an asshole.'" Now she opened her eyes and put her hand on her husband's arm. "You gave my client so much community service she lost her job, remember?" She ducked her head to murmur in his ear. "Ben, it's getting really bad. I think I need to—"

"Not now, Johanna," Ben said in a low voice. "We have to do this, you know it's required." Then he smiled at Shell and Colin. "Sorry. She's, ah, a bit tired from the trip. So, yeah, she called me an asshole. It was the first thing she ever said to me. How could I not fall in love with her, right? We went to lunch, dinner, then a drive along the Pacific Coast Highway. We stayed in a hotel room for the rest of the weekend. They left food at the door. We didn't come out." He grinned. Their story was done, Shell realized. Perhaps she and Colin were meant to imagine the rest, imagine these two nubile young strangers ripping each other's clothes off in some hotel room in Santa Monica. Shell kept a smile pasted on her face.

"Lovely," she said.

"How did *you* meet?" Ben asked.

Shell was silent. "We met at school," Colin said. "We were both studying geology, in British Columbia. Shell was—she was known for her opinions. Voted most likely to succeed."

"There were never any *votes*," Shell said, embarrassed.

"And I remember thinking, now, that is a strong woman. A capable woman. A woman who knows what she wants." He stopped talking. Shell thought he was just pausing. But no, he was done. She looked down at the table and blinked several times. It had felt like the most natural thing in the world, for the two of them to pair up. Similar backgrounds, equal in the looks department, same height, same major, both from Toronto. And they *had* fallen in love—only now she found it impossible to remember exactly what that had felt like.

"It's been twenty years," she said, as if that made things clear.

"Wow. That's a lifetime. Jo and I have only known each other for three."

Shell kept her eyes downcast. She thought about what Ben had just said about his wife: that it had been love at first sight. A modern fairy tale in a motel room by the sea. But did it make sense for these two people who barely knew one another to be in counseling? Three years? Three years was nothing.

"Shell?" Ben was saying.

"I'm sorry, pardon me?"

"Did you have anything to add?"

"Um. No. It was a long time ago, that's all."

The golden-orange sun was hanging just above the horizon like God had it on the end of a fishing line. And then, just like that, it sank below the surface and was gone. Johanna's eyes met Shell's.

"Time's up," Miles called out, and Johanna's expression changed. She stood, suddenly, and said, "I really can't do this. Ben, it hurts too much. I have to go." And she lurched away without saying anything more.

"I'm so sorry." Ben's expression, which had been momentarily smug—beautiful wife, meet-cute story clearly superior to theirs—was mortified. "She—she gets migraines. I should go after her. It was nice to meet you. Guess we'll be washing dishes this week." He shrugged but Shell knew he wasn't as philosophical as he was trying to appear. What would happen in their bungalow behind closed doors that night? What would happen behind all these closed doors?

"Unbelievable," Shell said, when they were both gone. There was still a clamor of voices around them, and at first she wasn't sure what Colin was saying. But then he stood, too.

"Come on," he said. "Before they get started."

"What?"

"I hung up on a safety board meeting when that Ruth woman dragged me off the bus."

"So?"

26

"So, I need to find out what's happening. It's really important."

"No way. We can't just walk out."

"It's pointless. This is a pointless exercise. If you keep your voice down, we can get out of here unnoticed."

"I'm not going!"

"Damn it, Shell. We're adults. This isn't summer camp. They don't get to dictate our every move."

"Do you know what dictates your every move? Your job." She was shouting now. All the other voices lowered and people stared. "It was your idea to come here!"

"You promised you would come here and try." He lowered his voice. "It was either this or—"

"How is *leaving*—"

"Come on. We can talk in our counseling sessions. Not here." The terrace was silent. Shell considered her options: stand and follow her husband meekly off the terrace or hold her ground. Who exactly did she want to be?

"I'm not leaving," she said.

He did. Shell lifted her chin and stared straight ahead. People were going to have to stop looking at her, eventually—weren't they? Miles and Grace approached her table. "I'm sorry," she said, her bravado dissolving and her cheeks tingling with shame.

"Don't be," Miles said. "Some couples are in therapy for months, even years, before they have a breakthrough—if they ever have a breakthrough at all. Most just give up, eventually, and go back to their lives of quiet desperation, or they separate, they end things, they tear their lives apart." He was speaking into his mic, but to her, only. Then he turned to his audience. "What Shell has so adeptly made us realize in just our first moments here is that layers must be peeled away quickly. And that's going to hurt. There's going to be conflict. But that's what we're after, especially at first. You did great, Shell. You were honest, raw and real. You have nothing to be ashamed of."

"Look around you, Shell," Grace said. "You're among friends.

We're all going to feel vulnerable this week, we're all going to feel exposed. But the important thing to understand is that we're all in this together."

Silence. Miles sat down at her table, taking the spot her husband had vacated. "I'll introduce you," he said. "I know who you are."

Day Two

Many of the couples we see in our practice have simply stopped talking to one another about anything except the bare necessities (*"Who is picking the kids up from school?" "Is there any milk left in the fridge?"* Sound familiar?). They've grown used to this lack of communication; it feels normal to them. But it's not! You must begin your journey with a commitment to the process of relearning communication with your partner. You must make talking to one another the norm.

But tread carefully.

After so much has been left unsaid, the truth can bubble to the surface, causing arguments that are counterproductive to your renewed commitment. Lay groundwork first. What is your husband's favorite meal? When Grace has something important she wants to discuss with Miles, she often has the chef at Treehouse prepare his favorite dish (chicken mole, in case you're wondering). Does your wife like flowers? Order some! (Grace has a soft spot for orchids, which, blessedly, are plentiful in Mexico.)

Marriage is not simply about taking. You must give to your partner before you can expect to receive. And you must do so when you are least inspired.

—from the *New York Times* bestseller *Revering Your Marriage and Renewing Your Love* by Drs. Miles and Grace Markell

Her: But where do I start? Do I focus on Miles, on how he was trying to push me away, and how I wasn't about to let him? It upset me at first, yes, but I got stronger. Or, do I focus on Johanna and Ben, her fragility, her headaches—how beautiful she was, how infatuated he was and how hopeless the entire thing was, what was really going on beneath the surface? Or on Shell Williams and the bottles of vodka and strong sleeping pills I found in her luggage—and confiscated, of course. Or her husband, who had not one but two spare phones hidden away? But Miles decided to let him keep those.

Him: Wait. You went through their things?

Her: Their luggage was always searched. Miles's idea. We had the porters do it while the guests went upstairs for the opening exercise. They'd leave any potential contraband out for me to deal with. It was in every contract, but none of them ever read the contracts, no matter how many times we asked them to. Johanna had something, too. A prescription that wasn't hers. I almost forgot about that, actually.

Him: That seems . . . extreme. You never mentioned that before, that their luggage was searched.

Her: The entire thing was extreme. That was the point. [Pause.] But maybe I *should* start with Miles and me. The love we shared—because we did love each other. As sick and twisted as our relationship was, as sick and twisted as he became, I did love my husband. And he loved me, once. When we first met. There's always love at the beginning. The problem is, I think I loved him too much. I made him think he could do anything.

*T*he morning sun in the restaurant filtered through palm fronds, casting shadow and light across Johanna and Ben's table. Huevos rancheros, yogurt and green juices. "And a side of bacon," the server said, setting it beside Johanna's plate. Her stomach pitched and rolled. "That's for him, not me," she said, sliding it across the table and wiping her hand with her napkin.

"You act like touching meat is going to contaminate you," Ben said.

She didn't reply. What was the point? She put down the napkin and looked around. The restaurant was called Treehouse. Two flights of wooden stairs led to the wide nook made of wooden beams and planks with a peaked palm frond roof and a circular view of the ocean, beach and resort grounds. There was a buzz in the air. Johanna noticed couples waving and greeting one another, stopping at each other's tables. The night before, while she was pinned to their bed in a blur of pain, Ben begged her repeatedly to return to the opening exercise. She had finally faked sleep, praying he would leave her alone long enough for her to take one of her pills, hidden in her bag. But, when she had crept out of bed to find them, the only pills that had ever worked for the blinding pain of her migraines, the ones that were so much more than just pills to her, they were gone. She hadn't been able to stop thinking about her, then. About Cleo, smiling, Cleo, crying, Cleo, dead beside her car. A nightmare, all of it. Eventually, just before dawn, the pain had retreated and she'd slept a little. Now she felt unsteady. Exhausted and wired at the same time.

In the restaurant, the only proper tables were in the center of the suspended room. The rest of the seating options were up on platforms:

cushioned lounge chairs that looked more like beds with small tables in their centers. Johanna and Ben were sitting at a regular table. Hammocks also ringed the room.

"It seems inappropriate," Johanna murmured.

"What does?"

"The hammocks, the weird bed tables. This is a restaurant."

"It's a couples' resort. A place designed for people to get close again. I think those hammocks and bed tables look fun. I hope we use one, later in the week." He inclined his head in the direction of a hammock suspended just outside the restaurant, perched on a ledge, the rocks and ocean and a set of stairs carved into the cliff below it. As he spoke, a gust of sea breeze caused one of the pillows to tumble and fall out of sight into the sea.

"I wonder how many of those they lose in a day," Johanna said. "That doesn't look very safe."

"Since when have *you* been concerned with safety?" He was smiling. He reached across the table for her hand, but she clenched it. She was so sick of holding hands.

He dropped her hand. "Can't you at least try?"

"I *am* trying," she said. Then she sensed a shift in the room, a sudden hum of energy. Miles and Grace were moving among the tables. Ruth walked behind them. It was as if they were larger than everyone, larger than life. They were now standing at the bar, speaking with the bartender, a young woman clad in black, dark hair to her waist. She handed them coffee cups brimming with froth.

"They wake before dawn, go for a run, eat breakfast and prepare for the day," Ben said. "They don't eat breakfast with the couples, only dinner."

"How do you know this?"

"From reading their books."

"Morning, guys." Johanna was startled to find Ruth at their table. "Feeling better today, Johanna?" Something in her tone and in the arch of her eyebrow made Johanna feel guilty, like the liar she was.

Suddenly, Johanna was certain she hadn't forgotten her migraine pills, the ones Cleo had given her, the ones she shouldn't have. She felt certain they had been taken out of her luggage—and she felt a chill.

"Yes. Much better, thank you."

"Great," she said. "Miles and Grace are about to make a presentation. I hope you'll manage to stay for the entire thing."

Shame flooded through her as Ruth walked away. It was so familiar.

"The Williams couple isn't here," Miles said, disapproval in his voice, and something else, too, something so rare in him it was almost alarming: nervousness. He liked things to go a certain way.

"I don't think we can delay it any longer," Grace said, glancing down at her watch. She was nervous, too. Sundays had to go like clockwork.

"You so rarely concern yourself with the details," he said, and she felt the needle of his words. But they were in public. He couldn't continue. "Very well." He put down his coffee and stepped to the front of the restaurant. "Good morning, everyone. How did y'all sleep? Enjoy your dinner last night? We've got the finest chef this side of the equator, haven't we?"

A smattering of applause. A breeze from the sea behind them lifted wisps of Grace's hair from her face, which was tilted attentively toward her husband. "And I'm sure everyone is feeling much more relaxed than they were last night," he said. "In fact, I can feel it in the air. And it's a beautiful thing. I just want to take a moment to thank you, and to thank you on Grace's behalf, for bearing with us last night. For baring your souls—because that was kinda what it felt like, yes? I know it was harder on some of you than on others. And we are truly, truly grateful."

She looked out at the couples, who were sitting with breakfasts now forgotten. Miles was so good at this part, at drawing them in and earning their trust. Meanwhile, she liked to recede into the background, watch and wait. From afar, she could anticipate the secrets she would uncover, and how she could tend to or dispose of them.

She walked among the tables in silence as her husband spoke and tried to feel as certain and confident as she knew he did. These couples would argue over laundry and cooking and the mundane details of daily life, at first. Or they would argue about larger things, about the big event that had severed them. People didn't come here without secrets, wrapped up and hidden even from their own view.

She couldn't hear Miles's words anymore, just the rich thrum of his voice. Grace stood behind the blond woman who had asked, the night before, if she and her husband had to speak publicly. There was a reason these two didn't like to talk, and it wasn't shyness. She glanced down at her clipboard and confirmed they were on her list of clients: Annabel and Max Robinson from Abingdon, Virginia. High school sweethearts. Grace would listen to them talk, and as she did, she would smell the mint in their garden and the season's apple butter simmering on the stove. She would hear their children clattering their way inside the house. She would become them, just for a little while. It would feel so good to leave herself behind, but they would have no way of knowing how much they were helping her just by being there. *"Grace Markell is the kindest, most skilled, most compassionate therapist in the world. She changed my life,"* one online comment she had recently viewed had said. *"She took the time to understand what was really going on in our lives. She saved us."*

"Don't read those!" Miles had snapped when he walked up behind her. "Why do you waste your time on that nonsense?" No mention of the fact that it was only she who was expected to cut herself off from the world, not Miles. A few days later, her laptop had disappeared. Her tablet and phone, too. This was a problem she had yet to solve. There was information on her laptop she needed desperately. "Handwritten notes, what more do you need?" Miles had asked her. What more, indeed?

Right now, the clients were nodding their heads along to Miles's words as if they were music. Grace knew most of their names, but preferred to label them by instinct. The man with the soul patch was Anger Issues, Possibly Verbally Abusive; his wife, Chief Enabler, sat nervously beside him, occasionally chewing on her hair, maybe without knowing she was doing it. The woman with the lank bob was the Criticizer; beside her, with his weak jaw and a fade haircut, was Mr. Resentful/ Anxious. A man with blond hair that had deteriorated into a crown of hopeful peach fuzz reaching over and squeezing his more attractive, taller wife's hand while she looked down and seemed to wonder how his hand had gotten there was the Great Disappointment and she, the wife, was the Irrevocably Disappointed. There might be no hope for them. A good-looking man with ruffled, sun-streaked hair and dark earnest eyes was leaning in, listening hard. He was Mr. Fix It. He wanted everything to be simple, to go according to plan. His wife was the one who had left the terrace, the striking red-haired woman who had departed on account of a migraine. Grace looked down at her name, then back up at her. She had to pull her gaze away, hard. Johanna Haines—Mrs.-Most-Likely-To-Be-Wishing-Herself-Somewhere-Else. Mrs. Painfully Beautiful.

Those were always the tough ones, the ones who didn't want to do the work. Ruth had said something about pills found and confiscated in Johanna's bag, during the luggage inspection. A prescription not in her name. And was it vodka that had been discovered in their bungalow as well? No. That was Shell Williams, the one with the husband who had stormed off the terrace the night before. Vodka and sleeping pills, strong ones. Grace remembered Miles, sitting down in front of Shell and staring deep into her eyes. He had known exactly what to do.

She watched her husband's lips and hands move as he spoke. When he was at his best, he made you feel as if whatever he said was what you'd always been waiting to hear. When he was at his worst, he made you want to die.

Miles saw her and smiled. She smiled back. *We are always on duty*, he often said. *We're supposed to make them want what we have.*

"I invite you all, and I invite you on Grace's behalf, as well—" Grace took the cue and walked toward him "—to commit to this work. This is your last chance." He had her hand now, they were standing before the guests, at the moment when the sun rose over the restaurant and lit them up. "Angel," he whispered in her ear, and maybe he meant it that time. Maybe the devil inside him was gone. She wanted to believe this, had believed it many times. But it never turned out to be true.

"The Williams couple, they still aren't here," he said into her ear, in a low, agitated voice. "And they didn't sign their contract yesterday, either."

"We can have the contracts sent to their bungalows. Don't worry."

"It's not how it's done."

"You're such a perfectionist. Relax. Darling."

He gritted his teeth into a smile back at her. "Did I mention how ravishing you look this morning?" His voice was too loud, or maybe just loud enough. Then he turned back to the crowd. "All right now, ready? I want you to declare yourselves. I want you to tell me, and Grace, and everyone here, that you will commit to working on your marriages, to healing what's broken, to doing absolutely everything that is asked of you here, in the name of a greater good. Yes? All at once, I want you to say it." He nodded his head, raised his arms like he was a conductor. "Will you do everything it takes to fix what has been broken? *I will.* Come on, say it: *I will.*" Miles was grinning now, as the couples did his bidding. "One more time. *Yes!* I will! Perfect." He lowered his arms slowly. "Now, as a reward for your good work, it's the question and answer period. Ask us anything. This is your chance."

Grace hated this part, but Miles insisted. "How many times do I have to tell you this isn't a clinic?" he would say to her. "We need to establish a connection, quickly. You'll never see these people again, so who cares if they know something private?" Ruth was the moderator, standing at the front of the room and pointing.

"Why didn't you choose to have children?" the blond-streaked woman in front asked. Ruth's eyes met Grace's for a moment, and Grace wasn't sure what they shared. Ruth looked away first. "Is not having kids the secret to your happiness?" Grace found herself struggling for air; her breath had snagged on the past. But Miles stepped in and spoke with ease. "We would have loved to have had children. The

Lord didn't choose to bless us with them. And in some ways, we have come to see *that* as a blessing." *"The guy is a little churchy,"* one of the online comments had read. *"But it seemed to work on my wife. We're still together."* "We wouldn't be able to do what we do with children," he continued. "We wouldn't be able to help people in the way we do. It's not the secret to our happiness at all, though. In fact, overcoming the disappointment was one of our greatest challenges." Grace shoved her hands inside the pockets of her long skirt and clenched her fists the way she had when she was in labor. Exquisite pain. Truly.

"What *is* our secret, you might wonder? It's that we don't have any secrets from each other. Not a single one." This was the naked truth and a blatant lie all at once. And *"the Lord didn't choose to bless us"* was the ugliest lie of all. But they were not the ones under the microscope. They were the ones in the spotlight. And a spotlight is full of light—yet it often reveals nothing.

*A*fter the question period was over, Ben and Johanna sat in silence. Finally, Johanna spoke. "When he had his arms raised up like that, like he was an evangelist . . ." She trailed off, unsure of how to finish the sentence.

"He's maybe a tiny bit crazy," Ben allowed. "But we need to do this. We need to be here."

"We do." She made herself sound certain, even though she had had to fight not to turn that short sentence into a question.

He reached for her hand. This time she let him and she kept right on smiling until her molars started to hurt. Then she said, "You know what? Why don't we just—" and she stood and picked up both their plates. The question and answer session had unsettled her, and it wasn't just because of Miles. She was sure Grace Markell had looked afraid, for just a moment, and she had felt afraid for her. Imagine standing in front of a group of strangers and saying, *"Ask me anything."* It turned her insides to liquid just to consider it. "Let's be a little crazy ourselves. Go sit on the damn ledge hammock. Come on."

"Are you—serious?" He was incredulous, then delighted, he was scrambling to his feet, grinning back at her, and the couples surrounding them were looking up from their meals.

Johanna felt lighter; the pain in her head receded. Everyone falls in love for a reason, and she knew exactly why Ben had wanted her in the first place. *She's unpredictable. She makes my life fun. She makes me do things I would never do.* She could say the same of him, but didn't because no one would understand. *He's my rock,* she would usually say, and people would nod because that was the type of guy Ben was: solid and steady.

Also: rigid and obtuse, but only if you lived with him or if you were on the wrong side of a court case. Like Cleo had been, always, every time.

On the hammock, to make up for the fact that she had just thought about Cleo, she fed Ben a piece of bacon. He spilled egg on his shirt and she dabbed it lovingly with her napkin. Everyone was watching. Even Miles and Grace Markell.

Johanna kissed her husband.

It was so much easier to say the right lines, to master the correct performance, when you had an audience.

—

Colin and Shell, their partner couple from the terrace the night before, were on the path in front of them as Johanna and Ben headed back toward their villa. "Oh, hell," Ben said. "This is so embarrassing. Maybe you should apologize."

"For *what*?"

"We just left them there."

"I wasn't feeling well! There was nothing I could have done."

"I think they're arguing."

It was true; she could hear raised voices on the breeze, first Shell, "We missed it! I can't believe you . . ." Then him: "Well, I *told* you . . ."

"Told me what? You were on your damn phone!"

They had perfect hair and perfect clothes. Johanna always got the same feeling when she saw people so flawless: a combination of envy, awe and a sneaking suspicion. Not all is as it seems when the surface is so shiny. Sometimes the surface is just a reflection of what you wished you could have for yourself.

They stopped walking and were unlocking the door of the villa beside Johanna and Ben's. "Oh, great," Ben said. "We're neighbors." The arguing went on.

Ben was rubbing the base of his palm against his jaw the way he did when he was upset.

"I'm sure they'll stop," Johanna ventured.

Ben shook his head but didn't say anything, just swiped their key card in front of the door. They entered their villa and were greeted by its strong scent of orange, lemon and cedar.

"What do you want to do for the rest of this morning?" he asked, sitting on the bed and taking off his shoes.

"I was thinking . . . there's an artisanal market I wanted to visit, just a few villages over. Want to come?" It was so fast, the twist of his lips, as if he had eaten something sour. She let it pass. "I read about it online last month. It's in the middle of the jungle. And there's a cenote in the back of it, one of those natural swimming holes. We can spend a few hours and be back in time for lunch."

"You want to *leave the resort*? We're supposed to stay here together," he said. "After last night, I don't think we should be breaking any more rules." The closeness she had felt to him at breakfast was a puddle in sunlight, evaporated. She turned away from him, meaning to search for the small cross-body bag she carried when they traveled but also because she didn't want to look at him just then.

"So, you're just going to *go*?"

"Do I not have your *permission*?" She turned back toward him.

"I'd been thinking we might just stay in our room and make use of this king-sized bed," he said. "At breakfast just now, you were so . . ."

Her stomach plummeted. Her hand went to the red leather bag again, her eye went to the door. She slid sunscreen inside the bag, found her black bikini and went into the bathroom to change into it. Silence in the other room. She came out, pulling a T-shirt over her head.

"I say I want to make love and you leave and change in another room," he said as she buttoned her shorts. "How are we ever going to get back our intimacy if you don't even try?"

"Stop telling me I'm not trying. I am trying. But intimacy isn't something you can get back just like that." She snapped her fingers; it felt like an absurd thing to do. She glanced at the door again, counted how many steps it would take her to get out of the room. This nervous habit had started after the incident at work. She hoped it would fade eventually. She grabbed a handful of pesos and shoved them in her bag. "I'm going to the market. That's all, just a market, and you're acting like I've just *murdered* someone!"

He stood and walked toward her. She knew it didn't make sense, this was *Ben*, but she still felt afraid. He had his arms around her now. The way he was holding her meant her neck was bent at an unnatural angle and she had to stand still, unmoving, until he released her. "I'll be gone only a few hours," she said. "Maybe I'll find a new painting for the dining room, to go with the walls that I *will* actually finish painting when we get back." She tried to smile.

A shadow across his face again. And a sadness in her heart at the idea of going back and fixing the walls she had impulsively started to paint one weekday when she should have been at work but couldn't be, when she was supposed to be at a therapist's office but had canceled, again. She had decided to go for a walk; it had been the first time she'd left the house in weeks. When she'd passed the paint store, a sign in the window had caught her eye: "Brighten your life with a fresh coat of color!" She had returned with a gallon of the brightest shade she could find: Mango Punch. But the gallon had been only enough to do half the room and Ben hadn't been pleased when he arrived home from work. "I'm glad you're up and about," he had said, standing on a drop sheet in front of the strokes of lurid orange on their demure gray walls. "But I really wish we could make decisions like this together."

He released her now. "I think I'll read for a bit and then go for a walk on the beach. You have fun at your market. Meet for lunch around one?"

"Perfect." As she took a water bottle from the minifridge, he reclined on the bed and opened a book—one written by the Markells. He picked up a pen and underlined something. When she said goodbye, he nodded in her direction but didn't look up.

race spread out the newspaper. To do so, she had to move the vase of orchids aside. The bouquet was larger this week than it was the week before. Miles kept looking up from his tablet, where he was reading news on websites that often seemed to have no bearing on reality, then back down again. Like he was waiting. She flipped a page of her newspaper, even though she wasn't registering any of the words at this point. Twenty minutes later, she said, "I should be going."

"I wish you wouldn't," he said, as he always did.

"I won't be long. I never am."

"But we should stay here. We should *be* here." His voice was like a boy's, petulant, rising. "We should go for a walk on the beach, visit the library—have lunch together. I hate it when you go." His voice had flattened now. It was an old argument; he was delivering these lines by rote.

"I'll be back in time for lunch. Rita's making your favorite." She lifted a hand to the nearest orchid and touched the pale purple flower. Orchids weren't her favorite. She preferred dahlias; she liked their layers. Orchids were too obvious. "And I need to go to Akumal and get more ointment for my skin condition. You know it's the only thing that has ever helped. They have to grind it from the *chaka* bark and leaves right there, or it doesn't work."

He looked up. "Yes, I know all that. You've told me many times. You go to a little holistic pharmacy in Akumal. Maybe if you didn't scratch at it, it wouldn't be so raw. Look, your ankle is bleeding. I don't want you to end up with scars. You need to go to a doctor."

As if you don't know better than anyone how fierce an itch becomes if you stop scratching it for a while. "I talked to the nurse," she said, a lie so small

45

he didn't seem to notice it, but so big it took over the room. "She's never been able to find anything that worked."

"A doctor, I said."

"Next week, then." She folded up the newspaper. Her heart was racing, but her tone was even. She met his gaze and was surprised to find no anger there. He was watchful, waiting, but not angry. "I promise. But for now, I need to get the ointment or our clients will think I have something contagious."

"The clients," he said, as if he had momentarily forgotten them. "We'll have our work cut out for us this session. You might need my help."

She bit down on her bottom lip. "I'll be fine," she said, keeping her tone as light as she could, even as the anxiety he planted began to sprout too easily. *You're nothing without me.* But he didn't say it today.

"At least the Williams couple is mine, Shell and Colin. A workaholic and an alcoholic. I'll handle them. But did you see that couple, out on the hammock at breakfast?" Miles asked. Grace nodded. "They're yours. Johanna Haines and Ben Reid. Ruth says the wife's got a prescription that isn't in her name. And Johanna's behavior so far has been unpredictable at best."

"I'll handle it."

"Don't be soft."

"Miles—" She closed her eyes for a moment and counted *one, two, three.* "Let's talk about it when I get back. You can help me with some strategies." She kissed the top of his head and her mouth filled with saliva, but she kept her lips there for the right amount of time, *four, five, okay.* He went back to his reading again. Grace stepped into the other room, keeping her movements as calm and fluid as she could. "I'll get you some of that natural bug spray you like," she called. "The sand ants were bad on my run last night." She stood in front of her bathroom mirror for a few extra seconds. In these moments, without her hair done, without her makeup on, without her carefully chosen outfits, she hardly recognized herself.

Silence, and then a distracted "And on mine this morning, too. Thank you." They never ran together, like their books claimed. They always timed it so they could have that time apart, too. It was yet another of their lies.

She piled her hair on top of her head, put on her Texas Longhorns baseball cap, a remnant from her college days, and her sunglasses. She disappeared from the room like a ghost, hardly daring to breathe until, head down, she walked along the cobblestone out past the main villa.

In the brush, two coatis digging with their snouts stopped what they were doing and stared at her as she passed. A big old iguana lounged in the sun, his markings familiar; he'd been here as long as she had and probably longer. Anticipation fizzed in her veins. At the top of the driveway she saw that she'd missed a *colectivo*, which would transport her to the market. But it wasn't long before another appeared in the distance. She waited in the shade of a frangipani tree.

"Akumal, *por favor*," she said to the driver, who was one of the regulars.

"*Sí, señora.*"

She sat near the front and held her colorful woven bag on her lap.

"*Usted va cada dos semanas. Como un reloj,*" he observed. *You go every two weeks. Like clockwork.*

"*Sí,*" she said, and nothing more.

The van picked up speed and she watched the scenery fly by, feeling hungry for it after seeing only the resort grounds, day after day. People often asked her and Miles what it was like to live in Mexico. Most of the time, she had no idea.

Grace said goodbye to the driver and got out of the van. She walked along the road, toward Akumal. But that was not her true destination. She turned a sharp left and walk-stumbled down the embankment into the jungle. She tore through the jungle and the thick brush at her feet—filled with stinging spurge and trumpet vine, both plants known to cause dermatitis—slashed at her ankles. She didn't slow, didn't stop, walked faster and let the pain come. She cried out only once. She would have relief soon from this self-inflicted agony. And because of this agony, she had her escape.

An hour later, Akumal was long gone and she was near the entrance to the Puerto Morelos market. She pushed her way through the bushes and out onto the road, then came into the market the way anyone else would. She walked toward the market tables, calmly stopped at one and turned a bottle of *copaiba* oil over in her hands.

It had taken some time before the women who worked at the market realized she wasn't a tourist, not exactly. But eventually they stopped showing her the key rings and handmade dolls they tiredly expected would be bartered for—Grace never did—and instead showed her their remedies and tinctures and lotions and plants, for which the price was the price.

One of the women approached now, the most familiar one. *"In l'akech,"* she said, a greeting she had quietly taught Grace a few months earlier, while Grace's heart had felt warmed and quieted. *"Ala k'in,"* Grace replied. Put together, the two phrases meant *I am you, and you are another me.* The woman had seen bruises on Grace's collarbone, the day she taught her that greeting. She had given her arnica and refused payment. Grace didn't even know her name, but wondered if this woman was the only person in the world who was an approximation of a friend.

Today, the woman dabbed something pale brown from a little pot around Grace's eyes and onto her shoulders. "Is *tepezcohuite*," she said. "Makes you look like Reese Witherspoon." Grace laughed. The paste smelled earthy and tingled on her skin. "I'll take it," she said. She slid the tube into her embroidered bag. She also replenished her stock of a tincture for the headaches she sometimes got during storm season, and a spray to prevent and treat insect bites. "And?" she said.

The woman nodded. "I have it," she said. "Just let me grind." She looked down at Grace's ankles and shook her head, then back up at Grace. Their gazes held. *Why do you do this to yourself?* the woman could have asked. But maybe she understood. She leaned down and lifted a stone mortar and pestle onto the table, then reached into a cooler and drew out a bag of bark and leaves. She tipped the contents of the bag into the bowl and added a drizzle of oil from a bottle beside her. Then she began to grind, her muscled arm moving in steady circles as a crimson paste formed. The smell of it, bitter and sweet at once, prickled Grace's nostrils.

"Perfect," the woman finally said. "Remember—keep it cold." Grace nodded. The woman scooped the paste into the jar Grace had brought with her, then offered what remained to Grace, who ran her fingers around the bottom of the bowl, then bent down and rubbed a score of deep red across her painful ankles. *"Gracias,"* she said, relief in her voice. The woman nodded, then moved on to another customer as if she were not Grace's savior. Grace slid the jar into the little cooler bag she'd brought with her, tucked inside her woven one, then walked among the tables, waiting for her moment.

She stepped into the trees. She would make an escape by blending in. By staying very still. She knew how to do this. The week before, Grace had seen a tourist try to walk down the path toward the cenote. The market women had shouted, they had clucked and explained that the swimming hole was not open, that it was not safe, that it was closed, *cerrado*, indefinitely. But they had never noticed Grace head toward it, not once.

She waited a moment, then moved toward the path in the jungle. As she began to walk quickly along the path, feeling the leaves of the plants at its overgrown border brushing across her already burning ankles and knowing they would make the rash even worse and that it would be worth it, as it always was, there was a flash of auburn in the corner of her eye. She thought it must be a bird. She kept moving.

She pressed forward down a path braided with tree roots. She could still hear the crackle of twigs behind her. Two steps across soft greenery and she was at the edge: there was the *Cuidado* sign and the more aggressive *Cerrado* sign, and the sign with the red-painted crocodile and no words at all.

She remembered the day she had discovered the swimming hole. She had wanted to swim in it so badly she ached for it and could hardly stop herself. She had gazed into the clear water and had seen no movement, no sign of a crocodile. She had thought about her childhood self, asking over and over how God could possibly exist if she couldn't see him or even feel him. Her mother's voice: *Just because you can't see something doesn't mean it doesn't exist. God is all around you.* She had jumped anyway.

When she swam in the cenote, she felt the possibility of the crocodile everywhere, the possibility of oblivion, too, a sweet release. But she never saw it. Maybe the existence of the crocodile was a myth. Maybe God was a myth, too. *I'll whip you if you say that again.* That was her father's voice. She put down her bag and her sunglasses on top of that. A loud snap in the trees behind her, probably an animal, but maybe not.

"Hello?" Grace called. No response. Swiftly, she peeled off her tank top, then her shorts, wincing as the fabric snagged on the aggravated skin at her ankles. She couldn't wait any longer. She jumped, a whole week's worth of angst burning to the surface.

Miles couldn't swim. She thought of this every time she jumped. His mother had never taught him. Once, Miles had told her that the day he had been baptized, in a particularly fast-moving and murky area of the Houston Ship Channel, he had been sure he would die.

"Did you think God saved you?" she asked.

"He did save me," he answered.

Sometimes as she jumped she thought about what would happen if Miles were to appear and she were to grab his hand just before she pitched herself over the edge of the cenote's ledge. She'd let go and he'd sink to the bottom. The crocodile, if it existed, would finally show itself, and—

But these were not the sort of thoughts a wife should have about her husband.

She dove down again, deeper, the cool water clearing her mind. It reminded her of summer afternoons spent swimming with her brother,

Garrett, in Jacob's Well, outside of Galveston. The sensation here was the same, of being shaken out of heat-induced torpidity, out of the heat of a Texan summer, out of the heat of her own body and her own thoughts. When she opened her eyes underwater, she half expected to see her brother's face. But she saw only fish black as onyx and no bigger than the tip of her pinkie. The rocks beneath the water were stained orange and yellow with minerals, green and black with algae. She saw the ancient-looking face of a startled turtle and felt her chest growing tight as she pushed herself farther, chased movement into a crevasse and saw mud-brown, army-green, a snake-like body swimming away from her: an eel.

She didn't know what she would do if she ever saw the crocodile. Miles was always talking about signs from God, about asking Him for what you needed—or at least, he had talked that way before he had learned to become his own deity. *Well, show me the crocodile.* That was her prayer. *Show me the crocodile and then spare me—and if you do, I'll know that my life is not worthless, that I am not nothing without him.* People tried to make the strangest bargains. Grace saw it every day. They did it without even knowing it, without even realizing that they really did believe in God.

Grace surfaced to gather air so she could dive under again but was distracted by a shadow from above, the outline of a person. She felt fear burn through her, a fear so searing even the cool water couldn't temper it. Had he followed her this time?

She kept swimming, back and forth, waiting for his voice to bellow down. *Come out of there, you Jezebel.* Silence. Nothing from above. She wiped the water from her eyes, she looked up, squinted to see clearly. It wasn't him. It was a woman. The sun was directly above her and her hair was a firebrand. The woman lifted her hand and she waved—Grace thought she did, at least—and then she was gone.

Grace treaded water and stared up at the now-empty edge of the cenote. Had her imagination just played a trick on her? She swam to the side and carefully climbed the rope ladder and then the decaying wooden steps, returning to her clothes. She forced them over her wet skin, looked around and around. *Was she here? Where did she go?*

"Hello?" she called out, for the second time that afternoon.

Nothing.

But, there: Grace's hat hung from a branch. She was sure she'd left it on the ground. It was a sign. *I was here.*

A trap door opened inside her. The truth emerged, first in her brother's voice. *Acknowledge me*, it said.

And then in God's voice: *I was here. I gave you your sign.*

Then in her husband's voice: *You are nothing without me.*

She looked down into the water and saw it for just a second: a ghostly white belly. She gasped.

Her own voice: *Spare me and I'll know my life is not worthless.*

Had she just been saved? And if so, by whom?

Despite the heat of the day, Grace shivered with cold. It burrowed its way inside her, along with a sense of loss. She'd gotten exactly what she wanted, her sign. But she couldn't help but ask for more. That was human nature, too. *Send her back to me. Make her real, and I promise, I'll—*

But she knew this God she couldn't help but believe in didn't want what she wanted for herself. What she wanted was a sin. She was an aberration. *Please, forgive me for what and who I am. I did not choose this. I am so broken.* They had given her tools she could use, words she could say, to wash the filth from her soul. But she was getting so tired of washing. She just wanted to swim. To be who she was.

Another snap in the jungle that sounded exactly like a tree branch under someone's foot. She turned and started walking back toward the market. She came out of the trees not caring that she was dripping wet, that it was obvious she'd been swimming.

The woman who had given her the herbs immediately approached. "Lady," she said. "You're all right?"

What was it in the woman's eyes? Fear. Warning. Understanding.

"I'm fine. I'm sorry. I shouldn't have been swimming—"

"That woman, she was your friend?"

A shocking jolt. Grace felt the way she did when she jumped in the water. "She was real?"

A frown. "Of course she was real. And the man, too—but he is not your friend. Is he?" Another jolt, this one less pleasant.

"Dark hair? Tall?"

The woman was nodding, her expression getting darker. "He's been here before. He's *not* your friend. *Diablo.*"

"No," she said, understanding now that there was no hiding from Miles, not ever. "He's not my friend at all."

"He's still out there. You should go. And you'd better not come back here. I'm sorry. There was something about him today. I'm afraid for you."

———

At the road, the *collectivo* was far ahead, already gone. The minutes until the next one came felt like an hour. Grace kept waiting to hear his voice, to feel his fingers clutch at her arm. That would be too obvious, though. That would accomplish nothing. Miles was going to save this secret, save this knowledge of her private life—a private life that consisted of nothing but swimming alone and wishing—for a moment when it would hurt her most.

When she got back to the resort, finally, limbs shaking as she opened the front door of their home, she heard the shower running upstairs.

"Is that you?" Miles called out as she walked past the bathroom.

"Yes!" Grace replied, trying to keep the terror out of her voice. "I'm home, sweetheart." He came out later, dressed in his Sunday clothes—chinos, a white button-down—and it was like it had never happened, any of it. Cold water. A woman with red hair. The belly of a crocodile. The snap of tree branches.

"Are you all right?" Miles asked later, slicing into his chicken with enthusiasm. She had left her plate untouched. "You seem shaky. Maybe you need to go back on your prescription."

It was waiting for her in her bathroom later, a microdose of lithium, just enough to dull her senses. She flushed it down the toilet, but knew that there would be one waiting for her every day, and that sometimes he would stand behind her and wait until she took it.

Day Three

Her: Anger is an adaptive response, you know. We inherited it from our ancestors. Fight or flight. I feel like flying right now. Of course, I can't go anywhere, can I?

Him: You can go wherever you want.

Her: Not after I confess. Then I won't be free anymore. But I'm still going to do it. It's time. No one can stop me.

Him: It's not about stopping you. It's about helping you.

Her: He had so many secrets, you know. So many things he thought I wasn't aware of. For example, I knew he had surveillance in all the rooms. So that he would always know, you see, exactly what was going on. I suppose in that way he was a little bit like the Wizard of Oz. Everyone thought he was a genius, that he magically knew everyone so well, knew exactly what their problems were, exactly what to do. But the truth was, he needed a little help. I understood that. I never said a word. I would have kept all his secrets, every single one, if only he had let me.

*S*hell opened her eyes. She didn't know where she was. Her mouth was dry. Her temples throbbed. But not from a hangover. Her vodka was gone. It had disappeared from her bags the first night, and she hadn't had the nerve to accuse Colin of hiding it.

Her eyes adjusted and roamed the octagonal villa with its vast white walls and large windows flanked by chocolate-brown shutters. A diffuser on the end table beside her piped out a lavender-citrus scent. There was a tiny bottle of essential oil beside it. She picked it up. It was called Harmony Blend.

"Use up to fifteen drops in a full tank of water to create a soothing atmosphere for you and your partner." The other half of the king-sized bed was unruffled, still tucked in tight. She had slept alone.

She could hear Colin's voice from the terrace. Two nights in a row spent like this. He was either sleeping on the couch in the other room, or not sleeping at all. She didn't care. She stood and donned the white robe. There were slippers, too, and she slid her feet into them. The sun was rising behind him on the terrace. She walked past the door and did not say "Good morning." There was a bowl of softening fruit still on a table near the terrace doors, a bottle of nonalcoholic champagne that had been sitting there, warming, since they had arrived. Now it was in a pool of tepid water. She picked up the phone. "Please bring me an egg white omelet, a pot of tea and a plate of fresh fruit. Small," she said to the attendant.

Colin's voice now: "Why the hell not? No. Don't do that. Yes, get him on the line. I'm here. I'm not going anywhere. Listen, guys, we have to get this right. It's not enough to be almost sure."

Papers had been slid under their door again, but she left them where they were. Just off the bathroom there was a deck with a saltwater hot tub. The view was of the beach and cliffs at the edge of Tulum, and a small portion of the main building. Shell had read in the property guide that there was a five-star restaurant, a spa, a gym, a yoga studio and an array of meeting rooms. "We are all in this together," Miles and Grace had assured her, after the embarrassment of the first night. She had believed that for about a minute before leaving the terrace, shamefaced. She still didn't know how she was going to face anyone. She wanted to be anywhere but here.

Shell slipped off her robe and let it puddle on the ground. She avoided looking at herself in the mirror as she walked naked over to the doors that led to the saltwater tub; this had become her habit. She didn't eat enough anymore, and in her twenties this would have revealed jutting clavicles and hips perfect for low-slung jeans and sexy shirts that hung from her frame as if they might fall off at any second. But she was in her forties now, and she knew her thinness just made her look older.

She lowered herself into the water and closed her eyes. Silence, brief, then her husband's voice, rising above all else. "For fuck's sake!" above the buzz of cicadas. "Goddamn it!" above the swooping flutter of a bird overhead. "Then call him again!" above the waves crashing in the distance.

They were due at their first counseling session in an hour. They hadn't spoken a word to one another in twenty-four.

The air-conditioning unit in Miles's office was too strong. Shell wrapped her arms around herself. When she did, Miles turned to Colin and raised his eyebrows as if he were on a stage and the people at the back of the theatre needed to be able to see his expression. "I wish I had a mirror," he said. "The two of you should see yourselves. You're behaving as if you haven't spoken to one another in days, as though you're both doing your best to wish the other person out of the room."

Silence from both of them. This was one of the things Shell had read about the Markells online, that their instincts were infallible. "I know who you are," Miles had said to her two days before. And now, she was sure, he was going to come to understand who she and her husband were together. Broken. Mismatched.

Miles sighed. "You're not giving me much to work with," he said. Shell heard sharp edges in his voice that hadn't been there on the first night. She thought of the other comments she had seen online, the ones she had written off because there had been only a handful compared with the hundreds of raves. *"Miles Markell is a charlatan. Travel to the 'last resort' at your own risk. My marriage is over now, no thanks to anyone at that place."* But some marriages simply didn't stand a chance, Shell had thought when she had read that. Everyone knew this. Shell knew hers didn't. She wasn't going to blame anyone else but herself and her husband, and the cruelty of life, for exactly why. *We tried everything*, she would be able to murmur, instead of the more painful truth.

"There's a huge amount of animosity in this room," Miles was saying. "Can either of you tell me why that is?"

Shell cleared her throat and tried to think of something to say to this man, the one she had met in the lobby two days before and felt she had known, the one who had marveled at her honesty, who had later so thoughtfully introduced her to the crowd as a wife and a mother who lived in the middle of a forest, beside a lake, whose husband worked at a gold mine while ignoring what he had at home. But now she couldn't speak. So she just sat, waiting for him to figure it all out, how ruptured they were. It would be a relief to be able to talk about it.

"We had an argument yesterday morning," Colin eventually said.

"And the other night on the terrace, in front of your peers," Miles said. "You argued then, too. About Colin's job, right? Did that argument continue, and now you're not speaking?"

More silence. Shell bit down on her inner bottom lip. Let *him* explain it. Let *him* get in trouble for constantly being on his phone, when that went against the rules of the place and everything they were supposed to be doing. Colin sighed and ran a hand through his hair. A clock ticked.

"I'll wait you out," Miles said.

"Shell got angry with me for being on the phone," Colin said.

"There it is," Miles said. "Not so hard, was it? Congratulations for being less stubborn than your wife."

Anger, sudden and fierce, no matter that this was goddamn Miles Markell. "*He* gets congratulated? He has a contraband device! And I'm not being stubborn. All of this is very hard to—"

Miles said, "I am an only child, and Grace and I were not blessed with children—but right at the moment, I'm getting a sense of what it must be like to have a sibling. This happens sometimes. Two people who were once in love become like roommates. They argue in an infantile way. There are a number of reasons this happens. Relationship ennui is incredibly common."

"Relationship *ennui*—it's a bit more than—"

"Listen." Now it was Colin who interrupted Shell. "I know I'm supposed to have relinquished all devices, but something happened at work just before we left for this trip and if I disappear, a lot of things could fall apart. There are safety issues at the mine, and it's my job to make sure they're taken care of."

Miles nodded. "I understand you have a high-pressure job," he said.

"Yeah," Colin said, relief in his voice. "And now, especially."

"You're a CEO . . ."

"Director of operations. The workers are preparing to start blasting the mine. But there are a few safety—"

"Excuse me?" Shell interjected. "Do you think about anything else, ever, aside from that damn mine?"

"You never listen to me when I talk about it anyway!" Colin said, days' worth of silence and anger bubbling to the surface. "Do you think this is what I would rather be doing? No! But it's my obligation. People's lives depend on it!"

"Why isn't your obligation ever to me? I need you to *see* me, I need—"

"I need you to stop shouting," Miles said.

"—you to actually look me in the eye and tell me you're hurting, too, that it's okay, that neither of us are over this and we're in it together—"

"*You threw a glass at my head!*" Colin shouted. "*You turned into a drunk!* I love you and I can't stand what you've become. It was either this or fucking rehab—"

"What *I've* become? You're a fucking workaholic! That's an addiction, too!"

"All right, that's enough," Miles said. But she didn't want to stop. She gathered more air, opened her mouth to speak.

"*I said stop!*" The sharpness of Miles's voice startled Shell. Reflexively, she glanced toward her husband, *help*, but he was staring at a fixed spot ahead of him.

"We are not going to get anywhere if you just sit here and argue for two weeks," Miles said slowly. He was holding up his hand, flat palmed. His wedding band glinted in the morning light. "And I may have learned more in these few minutes about the two of you than I would have if you'd actually attended the entire opening exercise together."

Colin was tapping his leg. Counting down the seconds. Shell knew him. *Tell him*, she willed. *Tell him why we're like this, Colin.*

"It's clear that you've backed your husband into a corner so many times he's shut down, and I'm here to tell you why."

She felt her rage, still coursing through her veins, but also a strange kind of relief after the outburst. The relief she had been looking for. "You think—you really think the reason my husband can barely look at me, the reason he refuses to see me is because I *attack* him? *Colin.*"

"I think we might need to do some one-on-one work before we can meet again as a threesome. You need help." Miles picked up his clipboard. "We're going to need to make some changes. I'm going to focus on working with Shell. And, Colin, you'll be moving onto Grace's roster. I'll double up with you, Shell. A session each morning and each afternoon, for the next few days at least. And, between that, anger management group."

"For both of us?"

"Just for you."

"What?" She laughed, incredulous.

"I believe you heard me," he said without looking up from his clipboard.

"*I* have to go to anger management?"

"Passive aggressive," he pronounced. He turned to Colin. "Your wife is a potential danger to herself and others right now," he said to her husband calmly, as if Shell weren't there. "And the drinking—you're right about that. She brought vodka to the resort. It was found in her bags. You are not to engage with her. You are to leave that to me."

"*You* searched my bags?"

"It's in the contract—"

"But we didn't sign that contract."

An expression on Miles's face she almost thought was uncertainty— and she could tell it was rare. But it passed. He shook his head as if to chase it away. "Really, Shell?" he said. "You want us to apologize for saving you from yourself?" She felt her body start to shake involuntarily.

"You can't just *search* our bags." She was embarrassed. But her anger was winning. This wasn't right. It couldn't be.

"You don't have to be here," Miles said, still even-toned. "Absolutely no one is forcing you. You are free to go. And we will, as is also included in the agreement you signed—or were supposed to sign—provide you with a full refund. Our satisfaction guarantee is one hundred percent."

Silence. Shell lifted her chin and waited for Colin to look at her but there was nothing, of course. Not a glance in her direction.

"How do I not engage with my own wife?" Colin asked, as if the previous exchange had not happened at all—and as if he didn't know exactly how it was possible to withdraw completely from the person you were married to.

"So, you're staying?" Miles said.

Colin nodded. "Of course."

"And what about you?" He looked at Shell. She struggled to recall what she thought she had seen in him, two days earlier. How comforted Miles had made her feel.

"Yes," Shell said quietly, but only because she couldn't imagine going home to their hollowed-out house.

"Okay. So let's move on. We're separating you for now. We do this in certain cases—rare, but it happens. Sometimes, facing the reality of a separation in a controlled setting helps couples understand what they stand to lose."

"So, what do we do?"

"Colin, go pack. A bellhop will be at your room within the hour for your bags. You'll be relocated to your own private villa."

She would be *alone*. She didn't hate this idea. Alone here was better than alone anywhere else. These beds held no memories. She had not tickled toes on any of the beds in any of the villas, had not attempted and mastered a complicated swaddle atop any of these sheets while her handsome, loving husband stood by and cheered her on.

Miles put down his clipboard and picked up the receiver of the telephone on his desk. "Shell, your anger management group starts in five minutes in the basement of the main villa, meeting room B. I'm going to send someone to pack up for you because you're moving to a new villa, too." This made her feel uncomfortable but she didn't speak. He wrote something down quickly on a notepad, then ripped off the sheet and handed it to her. "See you tomorrow."

There was a brown-and-white cowhide rug on the floor of the waiting area. It turned Johanna's stomach, so she looked at the bookshelves—except there weren't any books. The shelves were bare. She thought of her tiny cube of an office at work, the clutter everywhere, at her desk and everyone else's. Despite the stale microwave cooking smells in the air, the builder-beige walls, the constant noise—phones ringing, people talking too loud—she had loved that place. There was no greater punishment than staying far away from it.

She ran her finger along an empty shelf, then looked down. Her finger had encountered a rock a little smaller than her fist. She picked it up and examined it. It was heavy in her hand, rough textured. White, gray, brown, dotted with black.

"That's lava from Popocatépetl," said a familiar voice behind her, like a deejay's voice—a deejay on the night shift, running a show she knew might only be listened to by one desperate soul. In the moment before she turned around, she felt Grace come to stand beside her. She smelled shampoo and perfume, delicate spice. She turned. Grace's hair was smooth and shiny, flowing in soft waves down her shoulders. Her skin glowed with good health and likely good concealer, her lips shone, her smile revealed perfect teeth, snow-white. Johanna wished she had showered, at least, instead of tumbling out of bed late, pulling on the first clothes she found spilling out of the top of her still unpacked suitcase and shoving her hair into a ponytail. And she wished she didn't already know that the sheen on Grace was just a veneer. She closed her eyes for a moment. *You shouldn't have been there at the cenote in the first place. It was none of your business.* But it had kept her up the night before, all the questions she now had about Grace Markell. Now, Grace was smiling at her, expectant. It made her even more nervous. "Why are there no books?" Johanna said, her voice rushed and unnatural. "These are really nice built-ins. Look at the details. My dad was a cabinet maker. He would have—" She forced herself to stop the anxious chatter.

"Your father is gone?" Grace said.

"Shouldn't we be in your office for this?"

"Fair enough. But to address your first question, books are so subjective. I thought, *what if someone sees a book they really hate and it gets things off on the wrong foot?* So I decided I would collect things to put on the shelves. And then I thought about it too much. There are very few perfect items in this world." Her tone was thoughtful. "That lava rock—it's supposed to make anyone who touches it stronger. That's the legend. I love that there are so many legends in Mexico. And I liked that one in particular. I thought my clients might like that, too. But you're the only one who has ever touched it." Johanna looked down at the rock in her hands, then back up into Grace's gray eyes. She took in her entire face. Her heart was pounding too hard. She knew her next breath would be a gasping one if she didn't calm down. *Was it really you I saw swimming yesterday? Do you have any idea how seeing you like that made me feel? And who was he? Was that your lover coming down the path to meet you?* But, of course, she couldn't say that. She clamped her mouth shut. "Why don't you come on in," Grace said, and turned away while Johanna took in air as quietly as she could, then followed, still carrying the rock.

They walked down a short hall and into an office that had windows curving along a wall that faced the ocean. Grace indicated a heather-purple leather couch, then sat across from her in a matching swivel chair. There was a painting of a seahorse on one wall, all swirling strokes of paint, a prism of color. Her degrees were on the other wall: Department of Psychology, University of Texas at Austin. *Texas Longhorns*, Johanna remembered. She saw herself hanging a hat carefully on a bush, her own shaking hand and the water below.

Her eyes roamed the room again but there were no other personal effects, nothing except a pristine desk, all the drawers closed, their facings dotted with locks, and a box of tissues—the box was a blue argyle pattern—on the low table between them.

"Is it okay that I took it in here with me? The rock?" Johanna said, only just realizing she was still clutching it.

"Of course. I assumed you would," Grace said, smiling.

"But it's your one perfect thing."

"During your sessions, it can be *your* one perfect thing."

The rock had tiny craters in it, like the surface of the moon. Johanna imagined the heat of the fire that would have created the rock. "Thank you," she said.

"You're a social worker at a family services center in Santa Monica," Grace said.

"Was."

"Your intake file says you're on temporary leave."

"I don't know about that."

"About it being temporary?"

"Right."

"Do you miss your job?"

"I miss it a lot," Johanna admitted.

"What was it like?"

She remembered the longing she had felt for her old job in the waiting area when she had been looking at those empty shelves. "Chaos."

"Could you elaborate on that? What was chaotic about it?"

"It was messy and crowded there. The phones rang constantly, the waiting room was always full. Someone was always crying in the bathroom and pretending they weren't."

"Why not just talk to someone, if you were upset? Why pretend?"

Johanna ignored that question. "There was always junk in the lunchroom, donuts and cookies that everyone said they were not going to eat, but no one ever had time for lunch, so all of it always disappeared. And then, if someone took the last donut or cookie or whatever, someone would always leave an angry note. And we all thought it was hilarious." Johanna thought for a moment. It made her happy, to be able to talk about her work. Happy, and afraid. "Joking was a big part of it. Terrible jokes. It's hard to explain. You can't dwell on it too long, the way people hurt each other and themselves, and not be ruined by that. We were the helpers." Her throat ached when she said that. She fell silent and realized she had said too much without meaning to. She put the rock down on the table between them.

"I understand," said Grace. "Did any of your colleagues ever go to therapy, to talk about the things they saw—people hurting themselves, their families?"

The throat ache was getting stronger. Johanna could only shake her head.

Grace waited a moment, then leaned forward. "You do realize this is your chance, don't you?"

Johanna pressed her back against the couch. "What's that supposed to mean?"

"You can spend the next two weeks being closed with me, being defensive, maybe becoming confrontational because *you* are one of the helpers, and that means you don't go to therapy, right?"

"*Was* one of the helpers."

"But I'm a helper, too, Johanna. I can help you get out of this, but only if you accept that talking to someone like me will help you in all areas of your life, not just your marriage."

"I don't want to talk about it, ever. What happened in my office."

"Repressing trauma isn't healthy for the mind. It can lead not just to problems with intimacy, but to other very serious issues. Psychosis. Hallucinations. Manifestations of physical ailments. Have you experienced any of these?"

"That's not fair," she said, "for Ben to have written about what happened to me on his intake forms. It's my story to tell."

"Or not tell. Or avoid telling. I didn't get any of this from any forms. Your headache on the first night—"

"Was a migraine. I get them regularly and have for some time. Well before the—the incident at work." Johanna broke eye contact and looked down at Grace's bare feet, her perfectly painted toes. Johanna's own toes were painted apple red, and chipped. She hadn't even bothered to get a fresh pedicure before she came. She noticed a drip of Mango Punch paint on the nail of her big toe.

"When did the migraines start?"

"I don't remember," Johanna said automatically.

"Are you sure about that?"

Johanna looked up at her. "Listen, I don't know what you want from me. I just need a little more time, and it will all be fine."

"And you'll go back to work?"

"Not that. But I'll—I'll find something else to do. I'll move on, but in my own time."

Grace folded her hands on her lap. "My instincts tell me you've made suppressing your emotions a habit, in part because of the work you do and in part because of the person you are, because of your past—your childhood, maybe? I don't know, but we could get to the bottom of that together if you'd let us start."

"What happens when your instincts are wrong?" Johanna said. "What happens if I had the perfect childhood in a house with a picket fence and two perfect parents and—" Johanna realized she was about to cry. "Fuck," she said.

"Johanna. It's going to be okay. All you have to do is reach for what you need. What is it that you need? What is it that you want?"

Grace picked the rock back up and held it out, but Johanna didn't move. She saw the pool and the water ripples from the day before. She felt a chill down her spine. *Do you have a secret life, too, Grace?* But instead, "Why do you do this?" Johanna said. "Why is it so important to you? At this point, why do you even have to get down in the dirt with two dozen couples every two weeks? Why do you even bother?"

"Because without the work, we have nothing." Grace looked momentarily surprised, as if she hadn't meant to say that.

"But you two are so perfect. Aren't you?" She wasn't mistaken, Grace's eyes were guarded now. And Johanna felt guilty. Grace was a nice person. She shouldn't be doing this to her.

"We want to guide as many couples as possible toward what we have," Grace said, and it sounded like a script.

"Which is what, exactly?"

Grace looked down at the rock and was silent. "A happy marriage. A fulfilling relationship that helps us build the foundation we need to live the lives we want to live. But in order to achieve that, one of the first steps is getting in touch with what we really want." She looked up again and she seemed more certain than before. "Which brings me back to the question I asked you earlier. I'm going to keep asking until you can answer. *What do you want, Johanna?*"

She pressed the rock into Johanna's hand and their fingers touched. Johanna closed her palm around it and remembered herself at the market the day before, her hands on top of a pile of Frida Kahlo fridge magnets while she tried to get a better look at the woman a few tables up. The woman who had had dark hair, like Grace's, but uncombed and crammed inside a baseball cap, with wisps frizzing around her neck. She had been wearing mirrored aviator sunglasses, but her long, tanned limbs and her easy, white-toothed smile had seemed familiar. And her voice. A voice she knew. Johanna had moved toward her, pulled as if by a magnet. *Is that Grace Markell?* she had wondered. *Could it be?*

The woman who might have been Grace had seemed so at home at the market, so much more comfortable than she did at the resort, and yet completely out of place—which was how Johanna felt almost all the time. A stranger, no matter where she went, but desperate to find the one place she belonged. When the woman had suddenly started to move through the trees like a nymph, Johanna had followed instinctively, recognizing an escape route when she saw one, desperately wanting one for herself, too. She had ignored the underbrush that tore at her ankles. The skin was still smarting today, and Johanna had developed some sort of rash.

Eventually, Johanna had seen the woman's hat on the ground. She had bent over to pick it up. She had continued to move, staying as far behind as she could, wincing at the way the dead branches crackled under her feet and at the tingling pain in her ankles, as if dozens of fire ants were biting her.

And then, all at once, the woman had stopped and tilted her head up like an animal sensing a predator and sniffing the air. "Hello?" she had said, and Johanna had stood still, far behind her, closing her eyes and hoping to disappear.

A splash. Johanna had opened her eyes and the woman had vanished. *Was* it a splash she had heard, above the cracking of the branches, the pounding of her heart, the heaviness of her breathing? She had looked around and felt panic rising. What if she had fallen? Johanna had stepped forward and seen a wooden sign to her left, the writing on it faint: *Cuidado.* She had searched her memory for the meaning of the Spanish word. *Take care.* She had stepped forward again, until she was at the edge of the world, maybe. But really, she had been standing on a small platform jutting out over a swimming hole way down below. A crocodile was painted on a sign to her left. Foliage and vines plunged over the pool's edges and the sun flowed in and settled down there. A cave, but upside down. Johanna had looked beside her feet and seen the discarded tank top and shorts, the woven bag beside them. Her cheeks were a hundred flaming suns. She leaned forward, lost her footing for a moment and felt disappointed when she didn't tumble headlong into the water, taking away all confusion, all choice, forcing whatever was going to happen to just *happen.* The woman was swimming in the pool below, back and forth, determined. The sunlight illuminated her, like she was under a spotlight.

I want to be like that, Johanna thought, staring down at her. *I want to be that free.* She raised her hand to shield her eyes. She had no power over herself now. She couldn't have walked away if she had wanted to, even though she knew she should, even though she knew she was invading a private moment. The woman in the water had turned her body and started to swim in the other direction—and that was when Johanna got a clear view of her face. It had felt like a lightning bolt: it was her. It was Grace. She was almost sure of that—and she was certain Grace was terrified. Johanna had felt so sorry then, for causing that fear. She had backed away and fled the way she had come.

And then, as she ran: a man up ahead on the path. He had on a hat and sunglasses, too, and he bent his head down as Johanna passed. She was too embarrassed to look at him anyway, so the memory of him was nothing but a shadow—although she had been sure there was a cell phone in his hand, that just a second before she saw him he had been talking into it. She had started to run, had crashed out of the jungle and one of the women at the market had shouted at her as she ran. "The cenote is closed! You can't swim there!"

Out on the road she had chased a *collectivo*, her legs feeling heavy. She had been relieved when the *collectivo* stopped for her, and disappointed, too, as if she were being forced to wake from a dream. Back to reality and away from the strange and unreal world she had inhabited, for just a moment.

"Johanna?" Grace said.

"Yes?"

"Are you still in here with me?"

"Of course."

"Have you given my question some thought?"

"I'm fine." She struggled to make this seem true.

"That's not what I asked." Grace sighed, shifted in her chair. "A prescription was found in your luggage, and it wasn't in your name."

"What?" This shifted her thoughts, tipped them like a jug pouring out cold water. The memory of the cenote disappeared entirely. She tried to calm down. "I thought I'd just misplaced them."

Grace's tone was firm. "I know it feels like an invasion, but this is for your own good. It's time to confront the real issue. It wasn't a good decision, Johanna. Bringing a prescription across the border that's not in your name."

Johanna flinched. She put the lava rock down. It knocked hard against the table. "I hadn't even thought of that," she said, feeling foolish. "I'm just so used to—carrying them with me." She closed her eyes. She really didn't want to talk about this. Anything but this.

"You need help," Grace said, her voice gentle. "You shouldn't be taking prescriptions that aren't yours. If you get another headache and you need something, you can visit the nurse. Meanwhile, I have an idea." Grace wrote something down, then handed Johanna a slip of paper. *Anger management. Group therapy. 1:00 p.m. Main villa, meeting room B.*

Johanna blinked a few times. "*This* is what you think I need? Anger management?"

"Yes."

"But I'm not angry. I'm . . . something else."

Grace stayed silent.

"What if I say I won't go?"

"What if I asked you to trust me, just this once?"

Johanna thought of all the bargains she had made with herself, over the weeks, months, years. *Just this once* was a mantra. Maybe *just this once*, it would work.

A timer dinged softly, and Grace leaned over and touched a small Venetian glass clock Johanna hadn't noticed when she sat down. Another perfect item. Perhaps Grace had more of them than she knew.

"Our time's up." Grace picked up her clipboard. "I'm booking you in for an enrichment session with me later. You can talk about what you felt at the anger management group then. Do we have a deal?"

"Yes." *Just this once.*

―――

Johanna walked down the basement stairs slowly, like a teenager dawdling on the way to class. Two men passed her on the stairs, then a woman. She meandered down a hallway with wooden floors and terra-cotta sconces on the walls, each filled with a succulent plant and a dim light. Eventually, she stood in front of a door that said MEETING ROOM B until she realized that she was either going to have to go in or admit to Grace Markell that she lacked the courage to trust a stranger.

She pushed the door open and entered. It was like a college tutorial room: white screen up front and a large, U-shaped table facing it, with chairs lined up around it, half of them filled with people Johanna couldn't bear to make eye contact with. There was a window on one side of the room that looked out at a garden. There were benches, hammocks and a fountain, but no one was out there. Johanna took the seat closest to the door just as Ruth said, "All right, I don't think there are any more stragglers. It's time to begin." She rolled up the sleeves of the lab coat she always seemed to be wearing.

The windows opened out into the garden, but the air was stagnant in the room. Johanna wanted to pour herself a glass from the ever-present jug of cucumber-and-lime-infused water sitting at the front, but now that everyone was taking seats she didn't want to stand and draw attention to herself.

"Okay," Ruth said from the front of the room. Her lips were again painted bright pink, in contrast to her austere, clinical clothing. "Welcome to session one of anger management group therapy. You're brave, all of you, to be here. Can you say that with me? *We are all brave to be here.*" There were a few reluctant mumbles, but no one quite got the timing right and Johanna didn't even attempt it.

"We have an hour," said Ruth. As if having an actual hour were some kind of special gift. Johanna found herself scowling into her lap. "All the work is completed before we leave this room. Does that make sense?"

A few nods. Johanna picked chipped polish off a fingernail. Made perfect sense to her. She'd sent clients to anger management hundreds of times and it almost never worked. She looked out the window into the courtyard and felt frustration rising. You couldn't even see the ocean in here. What was the point of hosting these retreats in Mexico when, most of the time, they all could have been anywhere?

"There are no rules in here. This is your chance to talk, to get it out, to be angry if you need to, to cry if you want to, and this is also your chance to call each other out, to work with each other, to express it when anger manifests itself as hurtful or disrespectful, to be open about how you're making one another feel. This work is going to elicit an emotional response, but you're going to need to listen. Any questions?"

A pause that stretched, then festered.

"You're all very uncomfortable, I can tell. And that's normal. But anger is normal, too, guys." *Please stop talking to us like you're our volleyball coach*, Johanna thought. "Everyone feels it. In fact, most people feel it every single day." Behind her, there was the sound of a door opening and footsteps. "Oh—we have one more joiner," Ruth said. "Hello there—um?" She consulted her clipboard. "I don't think you signed up."

Johanna was surprised to see Shell, the woman from the first night on the terrace. Her burnished hair was tied back in a low ponytail and she wore white linen pants that draped over her legs as if they had been custom-made for her. She didn't look like she belonged here—not in this room of angry and confused people and not at this resort. She was too perfect. Except for the desolate sadness of her eyes. That was unmistakable to someone like Johanna.

"Miles sent me," Shell said. She handed Ruth a slip of paper similar to the one Grace had given Johanna, then walked around the table and sat beside Johanna. Their eyes met and Shell looked away quickly.

"Okay, let's get back to it." Ruth checked her watch. "Anger." She looked up at them. "It's an adaptive emotional response to hurt, injustice, fear and frustration. It's natural, but we still need to deal with it. Because anger can be destructive—especially in relationships.

No matter what, you can't attack the person you're in a relationship with." Ruth swiveled her head, looking each group member in the eye. Everyone looked away from her. "Who thinks they belong here?" she asked.

A few hands rose. Johanna kept hers in her lap.

"Okay—how many of you feel you need to hold *in* your anger, or a part of who you are? Hold yourself in until you feel like you might explode—and then, eventually do?"

Johanna didn't move.

"How many feel they are arguing constantly with spouses, children or co-workers?" Johanna clenched her hands into fists in her lap. This was bullshit. "Anyone experience reckless disregard for rules, physical violence, such as hitting, loud shouting, door slamming, threats of violence against people or property, out-of-control behavior, such as breaking things or reckless driving?"

Reckless. Johanna stared fixedly out the window, at a statue of a woman holding a jug at a benign angle; the water flowed slowly and the woman's marble head tilted downward to watch it with tenderness. The grass around her was brown in patches. What had this place been like before? She imagined wild beach and jungle, imagined things back the way they should be.

"Focus is important, everyone," Ruth said, and Johanna realized she meant her, that she was watching her pointedly. "I can close the blinds if the view is distracting," Ruth said.

"What view? Please no, we'll suffocate," Johanna murmured, and beside her she saw Shell Williams smile for just a second.

Then Shell spoke. "I have a question. I argue with my husband and I sometimes feel angry with him. But the rest of that doesn't apply to me, so why am I here?"

"Shelly, it's not productive to distance yourself from the group. You've just indicated that you *have* experienced one or more anger issue—"

"It's Shell. And I indicated that I have *one* of the issues."

"You don't have to experience all of them to potentially have a problem. Got it?"

Shell didn't reply. Johanna was sure that if they made eye contact again, they would both burst out laughing. She also knew there was a very thin line between laughing and crying.

"Okay, now, listen up. We're each going to share the last time we got really angry. What exactly happened, and why? But you have to be succinct. I've got a timer here." She held up a blue egg with a happy face on it. "Five minutes is the maximum. Let's start with you. Dave?" She indicated a heavyset man across from Johanna who was wearing a red golf shirt and khaki shorts.

Dave's chin disappeared into his neck when he opened his mouth. He said, "Oh, goodness, I get angry all the time." His voice, his North Carolina drawl, his gentle laugh, the hardness in his eyes—Johanna had encountered guys like him before, and her revulsion was instant. "The last time I got really angry, I stubbed my toe on a rock in our garden, cut it open, started yelling, caused a fuss. The thing is, in the moment, my anger seems like the only thing there is, you know?"

Nods from around the circle. "And I know it's not about the rock, I know when I start yelling at Christine to throw all the goddamn rocks from her *goddamn* garden—" a few laughs but Johanna could hear the anger rising in his voice and, she couldn't help it, her heart started to pound "—that what I'm really riled up about is maybe something that happened at work or maybe the fact that we've got three kids in college and I worry there isn't going to be enough to go around, you know? I never totally lose it. I don't *hit* her, nothin' like that, I swear, I would *never*—but the things I say. I'm ashamed of them."

Johanna's palms started to sweat. *I've lived with a man like you, I saw my mother hurt by a man like you and I hate you, I hate you. Why should anyone believe you, that you don't hit her?*

"I'm ashamed," he said again.

"No, you're not." It was her own voice, shaking with anger.

"Excuse me?"

Johanna looked straight at him. "I said, no, you're not. You are not ashamed. You think your wife is your punching bag."

"I told you, I don't hit her!"

"Maybe. But you know what verbal abuse is."

"Who do you think you are, exactly?" The man was shouting, turning to Ruth. "Can't you do something to shut her up?"

"Your words had an effect on her and she's explaining it to you," Ruth said calmly.

The room was now silent.

"Johanna? Perhaps it would be a good time to share your *own* experience with anger?"

Johanna shook her head. She was breathing hard, like she'd just run a race.

"You know what, actually?" A man's voice. He was sitting across from Johanna, beside Dave, and was probably about her age, with blond hair that thinned pathetically at the top and a pale beard that did not make up for it. "Honestly? That kind of triggered me, you going after Dave like that. It reminded me of my wife, and the way she overreacts—" As the man's voice wobbled, Johanna could hear it, all at once, the voice of the man who had walked into her office that afternoon, his voice quivering with impotent rage, reverberating with loss of control. She felt it then, the cold metal of it against her jaw, and the shock that it could have happened—even though she and all her colleagues had been making stupid jokes about something like that happening to one of them for years, that it was actually happening *to her.*

She stood, intending to leave the room and tell Grace later that she had been wrong, beyond wrong. But halfway to the door, she thought of Cleo. About how Cleo had needed someone to speak up for her and not even Johanna had succeeded, in the end. She turned, she stopped. "Do you all want to know what anger can lead to? All of you? Do you want to know?" She walked to the front of the room and stood beside Ruth, who now looked alarmed. "I'm a social worker and one of my client's husbands started the way you started, Dave, shouting at her, calling her a dumb cunt when he stubbed his toe on a rock, or whatever. Then it escalated. He started hitting her. Only in places that left bruises where no one could see—but then someone *did* see, and she felt pretty sure she might end up dead. So I helped her move with their kids to a women's shelter. I helped her find a subsidized apartment. I helped her find a job. Her life was starting to look up and a hell of a lot brighter. But that asshole went to Walmart, bought himself a rifle, waited for her outside her apartment, shot her dead, left her lying there beside her car, then drove to my office. He had the gun in a gym bag. He walked right in and pressed the gun against my jaw and he told me I was a piece of shit and I should be dead. He didn't kill me, though. He went out to his car and shot himself. So this is what your fucking anger leads to. This is what you get from it. And I'm not interested. I'm not interested at all. And no one in here should be, either."

She was shaking. But she didn't care. She was glad she'd said it. "Oh, but sorry. Sorry if I *triggered* you," she added as she looked at the men's shocked faces. Then she left the room.

She went to her bungalow. Her head was aching again, not as bad as the day before, but she knew it could easily get worse. She longed for the oblivion of those pills. Cleo's pills. She knew it was wrong. Grace had been right. They weren't for her and they were way too strong— barely even legal, or not legal at all, knowing Cleo. Johanna could see her raised eyebrow, her impetuous smile. *Come on, live a little. And you sure can't live with those damn headaches all the time.*

She felt the embarrassment again of Grace's gentle admonishment. Those pills had been all she had of Cleo, but what a foolish thing, to bring them with her here. Was it possible she had welcomed it? Had she been subconsciously willing to go so far to avoid coming to this resort that she would have risked a drug charge? She rubbed her forehead. *You really do need help.*

It should have been a relief that the drugs were gone, but it wasn't. Just their presence, just that canister, smooth in her hand, bearing

Cleo's name, had given her courage. Sometimes that was all it took, just to look down at them and remember freedom, or the idea of it. Gone, now.

For a moment, she imagined the lava rock, and herself telling Grace Markell the truth about everything. She couldn't. Not yet.

But maybe she would.

*S*hell was walking down the hallway, away from the room that housed the anger management group, when she heard Ruth's voice. "Shell! Wait up."

She slowed reluctantly.

When Ruth caught up, she said, "You didn't show up this morning for your appointment."

"What do you mean?"

"To email your daughter and your mother from my office?"

"Oh. Right. I . . . Oh, yes. Sorry. I overslept."

"I have a moment now. Would you like to come on up?"

"Oh. Sure. Thanks."

Ruth's high-heeled black pumps clicked against the floor, reminding Shell of the hooves of a horse. They headed down the hall toward a door that Ruth opened to reveal a spiraling staircase. "I'm on the top floor, and there are no elevators," she said over her shoulder. "Running up and down is how I get my cardio."

"Um. Great."

Her office was in a cupola, small and close but with windows on all sides. "This view," Shell found herself saying. "You can see for miles."

Ruth indicated the small mahogany desk. "You should be able to open the browser and log into your email, but let me know if you have any problems."

Shell realized Ruth wasn't going to leave the room. Instead, she sat down in a chair that faced Shell, took out a notebook and started writing. Shell logged into her email, then hesitated. Eventually, with no other choice, she opened a new email and typed in her mother's email address.

Dear Mom,

I miss you and Zoey so much. I hope the two of you are having fun. What did you do today? Tell me all about it, tell me everything. And please, give Zoey hugs and kisses from Mumma, and tell her I love her to the ends of the earth. Tell her Mumma's going to go swim in the ocean.

You always used to say I'd understand what true love meant when I had a child of my own, and I do understand that now, Mom. It breaks the heart, doesn't it? I'm sorry for all the ways I must have broken yours and disappointed you. I don't think that's going to change anytime soon.

I'll write again soon. Would you write back? I'd love it if you'd write back.

Yours,
Shell

Shell stood, legs shaky. "You must miss your daughter a lot," Ruth said.

She swallowed hard. "I do."

"Don't worry, it will get easier. It's only two weeks. It flies by. People don't want to go home, when the time comes. You'll probably be one of them."

Shell left, feeling unsettled as she walked down the stairs.

ou're a liar. You're a bad person. I should kill you. You should be dead. Johanna held the lava rock from their earlier session tight in her hand. Grace had handed it to her just before she sat down and welcomed her back for their enrichment session. She was at the end of the story she had already told earlier, in anger management group. But she couldn't go on.

"What did he say to you?"

"Why would you think he said anything?"

"Johanna." Gentle reproach in her voice.

"Isn't it enough to have a gun pressed to my neck?"

"Enough for what?"

The rock felt too small in her hands. She wished for an entire mountain. She put it down on the table in front of her, beside the tissue box.

"How do you feel when you talk about him and think about him?"

Johanna could see his face, and she could see Cleo's face. She felt like screaming. She kept her mouth closed.

"What is his name?"

"Was. His name was Chad Von Hahn."

"What does he feel like?"

She closed her eyes, too. "He feels too big. He feels bigger than he was. I can hear him."

"What did he say to you?"

Liar. Bitch. Whore. Dyke. "Nothing."

"Johanna?"

"Yes?"

"Open your eyes. Stay in here with me. No one's going to hurt you."

Johanna opened her eyes and she did feel better. Grace's face was becoming familiar already, her presence reassuring. She tried not to think of what she possibly knew about her, after witnessing her solitary swim in the cenote—and she was still grappling with the fact that she felt something like jealousy when she thought of the man on the path, the man Grace had surely been waiting for. But knowing Grace had secrets, too, was making it easier. Or, as easy as reopening an agonizing wound that wouldn't heal could be.

"What did he say?"

Johanna swallowed. "He kept saying it over and over. 'I should kill you. You—you fucking dyke.'"

"How did that make you feel?"

"Like I deserved to die."

"That man needed help. You understand that, don't you? He was mentally ill and he needed help and he didn't get it, and you paid the price for that. The things he said had no bearing on reality—only his own twisted one. You are not a disgusting person who deserves to die. You are innocent, Johanna. This man should not be allowed to have control over you. Get it out, and once it's out in the open, we can deal with it."

Johanna kept her eyes locked on Grace's. She thought, *You are the kindest person.* She thought, *But you have no idea.* She thought, *I am many things, but innocent is not one of them.* She was able to start speaking again. "Every time he said I was horrible and that I deserved to die, I thought of all the times in my life I really had wanted to die and how long it had taken me to stop saying those exact same things to myself, inside my own head. I wouldn't say I saw my life flash before my eyes, not exactly, but I saw my life as it could have been. And I didn't *want* to die. I wanted to start living. It was only later, after the shock wore off, that I realized I didn't deserve to be happy."

"Why are you so convinced that you don't deserve to be happy?"

Johanna just shook her head.

"What happened next?"

"I don't know why he didn't kill me. I really don't."

"What happened next? Tell me."

"The police asked me endless questions. Every time I explained what had happened, I thought maybe there would be a different ending, but there never was. They drove me home and I waited for Ben. I hadn't let anyone call him. I had lied and said he was in court and couldn't be reached. He came in and said, 'Hey, I heard something on the news just now,' and then he saw my face. And then—I told him we needed to separate. I told him we were over."

"Why, on that day, in that moment, did you say that to him?"

"Because I wasn't going to be such a coward anymore. I don't love Ben. Not the way he needs me to. I've always wanted to love him, and I've been able to imagine what my life would be like if I did love him, but I don't. I care about him, I admire him, but the way a wife should love a husband? I just don't." It felt like hitting water, cool and clear, not the hard, unforgiving ground she had expected. She'd never admitted this to anyone but now it was out.

"Why do you say that, the way a wife *should* love a husband?"

Johanna looked down at her hands. "I don't know. It just came out that way."

"Okay. So now, keep walking me through this day. This terrible, tragic day you had. You came home, and you told Ben what you wanted, and . . . ?"

"I was in shock, I guess. And so was he. Immediately, he was on the phone with the police, a psychologist, his parents, he was trying to solve it, the way Ben does. It all became a blur."

"Try to remember."

"A doctor came. He prescribed sedatives. I tried to go back to work a few days later—and I had a breakdown in the parking lot." Not exactly the truth. Not the truth at all.

"Can you describe your breakdown?"

Johanna saw herself sobbing into her co-worker Sandra's shoulder, crying, *I don't want to go home. Please, no. This can't be happening. I'm so sorry.*

"Johanna, you've allowed this man to convince you that you're inadequate. But he's a killer, and he's mentally ill, and he's dead, and you have to start living your life."

She felt cornered now. "It's not that simple."

"Will you give me the chance to help you see why it *is* that simple?"

In Grace's eyes, Johanna saw such kindness and such hope, such belief in Johanna as a person, such a deep desire to help her. It was familiar, all of it. She knew what it was like to believe in another person the way Grace was believing in her. And suddenly, all Johanna wanted was to make her happy.

Maybe she could.

Cleo was dead. Chad had killed her. He was dead, too. No one at this resort knew the whole story, no one but Johanna. And she didn't have to tell it. There was no one holding a gun to her head, not now.

"Yes," Johanna said. "Yes, I will give you the chance to show me how simple it can be."

Grace smiled and Johanna felt happy. It was the first time she had felt happy in a long while.

Day Four

Her: Everything would be different, he'd still be alive,
     if he had just chosen me. If he hadn't insisted on
     having more.

*S*hell picked up the room service menu, then put it down. She wanted nothing. She wasn't permitted in the restaurant—the rules of the separation had been left on her bedside table: walks and other recreation were permitted; meals had to be ordered from room service and consumed in the bungalow. But she had yet to order anything. What she wanted wasn't in this room. There was nothing here. No vodka. No more sleeping pills—strong ones her doctor had given her, the year before, offering instant oblivion that she had been parceling out for herself. Not even so much as a Tylenol. She wanted to be angry about this, but she only felt defeated.

As the first fingers of morning's light reached into the world, she dressed and left her empty bungalow and headed toward the beach. The clouds dotting the horizon were the color of an old bruise, the sky behind them was a band of gold, and every other inch of the sky was dull gray.

She walked for twenty minutes, until she couldn't see the resort anymore, until she could pretend it didn't exist. There was nothing up ahead but more rocks and more beach. Not a soul in sight. She sat down in the damp sand and stared out at the sea. How much time passed? She had no idea. She was stiff and sore when she finally stood. She was always misplacing tracts of time now. "What did you do today?" Colin would ask her when he got home from work. She never had any answer.

Mumma's going to swim in the ocean. She looked down the beach to ensure it was still deserted, then untied the scarf she had been wearing, slid down her linen pants, took off her sleeveless silk shirt, folded them all and placed them on a nearby rock. At the edge of the sea, she dipped in a toe. The ocean was as warm as the saltwater pools on the terraces of the bungalows. She began to walk into the water, feeling silken sand, tiny rocks, ribbons of sea grass as she went deeper. Soon, she lifted her legs and began to float. Then she turned on her back for a moment, the ocean holding her. The sun was still climbing and its light was still weak, but she wasn't afraid. She rolled over and started to swim again, away from shore.

"Shell!" A voice on the wind. "Shell!" She knew this voice.

A silhouette on the beach, that voice, her name, for a moment she thought it was her husband, come to find her, but *he wouldn't, he doesn't care.* She was treading water, staring at the shore. It was Miles Markell, and he was wearing running clothes, he was stripping off his shirt and walking into the water. She pedaled her legs slowly, made Vs in the water with her arms, but she didn't swim toward him because this wasn't happening, he wasn't doing this—was he? She watched in detached wonder as he walked through the water. Soon, his face came into focus and she realized he was angry.

"What are you doing?" he shouted. The water was up to his waist.

"Swimming," she shouted back. The ocean water no longer felt bathtub-warm.

"Come on. Back to shore."

"I can swim just fine."

"All by yourself, in the ocean, in the dark?"

"It's hardly dark. The sun is rising."

"Do you see how far you've gone?"

She thought she heard fear in his voice, in addition to the anger. She floated for another moment, then started to swim, obedient, back toward shore.

Soon, she could touch the smooth ocean bottom again. He was only a few feet away. "There," she said. "Fine. See?" She shivered and tried to pretend she was wearing more than a soaked bra and underwear in front of her therapist. He handed her his shirt. "Dry off with this," he said. "Get your clothes back on. This area of the beach isn't safe. It's full of jellyfish and lionfish and barracuda and sometimes worse."

She turned away from him and did as she was told, dressing quickly.

"You're a sad woman," Miles said, his tone and expression thoughtful.

"Well, shit. You could say that again, Doctor," she said as he pulled his shirt back over his head. This wasn't the voice of the bitter old crone she had become, she realized. It wasn't even the voice of the somewhat carefree woman she had once been. This was someone else entirely, a new person altogether.

He laughed. "Ah. Your bluntness. It's your greatest strength, and maybe your greatest weakness." He frowned for a moment. "But you shouldn't be vulgar."

His words pulled her in two directions. "Am I being analyzed, right here on the beach?"

"At Harmony, you can be analyzed anywhere," he said.

"I'm not going to another anger management session," she said. "If I'm saying what I mean, if I'm being blunt—you can forget it. It was a disaster."

He looked out at the ocean, then back at her. His expression was softer. "I read something once," he said, "about the very thin line between anger and desolation—between sadness and rage, even. It came to mind, when we were in our session yesterday. I could be wrong, but I don't think so. I *do* think you need to attend that group. But I'm also willing to trust that you know what's best for you right now. If you don't want to go, you don't have to. I see a strength in you I don't see in many others. Perhaps a strength I've never seen before."

She could feel her bra making a wet patch on her shirt, and, as if he could read her thoughts, he glanced down at her chest and she felt embarrassed heat creep into her cheeks. But he kept talking as if it were all perfectly normal.

"I know you were frustrated yesterday, and frankly, I don't blame you for that. I was thinking about it as I was jogging along the beach this morning. I lost my temper with you, and I shouldn't have—but there are moments with some patients when I realize two weeks might not be enough, when I long for the luxury of time, months and months to work together, maybe even years. And maybe I was testing you." He looked at her for a long moment. "It's a tradeoff, what we do here. I firmly believe we help more couples than we could if we had a more regular practice, but there are certain things we have to give up. Yesterday, I wanted to push you because I saw something in you, Shell. I understood what you needed. So I shouted, I pushed your boundaries— and I shouldn't have been so harsh, not yet. I'm sorry."

She felt shaky, a combination of relief and trepidation. *Not yet.* "I didn't feel comfortable," she said. "I didn't feel like I could trust you."

"I'm sorry," he said again. "I will earn your trust. That will be *my* work for this week. And maybe beyond?" They stood in silence for a moment.

"What do you mean?"

"It's all right. Not right now. Why were you swimming away like that?"

She hesitated. "It's probably a very good thing you showed up," was all she said.

"Did it help, the swimming away?"

"For a moment."

"Do you want to let me help you? So you won't want to swim away from your life anymore? So you'll have a life you love?"

She felt her eyes fill with tears and wished they wouldn't; she was surprised when he reached for her and pulled her into a spontaneous embrace. Her cheek was against his chest, against the shirt that she had rubbed over her body and now smelled like salt water and her own skin, and his. *At Harmony, you can be analyzed anywhere.*

"Why do you do this?" she said into his chest and she felt him stiffen. "I'm sorry. Maybe I should have asked you during the question and answer period, but we weren't there, because we were fighting. Why do you and Grace make this your life's work, helping people like me?"

At first she thought he wasn't going to answer her, but then he started to speak. "I was raised by a single mother. My father left my mother when I was very young and she was never the same. My whole life, I imagined what my childhood would have been like if they had actually tried, both of them. If my father had stayed, if my mother had made him want to. I imagined how different my life might have been."

"But you seem okay."

"I really have to work at it." He lowered his hands to her arms and held her away from him as he looked into her eyes. "It's almost impossible, to really know another person's inner life. And as for why I do what I do—some days, I'm not sure. I've been doing this for a very long time. Everyone burns out. I'm happy you're here, because what I see in you, it's making me want to get up in the morning and work hard." Another silence. She was almost smiling. Now she shivered and he rubbed his hands briskly up and down her arms before pulling her into another embrace that was confusing and perfect.

"It's going to be okay," he whispered. "You just have to be brave. I'm with you. I'm here. I want to help you. And I know you're going to let me."

She looked over his shoulder. There was a gap in the clouds and she could see the sun's rays casting ladders into the ocean. She stood in his arms and counted the rays, stopped when she got up to twelve. "I lost something," she said. "*We* lost something. I want to let you help me, but it's hard to talk about."

"Everyone here has lost something. We'll take the journey together. All will be well."

She could feel his chest moving up and down against hers. She kept counting the rays of the sun—ladders to heaven, someone had once called them. Maybe her mother? Thirteen. Fourteen. And then, suddenly, more than she could count and that was how much she missed Zoey and always would and she'd never be able to explain it to anyone, but she was going to try, she decided, eyes dazzled by those ladders of morning light she desperately wished she could climb. She was going to try it this way, Miles's way, instead of attempting to drown herself at the bottom of a bottle or an ocean. "Thank you," she whispered.

Movement on the beach, a figure jogging past, a blond ponytail, and Miles pulled back from her as Shell watched Ruth moving down the coastline.

"We should get back," Miles said. "Come on."

A knock at the door of Grace's office. She checked her watch. Johanna and Ben were a little early, but that was all right—Grace was ready for them. "Come on in," she said, rising from her desk.

But it wasn't the couple: it was Ruth, wearing her running clothes and breathing heavily. Even though she'd clearly been out running, she was still in full makeup. The year before, when Grace's mother had died and Grace had returned to Texas for a week, Ruth asked her to bring back a long list of cosmetics. The urgency of the request had given Grace pause, and she had brought it up with Miles. "Don't you think it's weird for her to request studio-grade concealer when I'm going to my mother's funeral?" she had asked. "She looks like a televangelist's wife. She looks like someone else. Is this what she thinks you want her to look like?"

"Are you really grieving?" Miles responded, ignoring her other questions.

"You still grieve a mother you haven't seen in almost twenty years," Grace said, and marveled for a moment at how much care they took to unearth their clients' secrets while burying their own. When she went home to sort out her mother's house, she'd found a letter in her mother's things. It was the only thing she brought back with her. *Dear Garrett, I'll get right to the point, I am the son you and a woman named Barbara Moore gave up when you were teenagers. I don't blame you, I swear, but I would really like to get in touch. Barbara Moore has yet to answer any of my letters. I just want to know where I came from.* Miles didn't know about the letter. No one did except her mother, and her mother was dead. They were masters, the two of them, at hiding the truth. Why did Grace even keep it? What was she going to do about it? It was a piece of her brother. It was all she had. It was family. It was a chance that, one day, Grace would be someone else, someone who might be able to explain to this young man where he had come from.

"Oh, good," Ruth said now. "I've caught you before your session. Johanna Haines and her husband, is it?" Her voice was like acid, full of innuendo that didn't belong in it and caused Grace to bristle, though she tried not to. She knew she had to be gentle with Ruth, especially now. It hadn't even been a year since the pregnancy, the baby. And she knew how long it took to heal from such a loss: forever. It never did heal. "I saw you had an enrichment session with Johanna on the schedule and I realized what you were doing," Ruth continued.

"What do you mean by that?" Grace said, startled now.

"How could you use my anger management group session, the first one I have been allowed to run on my own and something very important to my research project, for your own purposes, how *dare* you?"

"Is this about Miles, and the research project he took credit—"

"No! I'm not here to talk about that. Why are you always bringing up the past? This is about you hijacking my anger management group with your own agenda!"

"I don't understand. Please sit down." She glanced at her watch. "I do have a few minutes for us to discuss this, whatever it is you're trying to tell me."

"I am not one of your clients. Don't treat me that way."

Grace tried to temper the annoyance but couldn't. "No, you aren't. You're my employee."

Ruth gasped. "Your *employee*?"

"I'm sorry. No. I didn't mean it like that. It's not like that, you're family. Ruth. Please. Forgive me. Sit down."

Ruth sat, then leaned forward and gripped the edges of the couch cushions. "Just because you're the star, just because you're the *wife*, doesn't mean that *I* am nothing."

"Ruth, please. You're important, too."

"I haven't been feeling that way lately," Ruth said. There were tears in her voice and alarm bells in Grace's brain. Ruth rubbed her forehead, then her face. She winced as she did so. "I just feel so . . . overwhelmed."

"Do you think you need a break?" Grace asked gently. "Maybe a short sabbatical to work on your research project on anger and intimacy in a more intensive way?"

"You want me to leave? I've already moved into the main villa. You want me to *leave here, too*?"

"No. No! That's not what I meant." She felt like a bird flying through the air, mistaken—hitting a window, falling to the ground. She hesitated again. Ruth wasn't her department. She was Miles's. But clearly not. Clearly he had been neglecting her. "Ruth, I thought that move was temporary, just you taking some time to rest, after the baby . . ."

"Please, don't."

"I know it hurts. I understand."

"You have no idea. I didn't deserve it, not the way you did."

Grace gritted her teeth, glanced at her watch. "Okay, Ruth. I really don't have much time. Can we schedule an hour tomorrow to sit and really talk? I didn't realize you were . . . struggling so much."

Ruth's smile was bitter. "I don't want to have a heart-to-heart with you, thanks. What I'm trying to do is work intensively on my project by hosting those groups. But you just go ahead and send in your trauma-tized patient who messed it all up. She's paralyzed everyone. Now I've got a problem to deal with, but you'll get your glory because you'll have *fixed* her. And then what, you'll be Miles's star again?"

"I'm not trying to *fix* her, or get glory, I'm trying to *help* her. That's the point of what we do, all of us. And you're a part of that."

"No, I'm not! No one will let me be!" She sounded like a child, and Grace tried to imagine Ruth was her child, tried to extend the same compassion. It hurt, but she did it anyway.

"You have a generous soul, Ruth. You love to help people. And sharing that was probably an important step for Johanna. Try to make room for that."

Ruth narrowed her eyes, and they filled with tears. "Oh, what does any of it matter?" she cried, and suddenly all the anger was gone and she was sobbing, mascara staining her cheeks. Grace reached out, squeezed Ruth's shoulder, then held her hand, which was paper dry and shaking, like the hand of a much older woman.

"I saw him with her," Ruth said.

"What do you mean? Who?"

"Shell Williams. On the beach this morning. They were—" Ruth sniffled and wiped uselessly at the dark tears on her cheeks "—together on the beach. They were—it wasn't appropriate."

Grace closed her eyes for a moment, but couldn't find any words. *Not again*, was all she could think.

Another sob from Ruth. "Shh, calm down, don't cry," Grace said.

Ruth accepted a tissue and began to clean up her face.

"Ruth." She paused. How to say it? "Has your relationship with Miles ended?"

"He hasn't told you *anything*? Do I matter that little?" The words dissolved into more sobs. And the alarm bells that had been clanging in Grace's head earlier were full-blown sirens now. Ruth was wiping at her face, and she was sure there were bruises.

"You're so beautiful," Grace said to her, the way she imagined a mother might speak, the way perhaps her own mother might have spoken to her, if she had been different. "You shouldn't wear all that makeup. You don't need it." She leaned closer, reached up to turn on the lamp beside them, quickly, her hand flying through the air, her mind desperate to confirm her suspicions even though she had no idea what she would do if they were correct. But Ruth jerked away from her, eyes wide. She pushed Grace away. "Don't touch me! You're *disgusting*. You're just as bad as him. Worse."

Ruth fled the room, pushing open the door with a bang as it hit the opposite wall, leaving it open behind her. It had been so sudden, such a shock, and there was no one to explain it to, that Grace had only been trying to turn on the light, that she was worried for Ruth, worried about her safety. She pressed her hand against her mouth, appalled, filled with immediate self-loathing. Ruth had misinterpreted the situation entirely. But it didn't matter because it had awoken the truth inside her, which was now out and flying around the room. The success, the clothes, the shoes, the hair, the polished exterior, none of those things mattered. Two words, *You're disgusting*, peeled away Grace's layers. What a powerful girl Ruth was, and she didn't even know it.

Grace was catapulted to the past. Her present faded away. She became Grace Tyler, with her long ponytail and jeans, her sullied heart with hope inside it, still.

———

The church basement smells of burnt coffee, crayons and dusty Bibles. Plastic tables stacked against one wall, rows of chairs stacked against the other, a painting of Jesus on a shoreline on one wall, his cupped hands outstretched, the words "And Jesus said, 'And I will make you fishers of men'" stenciled across the bottom.

Pastor Kesey is praying. Grace Tyler's heart flutters in her chest. She's been in trouble before, for missing curfew, for blowing off schoolwork, for sassing her parents—but never like this. This is bad. Mom, Dad, I need to talk to you. I've been struggling with something.

As Pastor Kesey speaks, his words blurring in her mind, she feels the guilt and shame press itself against her chest, dance inside her stomach until she feels sick, literally. "Excuse me—" she has to say, and they bring her a bucket. She retches, but nothing comes out.

"Thank you, Lord. We thank you so much for your communion with us here today, for your support, for your grace and your mercy. Forgive us, Lord, for we are all sinners. Be with us, Lord, we pray. In Jesus' name, Amen."

Four voices for the last sentence: Pastor Kesey's, Grace's, a church elder, Don Cleary, and his wife, Janet. Grace isn't sure why Janet is there.

There is a tape recorder in the center of the table, beige, with a red record button, which Don pushes forward and presses. They don't ask if it's okay to record her. They don't ask if anything is okay. Normally, Pastor Kesey is in charge, but it is Don everyone looks to now for cues. He had been a psychotherapist; Grace heard this once. And he isn't anymore. She doesn't know why. She nudges the bucket away with her toe and looks at him hopefully.

"Grace, everything you say to us, everything revealed in this room will remain between us," he begins, and Grace knows he's lying. He reminds her of Grace's brother, Garrett, saying her family's presupper prayer. He could make dozens of words sound like one long one, eyes not closed but heavenward: "For what we are about to receive may the Lord make us truly grateful and may we always be mindful of the needs of others in Jesus's name amen." Don sounded just like that.

"Grace?"

"I'm sorry, yes?" A dry mouth, a thick tongue, she thinks of Jesus being deprived of water and made to drink vinegar before he was killed. No one is depriving her of anything, she reminds herself. Her mother, whom she still trusts, has promised this is going to help her. Her father—well, he's another story.

"Has anyone ever hurt you?"

"What do you mean?" Of course people had hurt her. People hurt other people every day. But this was not that. The question meant something else and if she answered it right, she could leave, maybe.

"Think, think back to your childhood. Tell us: Who hurt you? Perhaps someone in your family."

She had just been thinking of Garrett a moment before, of the two of them as little kids, only two years apart, in the backyard of her family's Galveston split-level with its garden, of golden afternoons that stretched and stretched, running on sunbaked grass and on warm asphalt, barefoot, soles of feet blackened, faces hot. Once, Garrett had taken the truck he was playing with in the dirt, a metal truck with one wheel loose, and smashed her on the head with it. She couldn't remember why. They fought once in a while, but it was normal, they were siblings. She feels weak from having almost thrown up, from the fear, from the certainty she is trying to push aside that these people are not here to help her.

"Garrett," she says, involuntary, wishing her brother was there, or better yet, that they were off somewhere together, swimming the day away in their favorite swimming hole.

All three at the table, Pastor Kesey, Don and Janet, lean forward, blurt a collective "Yes?"

"No! I didn't—I was just thinking of my brother. Something stupid, when we were young, he hit me with one of his trucks, but it was just—I mean, you asked if I'd been hurt. And I haven't been really hurt, no. That's all I could think of. The truck. He felt terrible."

"You played trucks with your brother as a child," Don says, writing something down on the notebook he holds. "Was this a common occurrence?"

"Playing with my brother? Yes. We're close to the same age."

"But was it often his games you played? With trucks, maybe with army figurines?"

She wishes she hadn't said that, about the truck, because now the memory, of a perfect afternoon, of all those afternoons, innocent childhood and no church basements because back then her family didn't go to church as much, is sullied by the tone of Don Cleary's voice. "What other games did you play with your brother?"

No matter what she says now, it's going to sound wrong. Dirty. Her brother got Barbara Moore pregnant and is, as she overheard her father saying, an adulterer. "Am I an aunt now?" she had asked her brother, and he shook his head sadly. "That baby is gone, don't you understand?" Then he left the room, carrying this new adult sadness on his shoulders. "It wasn't like that," she begins, then presses her lips together. Maybe it will be better if she doesn't talk, if she just listens. Wasn't that what her mother said? "Just go, please, Gracie. Just listen to what they have to say. They're not going to hurt you. They're your church family. You can trust them." But Don is leaning in, he has his hand on her hand, and his hand is warm and moist and it seems like he does want to hurt her, but he's holding it inside. "We need to talk about who hurt you," he says, his voice shaking slightly. "It was your brother?" The sickness in her stomach rumbles and boils like an earthquake from hell.

"I think I'm going to be sick again," she murmurs, and in an instant, there is that bucket again; it smells of bleach and sulfur. Janet is behind her, holding her hair back. She can hear Don's voice and Pastor Kesey's. "Depression . . . he came to me . . . not very stable . . . no, I wouldn't say this is a surprise."

"Praise the Lord," Janet says, rubbing her back. "Praise Jesus. Be with this child, we pray, as she expels this dirty demon from her soul."

The sound of a throat clearing. Grace snapped back to the present. She picked up the notebook and turned to the man in the doorframe. What was his name? Ben Reid. She struggled for footing in the present moment.

"Did we get the time wrong?" he asked, hesitant.

"No, no, sorry," she said. "I was just—my notes. Please, do go ask—" she swallowed hard "—Johanna to come in, too, and we can get started."

A moment later, Grace was in her chair, sitting across from Johanna and Ben. She smoothed her skirt across her thighs and was almost surprised to find that she was wearing silk and linen, not jeans and a T-shirt, that her hair was smooth and flowing down her shoulders, not in a ponytail, one that frizzed around her temples and neck, that went kinky in the heat. Her mind was still almost completely blank, aside from the shadows of the past. *Focus, Grace.* Panic nipped at her heels.

"Let's begin," Grace said.

The sun was behind Johanna, filtering through her hair. For a moment, Grace felt a grasping sense of déjà vu. The church basement receded. Something was here in this room, in the here and now, that needed her attention. Something that, just maybe, wasn't awful, wasn't harmful. "Let's begin," she repeated, and her voice was her own again. Too late, though, she noticed the two tissues there on the floor, the ones leftover from Ruth's tumultuous visit, blackened with mascara:

evidence. She picked them up, tossed them in the trash. Grace had missed half of what Ben had said.

"I love her so much," he was saying. "I just want her to be okay again, I just want *us* to be okay again."

"And what exactly does that mean, being okay again? What does it mean for both of you? What do you want?" Silence in the room. "I'll start with you, Johanna. What do you want?"

Johanna had a small frown on her face. *You asked me that already*, her eyes seemed to say. *When we were alone.* Grace tapped her pen on her page, tried to beat away the panic.

"That's a big question," was all Johanna said.

"Then give a big answer," replied Grace.

Johanna appeared to measure Ben up and consider him, as though she were trying to figure out what he wanted instead of herself. But when Grace tried to write this observation down—*Johanna seems more concerned with his needs than her own*—her hand was still shaking too much. Her pen made a black dot on the page. "I don't want to cause such stress anymore," Johanna finally said. "I don't want to be a source of pain for my husband."

"I appreciate you saying that," Ben said. "About causing stress. I really do. I know it's been hard for you, that the attack was . . . brutal . . . but something was taken away from me, too. When that man walked into your office, I lost my wife. I want her back." He looked at Grace expectantly, as if she were supposed to conjure up the wife he had lost.

Grace made a long, pointless line across the page. It wobbled. It reminded her of the road away from this place. "In what way, exactly, do you feel you've lost your wife?"

"In every way. I mean, come on, she asked me for a divorce, she pulled away completely—we haven't had sex since then. So when you say, what do you want? The first thing that comes into *my* mind is sex. I want sex. You told us to be honest, and that's me being honest."

Johanna was looking down at her lap.

"How do you feel about that?" Grace asked her. Silence. "Johanna?"

"I feel—" She looked up and now her eyes were different. Guarded. "I don't have any idea how to get our intimacy back. It feels impossible."

Beside her, Ben sighed. Grace turned to him. "Did you have something you wanted to say, Ben?"

"It's just that, the other day, our first morning here, we had a really nice breakfast together. And when we got back to our villa, I think it would have been perfect. An entire day ahead of us with nothing on the schedule except a bit of reading. A beautiful setting, a king-sized bed. And she . . . left. She went off to do some sightseeing."

"Did she ask you to go with her?"

"Sure. But markets aren't really my thing and besides, we're supposed to stay here, aren't we?"

Grace's head was still filled with fog but there was also that tug. *Pay attention.* "It's not a rule, no. You're free to come and go as you please. Did you argue?"

"Not really. Maybe for like a minute. I realized she really wanted to go, so I let her."

Grace managed to write the word *let* on her note page. The letters were shaky, like the penmanship of an old woman. Like the words in the letters her mother never sent. She had found them, in the end. *Grace, I'm sorry. Are you happy? Is he kind to you? You always deserved kindness. I was so afraid for you.* She said to Ben, "Why didn't you go with her?"

"Because I didn't want to. I wanted to stay where we were, make love, feel close again."

Johanna was leaning down and scratching her ankle. "Johanna, do you feel ready to move toward more physical intimacy with your husband?" Grace said in a voice that sounded like it was coming from another room.

Johanna refolded her hands on her lap. Grace prepared for what she was sure she going to say. *No, I'm not ready. No, it's too soon. I have serious doubts.* This was when the conversation would really start. And Grace would be able to help.

"Yes," Johanna said.

"You're—" Grace cleared her throat and blinked several times "—certain?"

"Yes."

Ben was smiling. "Okay. Great. So, what do you suggest, Doc? How do we get back on track?"

Grace closed her notebook. *You're disgusting*, Ruth had said to her. But she wasn't, was she? Surely, this was more disgusting, ignoring the truth of a person even when it was right there in her eyes.

"Yes," Johanna said, voice faint. "How do we?" And for a moment Grace had the sense that the person Johanna was trying so desperately to please wasn't her husband—it was Grace herself.

From where does my help come? It comes from nowhere. Grace thought of what she did, when Miles came to her demanding to have what was his, because her body was his body, to have and to hold. "Johanna, you know you're safe with Ben, and it's clear he adores you. Think of that and nothing else. Make that your sole focus. *I am safe with Ben, and he adores me.* And you . . ."

"Adore him," Johanna quickly finished, and only Grace saw the defiance in her expression, only Grace knew with certainty that Miles was right: she was not good at what she did. She wasn't strong enough. She had caved.

"Right. This is what you want." She tried to make the final part of her sentence sound like a question, but it was far too late.

"This is what I want," Johanna repeated, voice flat. Then she scratched her ankle again and Grace saw it, the fiery red skin, the irritated patches just like the ones she had. She closed her eyes for a moment. The jungle. The brambles. The cenote. The flaming red hair. Her prayer, her bargains. *The market*, Ben had said. Grace opened her eyes and the sun was still shining in through the window and lighting up Johanna's red hair.

The fog lifted. *Why didn't you do better for her? Why are you telling her to go back to her bungalow and do what her husband wants?*

Because I want to protect her. Because I don't know how to protect her.

Johanna met her gaze, and as she did, quickly drew her hand away from her ankle.

"That's all the time we have today," Grace said, even though they still had ten minutes. *I'm sorry*, she wanted to say. Instead, she stood and held open the door.

*S*hell waited outside Miles's office door for a moment. It was open a crack. Did that mean she should go in? A voice: "Please come in, Shell," as if he had read her thoughts. He was sitting at his desk, writing in a notebook. When she entered, he closed the notebook, put down his pen and took off his glasses. "Good morning," he said. "Or should I say, good morning *again*." A smile.

"Good morning," she replied, tucking her hair behind one ear. "Again." After their conversation on the beach, she had found herself in a mood so buoyant it felt foreign, found herself choosing her outfit even more carefully than usual. She felt dry mouthed and shaky, but she also felt ready. Ready to talk. Ready to let it all out. Ready to be seen.

"How are you feeling now?"

"I'm not really sure. Terrible?"

"Let's see what we can do about that. Have a seat."

She did, tucking her skirt around her legs. She had worn a floral wrap dress, one she had imagined wearing to dinner with Colin when she had had a single moment of hope that everything between them would work out.

"What do you feel in your body right now? Not an emotional feeling, but a physical feeling. Can you describe it?"

"My heart . . . it's beating a little faster than usual," she said.

"I make you nervous?" He smiled. "Perhaps I should be flattered. But more than that, go deeper. Close your eyes. How does the leather of the couch feel against your skin? What do you hear?"

"The leather feels smooth and cool," she said. "I can hear the ocean, and I can hear you breathing. I can still feel the beating of my own heart."

"Good," he said. "What else?"

"I can smell the sea, in the breeze through the window. And I can smell . . . I can smell you. Your cologne."

"Do you like it?"

She opened her eyes. "I . . ."

"I'm sorry. I shouldn't have asked you that. Sometimes therapists, we get insecure, too. I don't normally wear cologne at sessions, but there was something going on inside me this morning. I wanted to impress you."

"You . . . did?"

"We shared something intimate, on the beach this morning. Don't you agree?"

She found herself nodding, but she also felt a sense of disquiet. Her cheeks were starting to color. "Have you heard anything from Colin?" she asked. "Is he having any therapy sessions at all? What is he doing with his time?"

"What do you *think* Colin is doing? Colin is working."

"He isn't going to sessions with Grace?"

"He hasn't that I know of. But Colin is not your concern. How was your night, alone in your bungalow? Are you enjoying the time by yourself? Some women enjoy it, enjoy getting away from the bustle of family life. No one to look after."

Shell blinked a few times. "Well, we don't exactly have—our house is not exactly full of life these days." As she spoke, her throat felt like it was full of sharp rocks. "Miles, I—"

"I don't always feel such a connection to my clients. In fact, I don't think I ever have. I feel a real connection to you and I know you feel it, too—don't you? It's exciting for me. I think I can really help you because of this connection we share. But I need you to trust me. Do you trust me?"

"Yes," she said, quickly. She didn't know if the answer was really yes, not yet, but she knew she wanted to please him—because she wanted him to help her. Someone needed to help ease this pain inside her. She touched her hair again. The truth was that she was also flattered by his words. They had touched something deep and long neglected inside her.

He stood. "Do you mind if I sit here beside you? I always find it so clinical, the patient on the couch. And especially after the intimacy of our conversation earlier, I think we've moved beyond the regular patient/client banality."

He didn't wait for her to answer. Did it feel better, to have him there on the couch with her? Less clinical, more friendly? She tried to relax.

"Ah, that's better. I've always loved this couch. Maybe that's really why I want to sit here beside you. You have the most comfortable seat in the house." A wink. She sat still and tried to smile at him, and felt foolish for having to try so hard. It was okay. This was fine.

"All right," he said, when he was comfortable. "Why don't we begin—" he pursed his lips and looked up at the ceiling "—by talking a little more about last night. What did you do with your time on your own?"

She thought of the hours that had stretched before her, lonely and empty, of how ill she had felt, of what she had wanted: alcohol. Oblivion. It was the last thing she wanted to talk about. "I had a bath. I read a book on the terrace. I slept." All lies.

"Did you sleep well?"

"Not really," she allowed. "I've been having trouble falling asleep. I thought I might sleep well. I like how close my new bungalow is to the ocean. I like listening to the waves."

"Interesting," he said. "But it doesn't relax you?"

"I don't know . . . if that's quite the right word. I feel tired. Exhausted. But not relaxed."

"Why do you feel so exhausted?"

"I think being with Colin has become exhausting," she said. "When

I'm with him, it sometimes feels like we're trying to swim toward one another in a current but we're both . . . we're both just so tired. Just too tired to do it. And then it starts to get frustrating. I've been able to see that now, with a little distance. I was upset at first, but maybe it's part of what we needed."

"Maybe," Miles said, and Shell, who had been looking out the window at the waves, turned her head to look at him. She felt a prickle of something. All at once, his body felt too close and she wondered again where her husband was.

"I never thought about how infrequently we're apart," she said. "Some business trips, but often I'd travel with him, and then—" she swallowed "—Zoey, when she was born. The three of us would travel together. I knew a lot about what he did. I had a similar job once, too, until we started having trouble conceiving and I took time off. We were close, once. A family. A team." She paused. "Look, how's he doing? Can't you just—it would be really nice to know how he's feeling about this separation."

"You really do have a way with words, you know," he said. "It's refreshing. You know yourself. You know your relationship. I can see you. How deep you hurt, how hard you try. And I can also see your power. A businesswoman, you say. Impressive. Would you call yourself a leader?"

"Not anymore."

"You're incredibly strong."

"I feel weak, like a complete failure. Like I don't know anything about being a wife. Being a mother." Her voice broke. "I can't."

"It's all right," he said. "You don't have to do or be anything in here. You are not a wife or a mother. You are just yourself, in this room. *You* are the focus. The strong you." She was crying. She wished he would stop calling her strong. She looked up at him, embarrassed by her emotions, but he didn't seem to notice. She reached for a tissue.

"In this room, I want you to feel empowered to be who you are, to say the things you want to say. I want you to feel seen again, Shell. I want you to feel like the woman you are. Because I know how you feel. I truly do. We've all felt this way at some point in our lives. Invisible, inadequate, filled with needs and desires we just can't express. Because we're too afraid." He was leaning toward her and looking directly into her eyes and it was too much, like a spotlight swinging its beam across her body, invasive and overbright. It was what she had wanted, to be seen, but now she felt exposed, and not the right parts of her. She had seen Colin's intake forms, and he had written almost nothing on them. Hers were the same. Bare bones, a basic sketch of a marriage on the rocks. *Arguments? Check. Lack of Intimacy? Check. Resentment? Check.* But there was so much more.

Miles reached for her hand. "You don't have to talk. You don't have to say another word. Just look at me. Look into my eyes and stay here with me."

She looked into his eyes and felt a sickness spread through her, a sort of panic. He wasn't going to ask her anything, about Zoey, about her life, about any of the past that was burning a hole inside her. She took a deep, struggling breath. "Miles—"

"Relax," he said. "Breathe calmly in and out. Feel every single breath. Make it purposeful. *Feel* the leather against your legs, *hear* the ocean in your ears."

Shell did as he said because she didn't know what else to do. She forced herself to slow her breathing, to be conscious about it. "Repeat after me," he said after a few minutes, during which she noted his breaths had come to match her own, that their chests began to rise in mesmerizing unison. "I am broken."

"I am broken."

"I have failed and I have faltered, but those days are behind me."

"I have failed, I have faltered . . ." She echoed his words, closing her eyes. Were they praying? She couldn't be sure. When was the last time?

"I am going to allow myself to heal," he intoned. "I am going to allow myself to *be* healed. I am going to stop thinking about alcohol. I am going to forget about the sin of those bottles. I am going to turn away from the weak and sinful side of myself."

Her mouth went dry, but she repeated what he said. "And I am going to step forward into my new beautiful life. I will not be alone when I do." The sound of the waves and the sound of his voice were a comfort in the dark. "Open your eyes," he said. "Look at me." She did, and nothing happened. He stared into her eyes and she stared back, trying not to feel alarmed.

It felt like too much time passed. But eventually, she started to feel relaxed because there was nothing else to feel. Eventually, the ebb and flow of her emotions slowed, then stopped altogether. She was used to this, this sitting and staring. She had spent entire days this way. At least today she wasn't alone. There was that. At least she had eyes to stare into.

"Your soul is as deep as an ocean," Miles said. "Let me in. *Let me in.*" Shell found herself pulled out of the sense of relaxation by the intensity in his voice. She fought to come back to the surface, to push away the soporific sensations of sitting, staring. She had things she wanted, needed to say.

"Miles, there's something that—"

"Stop. You are always fighting, pushing, struggling in your life. I am asking you to sit and be still. I am saying you will heal. Let me in."

There was something in his words that scared her. But maybe she was the scary one. He was the expert.

She sat as still as possible, she made sure their breathing matched, and she kept her eyes locked with his. And she must have let him in, she must have done it, because later, when a timer sounded behind her, he smiled broadly and he said, "Wonderful, wonderful, excellent work, I'm honored to be your therapist. See you same time tomorrow."

"But what am I—what am I supposed to *do*? I mean, you haven't even asked me anything about—"

"Keep doing what you've been doing. *Relax.* You're a beautiful woman, Shell. I saw your great, intoxicating beauty, and I felt honored. Thank you for showing yourself to me." He pressed his hands together and nodded his head. "Yes," he said. "Yes. You are perfect."

She felt strange and numb. Colin felt further away than ever. And she felt as though she had just betrayed her husband.

―――

Inside her bungalow again, Shell walked to the terrace doors and opened them, stood and looked out at the same waves she had seen when she was in Miles's office, the same stretch of beach. She walked back inside. Through everything she did, she tried not to think about how much and how desperately she wished she still had the vodka. A sin, Miles had called it, and it was, wasn't it? For her, it always had been—and she had never talked about it to anyone.

She closed the curtains in the bedroom and undressed, then walked into the bathroom. She stood in front of the mirror. She was too thin, yes, but her stomach still had a slight roundness she had not been able to flatten after having Zoey, even with Pilates and yoga and random planks that would make Zoey laugh. There were stretch marks, too, low on her abdomen. These had lightened when she rubbed expensive creams and oils on them, but never disappeared completely. Wiggly silver bands, like handwriting. *You are a beautiful woman*, Miles had said to her. But these marks told another story altogether, one of a woman with a career who had realized, at almost forty, that she wanted a child. They had tried everything and she had told herself that no matter what, she had no regrets. And then, Zoey, a gift, a relief. Because there had been regret, even if she had denied it. Zoey had saved Shell from that—for a while. Now all she had was regret. She didn't care that she was considered beautiful. It was this other story she badly wanted to tell: how empty she was. How mired in what could have been. And yet Miles Markell, one of the best therapists in the world, didn't seem to be interested.

No. No. You must be missing the point. He doesn't need to be told what you're feeling. He just knows. She just wasn't focusing on the right thing. Maybe this path he wanted her on was the way to go. Maybe going over her trauma over and over again in her own mind was the problem. Was that it? She was just supposed to turn it all off to get better?

What choice did she have? She'd tried everything else. She had to trust him.

She walked naked over to the sliding doors that led to the pool. She slid in. Her body felt weightless in the salt water. Her hair floated out around her shoulders. She stretched her arms above her head. Her nipples rose above the water for a few seconds and she felt them harden in the sea breeze. She closed her eyes and she saw Miles's face. She opened them again, because his face was not the one she wanted to see. She was lonely. That was all. She wasn't used to allowing someone to get too close. It had been a year—386 days, to be more precise—of keeping herself locked away. She was frustrated, she had expected release, and it felt instead as if everything was being forced deeper and deeper inside. But she just had to do what Miles said and the agony would stop.

She closed her eyes and ducked her head under the water. In the total, womb-like silence, she felt a strange form of peace. But it didn't last. Under the water, her body trembled. She breached the surface and gasped for air.

"A re you ready?" Miles said into his microphone, his voice an exuberant shout.

"He's enjoying this a little *too* much, don't you think?" Johanna said under her breath.

Servers were moving among the tables with rolling carts. They were placing a box on each table with a board game inside. Johanna pulled the box toward her side of the table and read the top. "The Marriage Retreat Game. That's an original title." She shot a wry look in Ben's direction. "Can you read the rules? I don't have my glasses."

Ben shook his head and smiled. "When do you ever have your glasses? Did you even *bring* them?"

She smiled, too, she made herself do it and the smile reached her heart and warmed it somewhat. Wasn't it true that you could grow to love someone? It just took time. She didn't need a counselor to teach her that. When she was alone with Grace, she felt the opposite. Out here, she saw what could be possible. The life she was supposed to lead. "Of course not. You know me so well. I don't even know where my glasses are."

Grace had arrived. She was standing beside her husband in a long dress, burgundy with smoky gray flowers. Her hair was piled and pinned atop her head. Miles took her arm and said something and Grace smiled, and it felt familiar to Johanna, a smile that moved over her face slowly.

She turned away from Grace and focused on the task at hand. The game. Her marriage. It was going to be easy. It had to be easy. All you had to do was close off your true self, hide it in a box somewhere inside. The simplest thing. She'd been doing it for years.

Ben opened the box and lifted out the game board and instructions. "Increase your communication and deepen your intimacy with a roll of the dice," he read, then looked up at her. "Okay, I can admit, this is a little cheesy."

Johanna picked up the dice and shook them in her hand. Ben looked nice tonight, she told herself, with his hair tousled and still damp-looking, his shirt buttoned down. She thought about how it should make her feel, to see him sitting across the table from her—and then she did feel it, she was sure of it. *I adore him.* She had said that earlier today. She could make it true. And every day, she would get more strategies to take home and use to make her life easier than it had ever been.

"Love you," she said, reaching across the table to squeeze his hand.

"Love you back. Okay, so I think we roll the dice and answer questions. And whoever gets to the end first . . ." He read the rest of the instructions and laughed. "I don't actually know. There *is* no winner or loser. Apparently this game is 'all about the journey.'"

"Who gets to go first?"

"Doesn't matter."

"Any other rules I should know about?"

"Nope."

"So, basically, this game is entirely pointless."

"We're supposed to learn things about each other."

"We know *everything* about each other."

"Maybe not."

"Okay, let's see. You go."

He rolled the dice, moved his marker—he had chosen blue—six spaces and lifted a card from the top of the deck. "Funny, I don't actually know the answer to this question," he said. "So maybe we *don't* know everything."

"What is it?"

"Who was your first love?"

The smile disappeared from her face. She pasted it back on. "I know *your* answer," she said. "Denise Morris, in third grade."

"Wow, you have a great memory. But I wouldn't exactly call her a first love. I was eight."

"Okay, well, who then?"

He thought for a moment. "My girlfriend in college, Maya—but truly, Jo, it was nothing compared to the way I feel for you. Anyway, aren't you supposed to be answering this question?"

"You," she said. "You were my first love. My only love."

"Come on. There were guys before me."

"Yes, but none I loved the way I love you. Truly, you are the first guy I've ever loved."

"First boyfriend, then. First guy you . . ." He raised an eyebrow, and she remembered how he used to like it, when she would tell him sexy stories. Back when they used to have sex.

"His name was Matt," she said. "It happened at a high school party, in someone's parents' bed."

He leaned forward. "I bet you were so hot in high school."

"I bet you were, too," she whispered. She took her foot out of her sandal and ran it up his leg. Then she leaned toward him and whispered, "Let's ditch this pointless game and go back to our room."

"We can't just keep taking off on these things—"

"We can do what we want. We're not children." She moved her foot higher. She was a star pupil.

"We certainly aren't," he said.

"So . . . ?"

"I'd be a fool to say no to you." He stood. "Let's make our escape."

She saw Miles Markell watching them and frowning as they joined hands and walked quickly away. She didn't see Grace anywhere, and wondered if she was watching, too. Johanna tilted her head and kissed her husband as they walked. A few couples were whispering, eyebrows raised. The fire that had been smoldering ignited in the base of her pelvis, she *wanted* this now, now that it wasn't just the two of them, now that there was room for fantasy—and the idea that maybe later, people might be fantasizing about *them*.

"I want you inside me now," she purred into his ear, then tried to think of something else. "I want your cock. You should lift my skirt, bend me over and fuck me, now, up against that tree." Her mouth was on his earlobe.

He groaned and said, "Come on, let's go to the villa," and they started to walk even faster.

He fumbled for his key, opened the door, pressed her against the wall with his hands and his mouth and kicked the door shut behind him. She closed her eyes, closed them tight, ran her hands down his back, then stopped and said, "Blindfold me, tie me up."

"I don't think I have anything to tie you up *with*," Ben was saying into her mouth, as she felt the fire inside her dimming slightly.

"Nothing?"

He had his hands on the waistband of her skirt. He pulled it down, then her panties. "No," he said, "and I don't think I can wait."

"Against the wall," Johanna said, but he was lifting her onto the bed and then he was on top of her. She closed her eyes.

"You feel so good," he said, but she heard him as though he were miles away. She was thinking about something else, someone else, somewhere else.

"I want you. I always have." It wasn't him, but she tried to make it so. The body she was imagining was much softer. "Please . . ." She squeezed herself around him and felt the waves coming. She made the appropriate sounds and compliments, all directed at him, but she could already feel the hollow regret swimming its way toward her. She shut her eyes tighter.

"Jo," he said. "Oh, yes, Jo."

"That was amazing," he said afterward, breathless, climbing off her, and she wondered how it was possible to be inside someone's body and not realize they were gone.

"Ruth, could you please clean up that table?" Miles snapped, even though it didn't matter, even though the staff would do it. Ruth did what he asked, her mouth a slash of hot pink unhappiness. Eventually, Grace watched her walk off alone into the night.

"Ready?" Miles said, beside her now. She followed. The night air was calm, warm on her skin. Above, stars spilled out across the sky, lawless and yet mapped out and analyzed for a millennia, even more rigorously than people had ever been—even more than the people Grace treated week after week, year after year. Grace had often wondered what would happen should a star fall out of Orion's belt, should one of the Seven Sisters plunge into nothingness. Some nights, she stayed outside and looked at the stars and indulged in thoughts like this. Tonight especially, she needed time alone, to think. It had been easier to do that, she realized, to take time for herself back when Miles and Ruth would spend their evenings together. She had sanctioned an extramarital relationship, yes—but she had had her reasons. It was out of her mouth before she could really think about it: "What's happened between the two of you? You and Ruth?"

He didn't answer her. They left the poolside lounge behind; it was empty of couples now. Grace could see a few of them, walking along the beach, talking. The game didn't seem like much, but it generally didn't cause any conflict, and often did do what the box said: foster a sense of intimacy. She had walked past Johanna's and Ben's table a few times, had tried to get a look at Johanna's ankle and that familiar-looking rash—but there had been no way, and then they had left. "The game certainly seemed to work with the Reid couple," Miles said, as if reading her thoughts. "A little too much. Shameful behavior."

Just then, a loud voice erupted from the bar area, one of the husbands, a large man from North Carolina, shouting "Jesus, I could really use a scotch right now!" to raucous laughter.

She winced and didn't look at Miles.

He stopped walking and turned to her, his face a bitter mask. "Really, Grace?" His voice was a low growl. "How long has she been out of my bed and you're just noticing and asking *now*?" He began to walk again.

She caught up. "I noticed, but I thought you were just giving her time, after what happened with the—"

"*NO.*" This time, his voice was a roar. They were far enough away that the guests wouldn't hear, and if they did they'd think it was the ocean, or maybe an animal in a jungle that they somehow believed still existed here, whose habitat they didn't understand had been bulldozed to make way for resorts like this. Paradise, Miles called it, but it wasn't— it only had been, once, and well before their time.

She let him walk away. She waited until she heard the front door of their villa slam far ahead of her before she began to walk again. She stood outside their home and looked up at the stars but found no comfort or distraction from her thoughts, which strained against their tethers in so many directions. Ruth. Miles. Johanna. Her own fears, her own past, like a creature in the walls of a house, ignored but unmistakably there. Finally, she went inside. Silence. She was afraid. She took the stairs as quickly and quietly as she could, entered her office and closed the door. It had no lock. She wished for one but it was no use: he had broken two already.

She walked to her bookshelf and her eyes roamed the titles, mostly psychology texts, filled notebooks, the white leather-bound Bible Miles had given her as a wedding gift. A few spines away was a battered volume of *Leaves of Grass* by Walt Whitman, the spine cracked so many times that deep groves now obscured the title. This was a book she had once found on the shelf in her childhood home. In it was an inscription written for her mother from someone who was not her father. *Dear June, there is more than one way to see the world. Enjoy these poems. Love, your friend Eli.*

When Grace had asked her about it, June had blushed and said, "Oh, he was a boy I knew in high school. He was—" but her father walked into the room just then. "What about Eli?" he had barked. Her father had been a lieutenant general in the Vietnam War. Garrett was born two years before their father even met him; it was in the local newspaper, a black-and-white photograph of her father's expressionless face as he saluted the flag while his wife stood before him, holding up their child for him to see, or even just notice.

Her father flipped quickly through the pages of the book and, as was his custom when he didn't understand something, assumed it to be immoral. He called it lewd and threw it in the trash. Later, she had heard him calling her mother's friend Eli, whoever he was, a faggot.

Grace was only eight at the time. She had read some of the poems earlier that afternoon and not understood what was lewd about them. Later, she took the book out of the trash. She read more of it, read words she had been taught were evil and dirty, words like "sex" and "crotch." There were other words, too, that made her laugh, words like "belch." She showed her brother, Garrett, and he laughed, too, but told her to hide it or put it back in the garbage or her father would whip her with the belt. She didn't throw it out. She kept it hidden for years, pored over it in secret until she was able to understand what her father had found so lewd. It spoke to what she understood to be lewd inside herself. It didn't make her feel any less tainted, but it made her feel less alone.

She took it with her when she left home, the only thing aside from a few changes of clothes that she had packed into a bag. Her parents had been glad to see her go. Relieved, muttering grateful prayers as they signed papers to release their daughter from their home. Only a moment of doubt, and Grace had seen it. "A minister's wife," her mother had begun, and she had been about to say one other thing when Grace's father had walked into the room.

"What's that?" Miles had asked her once, about the book of poems. This was later, after he had left ministry and they were studying to become therapists because, Miles had said, they would be able to help more people—and make more money while doing it. "Money we can use to change the world," he had said, though that part of it had never been clear. Really, they had only ever used the money they made to change their own worlds. Really, they had only used it to turn a patch of jungle and oceanfront into a place that Miles had dominion over. "It reminds me of my brother," Grace had said, thinking it might be okay to talk about Garrett now. But Miles had frowned and turned away. That was it for the topic of the book. Garrett or no, Miles didn't concern himself with poetry, not even the Songs of Solomon. He preferred the fire of Exodus, the rule of Deuteronomy. And lately, it seemed, the gospel of Miles.

She had no photographs of her brother, but when she looked at this book, she thought of him, his easy smile and then his urgent whisper: *Hide it, Gracie. You don't want Daddy to whip you. Hey, want to go swamp fishing?* This book had become the golden afternoons with her brother that had begun to grow fewer and further between, it had become the moments when he had discovered girls and she had started to fall into trouble, internal trouble, nothing she had acted on, but still, it had landed her in that church basement, her hair held back by a stranger as she vomited her life into a bucket. And she had never mentioned that book of poems. It was one of the greatest regrets of her life. Because what if she had said it was the book that had corrupted her and not allowed them to believe it was Garrett? They would have destroyed the book. Not her brother. If only she'd thought of it.

She ran a finger over the worn cover of *Leaves of Grass*. Miles turned to the Bible for insight and inspiration, found lines like *"To the woman he said, 'I will surely multiply your pain in childbearing; in pain you shall bring forth children. Your desire shall be for your husband, and he shall rule over you.' "* to gild and justify what he believed. She flipped to a page in her book now, lay a finger down at the start of a Whitman verse: *"I am not to speak to you,"* she read. *"I am to think of you when I sit alone, or wake at night alone. I am to wait. I do not doubt I am to meet you again, I am to see to it that I do not lose you."*

She left the office and crept next door, into her bedroom, carrying the book with her. She changed out of her dress into a peignoir and bed jacket, then walked to her en suite, book still in hand. She slid it into her cosmetics drawer, closed it and began to unpin her hair. She listened, but still heard nothing. It had never bothered her, when she had heard Miles and Ruth together, when she had passed the door to his suite of rooms and heard laughter, even moans. She realized now there was comfort in it for her. She was free on those nights, safe. On those nights, she didn't have to think about how repulsed she was by her own husband's touch. But it was sick, wasn't it, to find comfort in the sounds of your husband taking pleasure from and giving pleasure to another woman? To allow it to happen under your own roof? It was abominable, wasn't it, to pretend to be the ideal couple when, really, you lived separately, under the same roof, when, really, the moment you saw how besotted your intern was, you had encouraged your husband to solve the fact that the feeling was clearly mutual by taking a second "wife" because you were too afraid to stand up and be who you really were?

Miles. Behind her. Standing reflected in the mirror, and she hadn't even noticed him come in. A sharp intake of breath, but she tried not to show her fear. "The behavior I witnessed tonight," he said, and she glanced at his hand and saw the intricate pressed-glass tumbler, a wedding gift. It was almost empty of its clear liquid. Not water. Vodka. He would have taken one of Shell Williams's bottles. He did that sometimes, if Ruth didn't hide it first after the contraband-gathering missions. He saw her looking and his eyes narrowed. "You made me do this," he said. He had been saying that to her for years, whenever he faltered. Sometimes it was drink. Sometimes it was pills. Sometimes it was women. Or a combination of all three. All things that could be found if you combed through the resort in secret. A kingdom of riches, a mine of temptation. "You upset me so much you made me do this. And her. That woman. *She* did, too. I can't stand women like her."

He was slurring. The vodka smelled like surgery. Grace didn't reply, just kept unpinning her hair and trying to stay calm. He had always called her hair her crowning glory. She wondered, suddenly, what it would be like to take the kitchen shears to it while he watched her in the mirror, wondered what he would do. Wondered what it would be like to stand up to him, instead of trying to fly under his radar, instead of suffering through nights like this every few months. There was a change in him tonight, an intensity she had seen building, along with a restlessness she should probably have been fearing instead of trying to ignore. *You should have left yesterday.* She said this to herself every time he got like this—every time it was far too late.

She finished with her hair and ran cool water over a cloth, lined up her creams. But then she put the cloth down instead of raising it to her face. She looked at herself in the mirror, at her husband behind her, at the pure, distilled hatred in his half-closed eyes. Everything she had— her marriage, her work, her self—was a lie, and she could see it all at once in the crystal clarity of the fear that hung in the room. You could ignore the truth, but it would come for you eventually.

"Please explain to me what happened between you and Ruth," Grace said, and as she spoke she remembered Ruth's arrival as an intern, three years before. She had been so starry-eyed. *I can't believe I'm actually meeting you two*, she had said, over and over. And meanwhile, Grace had felt she and Miles were at the edge of ruin. A maid had come to Grace with a story about Miles's advances getting out of hand. Grace could still practically feel the sting of her stony glare directed at the young woman. Who had she become, in that moment? It was a familiar person. It was a person she had met many times at the church she and Miles had attended. A woman willing to fall on her sword in the name of her beliefs—or, a woman willing to use her sword to hurt anyone standing in her way. "No one will believe you," Grace had said to the maid. Such simple words, such awful truth. "What, the world will ask, would a man like Miles Markell, who has money, success and one of the most renowned marriages in the world, want with a maid? If Miles says he didn't do it, people will believe him." *Oh, Grace.* Her eyes were filling with sorry, regretful tears. She had given the young woman money to be quiet, but it was really money to make Grace feel better and it hadn't worked. It had been money from her own personal stash, a portion of her inheritance from her mother she had managed to hide away from Miles and had never imagined using in this way. It haunted her, still, what she had said to that maid. And she feared her, saw her in her nightmares. She could still come forward, and when she did, it would be with her finger pointed directly at Grace, she knew it. *I am not innocent. I am the person who stands by and allows him to do this to people. And, I am broken. I am so, so broken.*

The next year a client came forward and this time Grace and Miles worked together to secure her silence. It was expensive. And, Grace believed now, it had cost her a portion of her soul. The recession hit and she wondered if there would be enough money to pay the next woman who came forward. She imagined what the world would think of her, when the truth about her, about their marriage, came to light. She knew the things Miles would say about her to save himself, the secrets he would reveal. She saw her secret shame hung out to dry, heard the taunts and the curses. And people would see, wouldn't they, that she was the liar? People would see that she had never been a wife to Miles, and because of that she had ruined him. Not everything Miles said was true but this was: she was broken and he had tried his best to fix her, once. She had been working her entire life to do this one thing he had told her: to avoid turning her brokenness into sin.

Most of the time, it felt like *that* was the sin.

It was when Grace had been standing at the precipice of her deepest fears and shame, afraid of who she was becoming, that she offered Ruth to Miles.

Grace looked at Miles now, met his hateful eyes in the mirror and remembered the calm that had existed there, for a while, at least. "She's perfect," Miles had said to Grace, back then. "She's the one. The one who will bear my children." And Grace hadn't felt jealousy, only a flood of relief. It had not lasted. All of the women who had come into Miles's path were distracted by his fame. She knew now that Ruth was just the next in a long list of women who had been, as she had, seduced into serving him. All of them blurred together. What was clear was that Grace had been willfully ignorant. She had been throwing women into Miles's path for years. She was just as bad as he was.

It had to stop.

"*Miles.* Ruth loves you. She's heartbroken. You need to do something."

"Ruth isn't worthy of my love." He said it slowly, as if explaining something to a child. "She lost one of my sons, and so did you. Neither of you are worthy. I need to find someone who is."

His words crackled between them. "Not Shell Williams," she said. She met his eyes in the mirror and lifted her chin. But it was there: the tremble. He saw it, heard it. He put the glass down on the counter. She lifted the cloth, tried to pretend nothing was happening, that they were just a couple having a conversation about their shared work. "She seems fragile. I don't think you have a clear handle on what she really needs yet, and you should—"

"Don't tell me what to do! Don't try to *mother* me, damn it!"

There it was. There it always would be. How simple it was to trace back into childhood and find the moments, the environment, that had created the adult. His mother was a woman abandoned by her husband, turning to a church with rotten foundations for comfort and strength, and then—people speaking in tongues in their parlor and writhing on their living room floor, Miles soaking all of it up like a sponge. Acts done to Miles in the name of the Holy Spirit that should never have been done and which he spoke of like a robot, devoid of all emotion. He ran away from home, he told her after they met, and he didn't talk about what had happened to him during the years he was lost—but she came to understand the addictions he had cultivated and the hatred he had nursed. Hatred of the mother who had hurt him that had blossomed, dropped seeds. All he said about his past was that he had eventually been found, saved, put on a path that landed him at the doorstep of her family's church, a reformed young man ready to save other lost souls.

"Miles was once broken, too," they said to Grace. "He sinned in other ways, but still, he sinned. And then he was found. And then he was saved. Let him save *you*, Grace. Let him in."

Miles moved in on her. He picked up a strand of her hair, lifted it to his nose, dropped it. She tried not to tremble anymore. "I know better than you. You fumble through your days and it's sheer luck when you actually get it right, isn't it? How often are you coming to me for advice? You would be nothing without me!" His words were angry but his touch was gentle, first on her waist and then, drifting up to her breasts. She eyed the wastebasket in the corner but prayed she wouldn't be sick because it always made it worse for her when she was. "That woman," Miles said, his voice now soft. "The red-haired one. Johanna. The way she took her husband by the hand like that. She might as well have screamed, 'Hey, everyone, we're going to go *fuck*.'"

Grace tried to pretend he wasn't touching her the way he was. "We're encouraging intimacy. That's the point of the game, isn't it?"

A grin, a smile on a wolf. Once, she and Garrett had seen a wolf in the swamp. Garrett had thrown rocks at it until it slunk away. Grace wished her brother were still alive. "The way *you* were looking at her, too. Did you know you appeared so hungry? Did you feel it, Grace?" He squeezed her breast hard and she tried not to wince or even move or even think about what he was saying. "Did you want to fuck her, too, my darling, my love?" Then he had her by the wrist, so fast it took her breath away and she stood, gasping, as he twisted her arm behind her neck and the hairbrush clattered to the floor. *"Answer me!"*

"Let go."

"Wives obey your husbands," he hissed in her ear. She closed her eyes.

It hurt so much. "You will always be broken. Maybe I should break you for real."

She heard a scream. She realized it was her own. He let go. He wasn't the type to break bones, only the type to threaten it. He stepped back from her and reached into his pocket. A white tablet. He pressed it into her other hand. "Take your fucking pill," he snarled, and he waited. She put it in her mouth and tried to parcel it into her cheek. "Swallow," he commanded. She did what he said. He left the room, left her staring at herself in the mirror, a metallic taste in her mouth and a deadness already setting in as she rubbed her wrist.

She needed ice but she couldn't risk leaving the room. She saw his glass on the counter and knocked back the last sip. The vodka burned down her throat and set her chest on fire, but did nothing for the cacophony of pain in her wrist. With her other hand, she locked the bathroom door, then opened her drawer. The book of poems was still there, a silent witness to all this. Her finger found the right page. *I am to see that I do not lose you*, she read.

She slid to the floor, a woman with nothing left to lose.

She slept in the tub.

Day Five

Her: He was my everything. As much as I came to hate him,
     he still had such power. Such charisma. I regret
     what I did. My heart was broken, but it's no excuse.
     It's just—those final weeks were hard. Those people,
     all of them—it's like they were slowly killing him.
     And he was trying so hard to play God. We'd done it
     before but it didn't feel right, not that time. I
     should have known. I wanted to try to save *him*. He
     refused to believe he needed to be saved. If only
     he had really listened to me. If only he had really
     wanted what I wanted.

Him: You're dwelling on the past.

Her: It's all I have.

*S*omeone left one of her sleeping pills on her bedside table. Shell recognized the smooth beige circle immediately. And instead of questioning where it had come from, Shell almost cried with relief when she saw it. She took it and slept for almost twelve hours, and she still barely had the energy to get out of bed to order a breakfast she couldn't eat because of nausea and trembling hands and a mouth so dry nothing could slake her thirst. She drank glass after glass of water that wasn't cold enough, and scalding black coffee that cooled in her cup too quickly. She showered and dressed, then took the stairs to Ruth's office because she didn't know what else to do with herself except sit in the villa and wish for things she didn't have anymore. The ones she didn't have anymore. Her next session with Miles couldn't come soon enough.

At the door at the top of the stairs, she forgot to knock, just walked in. Ruth jumped and minimized what she'd been reading on her computer screen. "You scared me," Ruth said.

"I'm sorry. I'm here to—"

"Yes, I know why you're here!"

"Sorry," Shell found herself mumbling.

"I'll leave you alone today," Ruth said. "I just need to gather my things."

Shell looked out the window while she waited. It was a gray morning, still hot, but there was a strong breeze off the ocean. A man far down below on the cobblestone path walked in a familiar way, hands in pockets, head bent. *Colin.* She found herself stepping toward the window, lifting her hand to touch the glass. Where was he going? He was walking fast. She realized his speed and sloped posture was because it had started to rain. He disappeared down a path. She willed him to appear again and give her a clue about where he was heading, but he didn't. *Colin is not your concern*, Miles had said to her the day before. It seemed strange, the idea of there ever being a time when Colin wasn't her concern, the idea of that time being now. She missed him. It was sudden and acute. She missed the way they had been *before*.

She turned from the window. Ruth was standing near the door, a large folder in her hand. "What bungalow is my husband staying in?"

"I'm afraid I can't tell you that."

"But why not?" Shell felt the flare of anger, so customary in her life. It was welcome this time because she had grown so used to it and so many things were unfamiliar now. But she couldn't sustain it. Almost immediately she felt tired again.

"You've been separated, haven't you?" Ruth asked her.

"Yes, but—"

"Then that's the rule."

Ruth narrowed her eyes and Shell felt as though they were squaring off. Why? She thought back, tried to remember—oh. Yes. The morning before, on the beach. Her heart thudded a few times as she considered what it may have looked like to Ruth, her and Miles embracing. Surely he would have explained it, though.

"I'll be back in ten minutes. Is that enough time for you?"

Shell didn't reply, just sat and swiveled in the chair, then logged into her email. But she found she couldn't focus on the pointless and macabre task ahead of her, the only task she had, aside from seeing Miles, to fill her day with. Instead, she pictured Colin again, walking in the rain. Ruth's voice: *You've been separated, haven't you?* She hesitated for just a moment, then picked up the phone beside Ruth's computer. She tried his cell phone and was surprised when it went straight to voicemail. The same for his work phone. Both, off.

There had been moments at home when Shell was sure this was what she wanted: to be separated from her husband, to eventually be severed from him altogether, to leave behind the part of her life where she relived a single moment over and over in her head. It was that or to die. To die alone and let him have another life. *Are you trying to kill me?* he had asked her that night as she stood in their kitchen, an empty bottle in her hand and broken glass everywhere. *No,* she was sure she had said. *No, I am trying to kill myself.* Had he not heard her? Had he not believed her? Had her words been so slurred he didn't understand?

Her fingers were still on the keyboard. She typed in Colin's email address instead of her mother's.

Dear Colin,

Maybe we need to talk. This doesn't feel right. What bungalow are you in?

Seeing Colin out there—he hadn't always been a stranger, walking in the rain. Had he? She rested her fingers on the keyboard and tried to remember the Colin she had first met, years ago, the man who had been a stranger, had at one point been entirely unexplored terrain, uncharted territory that made her breathless with each discovery. That was what love was like, at first, always. Theirs had been that, too. And these memories were what she had been searching for, that first night on the terrace when Ben had been going on about his passion for his wife, Johanna. Her story was different, but it had still contained love, once. And more than love: tacit understanding.

"We shouldn't drink anymore," she had told Colin, back when they were new, and he hadn't asked a single question or said a single word except, "Okay, let's stop." And they had. This had meant more to her than a stranger could ever understand. This had made her sure that he was the one. And, of course, there had been more to it than just those two sentences. But they'd never had to rehash it. Until now.

It had been after a night out with friends, the weekly university pub night they went to religiously to drink jug after jug of watered-down beer, or shots of tequila, or—Shelley's preference (she still went by

Shelley back then; now it seemed like the name of a child she had once been)—tiny and cheap glasses of vodka and water with lemon because she was trying to avoid the freshman fifteen but also because, and she remembered this so clearly, the vodka made her drunk faster, did something to her that other drinks didn't. She could tell, even then, that she wasn't experiencing the parties, the drunkenness, in the same way her friends were. It wasn't harmless—or, at least, it wasn't going to stay that way. But she was young, and consequences weren't a necessary concept yet.

This night, the one she was remembering now, Shelley was on the dance floor with her friends. She had been trying to ignore the fact that she wanted to throw up or pass out or both, when a group of young men they didn't know, rowdy and over-refreshed, approached their group, hands outstretched, to place on their waists. Strong bodies ground up against their unsteady ones. Some of her friends, the ones who were single or whose boyfriends were long distance, paired off with these forceful boys and danced with them and batted their hands away until they grew too tired and relented, but she pulled away entirely. One of them followed, putting his hands on her over and over. She stumbled away, and her eyes searched the crowd at the edge of the dance floor for Colin. Finally, she saw him, his expression dark as he moved across the room toward her. This darkness was unfamiliar; Colin was known in their fledgling group as the easygoing one.

"Get your damn hands off her."

"Why should I?"

"Because she wants you to leave her alone. And she's too drunk to tell you."

"How do *you* know what she wants?"

Colin had grabbed the young man's collar and pulled him close. "Put your hands on her again, I'll kill you," he'd said before abruptly letting go. The stranger fell into the crowd, then reemerged, fists clenched. She remembered gasps, grunts, curses, fear.

The painful light of the next day had revealed a black eye for Colin and a difficult truth for her. Suddenly, the word "consequences" had meaning, as did the idea of a future. She knew she did not want to see him like that again and that she never wanted to feel like that again, either: helpless, tarnished. She had stayed silent beside Colin in the single bed of her dorm room and imagined their future life. She could stop now, draw a line in the sand with alcohol, or keep on going and never be able to stop. But she needed his help. She needed him to stand with her if they were going to go forward. So she took a chance, because she had a feeling he would understand. "We need to stop drinking," she said. "I can't anymore." This was the only time in her young life she ever discussed the problem she had with anyone. Shell came from a good family. She was an aberration. Who knew where these things came from? Better not to talk about it. Colin took her hand. "Okay," he said.

He came with her to AA meetings, and held her hand throughout those, too. "My name is Shell and I'm an alcoholic," she said at the second one. They went to dinner. He called her "Shell" that night, and she felt she had become a new person. And she had known: this was the man who would love her, always. This was the man who was strong enough to stand beside her through anything, everything. *That* was the story of Shell and Colin. But what a fool she had been to believe that was the happy ending, that life was always going to be easy and she'd never be hurt so badly she'd hit the bottle as hard as she could and beg for it to hit her back.

No.

She deleted the words on the screen before her. *Stop. Enough dwelling on the past.* No one was strong enough for what had happened to her. No one. And Miles knew what he was doing. She had to do what he said, if she wanted to be all right again. That meant no contact with her husband.

Dear Mom, Dear Zoey,

I wish you were here.

I know it's not Colin's fault–Zoey, I know that. And I know I've said some awful things to him, and he's said some awful things back, because, if only–but I just don't think I'll ever be able to forgive either of us for not making different choices that night. So we've separated. I'm sorry. I wish it could be different, but it isn't. We loved each other once, so much. And now that love is broken. Don't be sad. We love you so, so much.

My only hope now is to make myself okay. Then maybe I can start living in a way that would make you proud.

Tears blurred her eyes until she couldn't see the screen anymore. She wondered if there would ever come a day when she recollected the night their daughter died and didn't fall to pieces. *Stop, stop. Save it for your session with Miles.*

Yes. She would tell him everything. She had so much to say. And he would help her.

"Shell?"

Shell turned her head and saw Ruth standing before the desk again. "Yes?"

"That's the third time I've said your name. Aren't you finished? You're due at your appointment with Miles soon."

"Oh. Yes. I'm done now." Shell hit send. She stood. She couldn't feel anything. She would, though. Soon, she would.

"Is it getting any easier?"

"Is what?"

"Missing your daughter. Is it?"

"No."

"Well, it won't be long now. And then you'll see her." A strange pause. "Right?"

Shell backed out of the room. She ran all the way down the stairs.

"We made love last night." Johanna's voice in Grace's office sounded as hollow and empty as she felt. "Things are good now." Then she leaned down and picked irritably at the itchy scab on her ankle. This wasn't Grace's fault, the way she felt inside, but Johanna still felt frustrated with her.

"Did it feel right to you?" Grace said in a voice that was even more throaty than usual, as if she had a cold. Or had been crying.

Johanna leaned up and looked at her, hard, trying to chase away her sudden concern for Grace when, really, the person she needed to worry about was herself. "Why wouldn't it? He's my husband. It's what you told me to do. Why does it matter to you if it felt right or not?" Their eyes locked and Johanna lifted her chin in defiance.

Grace sighed. "During our last session alone, we talked about my showing you how simple it could be, to find your way to happiness again, to be okay inside yourself again after all you've been through. And I think in that moment we both felt good about what we could accomplish together. Am I right about that?"

Johanna nodded. She hated that she wanted to cry.

"But we didn't do very well in the couples' segment of the therapy, did we? *I* didn't do very well." Grace leaned back in her chair and put her notepad on her lap. She had on a long-sleeved blouse and she pulled the sleeves down as if she was cold. Johanna squinted at the notepad, thinking that if she had brought her glasses with her, she could have read the words, could have read what Grace thought she knew about her or what she wanted to say to her next. But from there it just looked like a squiggle. "I'm really sorry. Forgive me," Grace said.

Johanna was caught off guard. "For?"

"I stopped listening to you, when you were in here with Ben. I stopped seeing you clearly. To be honest, I was having a tough day. It can be a challenge to treat the individual and then the couple. Miles thinks—" but she shook her head slightly and stopped, then began again. "What you are going through is very personal. It is not just about your marriage. I knew that, but I became focused on the task at hand—on the marriage part. That's what we do here, but that kind of focus is not what you need right now. Am I right?"

Johanna could only manage a slow nod.

"Can we start over in here today? Can we attempt to rebuild the trust we had started to establish?"

"How do you know?" Johanna asked.

"How do I know what?"

"That it's not just about my marriage? That I'm not feeling good about last night? How do you know?"

Silence. Then, "Are you?"

"No."

"Did you feel conflicted last night?"

"Yes. Not exactly. I don't know." Johanna laughed self-consciously, although none of it was funny to her. It was a reflex that felt like it was left over from another lifetime. "Okay, yes. I felt like I knew just what I had to do. I felt like I was giving myself a prescription. And it didn't feel right, even though I wanted it to. I tried too hard last night, but instead of feeling safe with him, I came very close to feeling . . . exposed."

"What was it that made you feel exposed?"

"It was the board game," she said. "That one question."

"Which question?"

"Who was your first love?"

"Did you tell your husband about your first love?"

"I said it was him."

"Is that true?"

Johanna felt the softness of the leather couch beneath the palms of her hands. "No."

"Will you tell me about who your first love really was?"

"Yes."

———

Her name is Amy. She has long dark hair. She always wears nude lipstick with dark liner. Like most best friends their age—fifteen—they brush and braid and crimp each other's hair and they borrow each other's clothes and they sleep on the floor beside each other's beds, or sometimes in the same bed, and they call each other on the nights they're not together and they talk for hours and meet each other before school and walk there together, and walk home together, and make cheese and mayonnaise sandwiches after school, but only with each other. When they're together, time moves too fast.

When they're not together, Johanna has peanut butter and she hates the taste of it, of anything, when she's alone in her trailer without Amy. "That song makes me think of you now," said Amy of a cheesy nineties techno tune they both loved, something about Saturday night and liking the way a person moves, so be my baby. "Remember that time you danced like an idiot in the kitchen while you were making us sandwiches?" Amy said. "Remember you added sliced green onions and mustard and how gross?" The word "gross" reminded Johanna of Amy's cruel older sister, Marybeth, who would say that about almost anything they did or said or wore, but most especially when they would go to the store to get the pasty white bread and plastic-wrapped cheese slices they adored. "Gross. We actually have real food here, we're not trailer trash like she is."

It stings, when Marybeth calls Johanna trash the first time, but then it becomes another thing she and Amy are united against. She focuses on the things they agree on. Holes in the ozone layer are bad, alongside George Bush, and eating meat. They don't like to eat meat because of Johanna's mom's boyfriend, who works at the butcher counter at the grocery store and always smells like blood. Sinéad O'Connor is great, and they watch that video with the tears falling down her beautiful cheeks in silent reverence, maybe each for different reasons. Johanna squeezes her hands into fists at her sides when Sinéad sings about how she could put her arms around every boy she sees. When they sing it out loud, Johanna screams that part and Amy laughs. "Whenever I hear this song, for the rest of my life, it'll only remind me of you—your terrible singing voice," Amy says. "We'll be best friends forever, right?"

"Promise," Johanna says. "Cross my heart, hope to die, swear on my life." Where do promises like these go, when they're broken? Johanna wonders this later and she tries to never make promises like this again.

They want to be different than their friends, they decide, so they start to listen to eighties music instead of nineties, discover the song "Asleep" by the Smiths and listen to it over and over, crying into one another's shoulders. They don't write songs like this anymore, they moan. They turn up their noses at Nirvana—it's just music for boys to jerk off to, Amy says, and Johanna agrees because they always agree and then Amy asks Johanna if she would ever touch a boy's penis and Johanna shrieks and says "No way!" They listen to "Asleep" again. They cry into one another's shoulders some more and Johanna revels in the smell of her friend's skin when they are close like this. Johanna saves her money and buys her the Sunflowers perfume gift set she so wants for her birthday, the one with the body wash and the body lotion, too.

The difference between Amy and Johanna's friendship and the friendships of other girls their age, though, is that Jo is in love. Not platonic love. Not that at all. She doesn't know when she realized it but she knows it to be true, and the reality of it, of finally being in love with someone, is a revelation. All of her friends have been deeply, irrevocably in love by this point, some of them more than once. These crushes started up in grade six or seven, and Jo had never felt them, had felt only a subtle revulsion for boys she had assumed she would eventually "grow out of." When she didn't grow out of it, she started to pretend so she'd have something to talk about when the other girls were talking about their crushes. "Oh yeah, he's totally cute, yeah, he smells totally good," she'd say to other kids her age, when really she thought the boy in question smelled like the rotten beans her mother threw in the compost. "Oh, yeah, I have a major crush," she would say to their friends, as she started to fear she was incapable of love.

But then there was Amy. It was around the time Johanna's dad died that they started getting close, and maybe that's what cemented it, that Amy was the one beside Johanna at the funeral, the one at school who linked arms with her in the hall on the hardest days, the one who guarded her and her grief at school, proudly, dramatically, as teenage girls do. "Not right now. She just needs some space."

Nothing compares to Amy. Especially with her father dead and her once warm and caring mother so distant and sad, she longs for love the way a drowning person longs for air, with no way to get it. She is paralyzed by fear, swims toward the light and then realizes she's gone in the wrong direction. The only time she doesn't feel like she's gasping for air is when she's with Amy.

She tries not to worry, tries to focus on the fact that at least there are times she is okay, that at least she has a friend. She tries not to mess it up. Amy hugged her so hard when she gave her the perfume. For her birthday, Amy bought Johanna a silver ring with a heart of turquoise. The color of the ocean they were going to see one day, together. "You can come with me, on our next family trip to Naples," Amy said. She meant Florida, where Amy's mother was from, they went every year and all Johanna had to do was pay for her flight, but there was no money for that. And by the time the next spring break rolled around, even though Johanna had saved and saved and almost had it and Amy was going to secretly loan her the rest, it was too late. She wasn't invited anymore.

"Morrissey is so hot," Amy would say, and Johanna would say, "Totally hot," but she felt broken inside, hollowed out by her own lie. "I wonder if Morrissey's gay?" Anna said once, and all Johanna said was, "Ew. No way." And she had wished for her father's wisdom then, and her mom's easy understanding.

Johanna writes letters and throws them away. She drops hints, to no avail. She wants what all teenage girls want, just to fit in, but she doesn't; that's just the way it is. She decides she will be brave, because if Amy is deserving of her love—and she is, she knows it—she will understand. Maybe even feel the same. And then, Ivan, her mother's new boyfriend, their relationship a symptom of her mother's brokenness, invites them to move in with him. He was bad when he was always around, but it's worse now that it's officially his house. "Your mom couldn't have picked someone more different than your dad was," Amy has observed. Johanna can't talk about it. She just rolls her eyes and feels her heart break a little more.

When he walks in one afternoon, the girls are curled up on the couch together like kittens watching a movie. Johanna hates it, the way he looks at Amy, the way he looks at her.

"What are you, some kind of fuckin' dykes or something?" he says, and she longs for her trailer, for her real home. His place is bigger, but there's nowhere to hide.

He makes it sound so ugly, what he calls them. He dismantles all the work Johanna has done inside herself, convincing herself that it's going to be all right and that, someday, people will accept her for who she is. After that, they don't sit in the living room anymore. After that, Johanna says they should stay in her room when they're at her place. He takes to banging on the door. "What the fuck are you doing in there? You two dyking it out again?"

"Fuck you, asshole!" Johanna screams one day. Silence. And then he breaks down the door and tells Amy to get the hell out. Later, her mother doesn't defend her. She says she shouldn't have spoken to Ivan that way in the home he was kind enough to let them live in after they lost the trailer. Everything changes because of him. He ruins everything. Johanna fantasizes about killing him, but it's idle, how could she? She even goes so far as to research poisons at the library, but, in the end, she doesn't have the courage for that or anything else. It scares her how much she hates this man. And it scares her even more that her mother doesn't seem to notice, no matter what he does, no matter how many times he hurts her. Her mother doesn't hate him at all. She's grateful to him.

A good summer, endless days spent at Amy's and away from Ivan, and then—

"Johanna?"

"Yes?" She blinked a few times and there was Grace Markell, who had probably never had a moment of such uncertainty and self-revulsion in her life. Grace Markell, who swam naked in cenotes with her lover. Grace Markell, who was free, even though she didn't always appear to be. But Johanna knew.

"You've been silent for a while. What happened next?"

A sigh. "I told her I was in love with her."

"And she . . ."

"Told me to go home. I was lying on the floor beside her bed at the time, where I always slept when I slept over at her house, on an air mattress we would blow up. She told me to leave and I did, went home in the middle of the night and told my mom I felt sick and when I went to school on Monday everyone was whispering about me because Amy told Marybeth." She pressed her lips together, but then forced herself to keep talking. "That was when I decided it wasn't who I was going to be. I just—decided. By the following year, I had a boyfriend." Johanna wiped her eyes, then put down the tissue and carefully watched Grace's face for signs of surprise or revulsion, but Grace appeared neutral, and when she caught Johanna's exploratory gaze, she nodded encouragingly.

"You're being very brave," she said. The lava rock in Johanna's hand was burning hot. "I know this is hard for you to talk about."

Johanna put the rock down. "It was probably just a phase," she said, because it felt better to say that. It had always felt better to say that. She was such a coward. Other people weren't such cowards, and Johanna had never been one of them. She always heard Ivan's voice in her head, calling her ugly names. She had never been able to chase that voice away. She opened her mouth to say something like this but then, the timer. The damn timer.

"I'll see you tomorrow morning. We'll continue this then," Grace said to Johanna. Johanna stood. Her legs were wobbly. She needed something to hold on to; she thought for a moment that she would keel back onto the couch. But she managed it. She stayed upright.

"It's going to be okay, Johanna," Grace said, standing, too. "I promise it is. You'll get it all out and then we can pick up the pieces." She took a step closer and looked down. "Wait, though. Just one minute before you go. That rash on your ankle looks bad. You should go see the nurse about it, okay? And let me know what she says."

*S*hell and Miles were sitting beside one another on the couch in Miles's office. Shell felt jittery and expectant. She badly wanted to sound the right note. She could hardly focus on what he was saying, so intent was she on choosing her next words, on explaining it all to him in a way that would be clear, in a way that would not cause her to fall apart in front of him. *My mother came to visit. I was tired, but I shouldn't have been. For years, we tried to have a child, and that's the way I acted—ungrateful? And Colin, too. How could one night in the house alone together be so important to us? We should have been the ones going out to dinner, but I said I just wanted a quiet evening in. We sent my mother out on roads she didn't know. We could hardly wait to get them out the door; we mustn't have even given her proper directions into town. And those rural roads, when it gets dark—we should have known better.*

"Did you know," Miles said, "that of the five senses, sight is the strongest one?"

"Um. No," she said.

"It's very interesting when you think about it. In order to perceive touch and taste, we need to be in direct contact with an object. The same with smell or sound—we need to be close to hear, to smell. But our eyes can see for miles and miles. And our eyes can see inside things, the tiniest of details. Like, for example, I am noticing right now that your eyes are amber, ringed with dark brown. I thought they were brown. They're beautiful. A very unusual eye color."

She blinked. He kept staring into her eyes. "And I see sadness. Such sadness. And I think I know why you're so sad, why you're so lonely, just by looking at you." She opened her mouth to speak. "What do you

147

see?" he asked. "When you look into *my* eyes?" He took off his glasses and held them in his lap.

She hesitated. "Your eyes are dark blue," she said. "Navy. You look . . . you seem . . . confident."

"Anything else?"

She shook her head. "Not right now."

"Do you remember yesterday, during our session? We were trying something new. It's a technique I've wanted to try for some time but hadn't had the courage. You gave me the courage. You say you see confidence in my eyes but I'm actually quite nervous right now."

He seemed nervous, it was true. It was disconcerting, but also made her feel she possessed a power she hadn't realized. It was calming, to be focusing on something other than her own pain.

"I suppose this could be called a consciousness experiment. I've been feeling a little disillusioned with myself and my practice."

"But you're so successful. You and Grace. How could you feel disillusioned?"

His eyes moved away from hers at the exact moment she said the name *Grace* and then back again. "It's the human condition, I suppose, to chafe against what we have, to seek more. And I'll be honest with you: the moment I saw you, the moment I looked into your eyes, I felt a connection. Did you feel it, too?"

She thought about that moment in the lobby when she first met him. She *had* felt a connection, but to his voice, not his eyes. She nodded. She felt like a student seeking approval from a teacher. Something didn't feel right, but she never felt right, so she ignored the sensation. As she continued to stare into his eyes, she found she was losing touch with the physical symptoms she'd been experiencing that morning, the ones she didn't want to talk about. Maybe this was a sign of improvement, that she no longer felt a searing urge to kill herself? That was another thing to talk about. That was something to tell Miles. When he asked.

"So, are you ready?"

"Ready for what?" she asked.

"The experiment. It's called EMDR—eye movement desensitization and reprocessing. Studies have shown it's very effective for treating trauma. And yesterday, during those moments we tried it without even knowing it, it felt so right, didn't it?"

Trauma. So he knew, and this was his way of leading. She felt herself relax then. Why was she so suspicious all the time? *Just relax and go with the flow,* she thought to herself. *It will all come out in its time.* Her eyes filled with tears in anticipation.

"Thank you," she whispered. "Yes. I'll try it."

He stood and walked over to his desk. "I think it might be best to have a little help at first," he said. He had a glass of water in one hand and his other hand was held out, palm up.

A pill.

He put it in her hand. A current ran through her body. Alarm was drowned out by her own need. At the sight of it, her hands started to shake—whatever it was, that pill, she *needed* that. If she couldn't have vodka, she needed it. She swallowed it, dry.

"It's a mild relaxant," he said. She tried not to be embarrassed by grabbing for it, and then it didn't matter. The sedative wasn't so mild. She felt her senses dull and then heighten. "Colin," she said. It was almost involuntary.

"Don't think about anything right now. Not your husband, not the past. Just us, right now. Focus on this."

She stared into his eyes. Time passed, and then more time. She stared so long his face distorted. He didn't move. It was almost like being asleep. Then she heard a sound. Tibetan chimes, from his phone in the corner. Was he supposed to have a phone? Was he supposed to—

The chimes were still ringing, she was still staring into his eyes while inside her a torrent of unanswered questions begged for answers. It took her a moment to realize his lips were on hers, but then he was kissing her so forcefully she had to pull away and gasp for air.

"Oh, forgive me," he moaned, putting his head in his hands. "Look what you've done to me—I'm powerless. Oh, Shell, I'm so sorry, but our connection was so intense. It felt like an out of body experience."

She was stunned and heavy, as though she was underwater. "This is what you think I need?" Her tongue felt thick as she said the words. The pill was too strong. But *she* had taken it. *She* had grabbed it out of his hand. Hadn't she? Now she didn't remember.

"I'm sorry, I'm sorry," he kept on saying.

"It's okay," she found herself saying, more to herself.

"Did you feel it? The connection."

She thought about all the things she had wanted to say before, but came up empty. She felt vaguely nauseated.

"This is what I know you need. To be seen. To *see*. Don't you feel it, too? Don't you feel this?"

"You keep asking me that." Her voice was dim.

"Because I want you to say yes."

She touched her lips. Wait. What? Had he just kissed her, a minute ago, or had she imagined it?

"You wanted that," he said, his gaze on her hand, her hand still at her lips. "That was what you needed. You didn't say it aloud, and I didn't hear it said, but in our moment of connection, your body sent mine the message. You asked for that, and more. This is what you want."

She opened her mouth, tried to say no, but he said, "Say yes. Because your mind and your body have already said it. This is what you want. Say yes," and so she stayed silent.

Too much. What was she supposed to say? "Yes," wasn't that it? Except she couldn't remember why she was saying yes and then he was kissing her again—and it couldn't have been to that, he was her *therapist. What is happening?*

She wished she had said no. It seemed to be too late.

*J*ohanna dove down, pushed the crown of her head forward and up, stretched her body, first curving upward and then into downward dog, a position she had never liked the name of particularly, not even when a Buddhist friend of hers from home had once explained it had just as much to do with letting go of pride than anything else. She knew enough about letting go of her pride; she didn't need to call herself a dog in order to do so.

She rose and twisted, dove down again, repeated the sequence. She turned her attention to her mat, and then to the front of the room and the yoga instructor, who said, "Remember to breathe."

Dyke bitch. That voice was everywhere and she couldn't tell whose voice it was anymore. Talking to Grace had helped, but only when Grace had been there with her. Now she felt scared. Grace hadn't said anything. Grace had just listened. What was Johanna going to say to her when she saw her next? What would Grace do if Johanna kept going, if she finished the story? Because that had just been the beginning, the very beginning of a long story. There was still Cleo. There was still the real truth, darker and worse. She had vowed not to tell—and now she wasn't sure she was going to be able to stop herself.

The teacher instructed them to move into warrior two. Johanna liked the warrior poses best of all; they were the chief reason she did yoga, to feel that momentary strength and forward-moving purpose. But she didn't feel it this time.

At the end of class, the instructor said, "There isn't another class after this, so if you would all like to stay in *savasana* for a while, please feel free." But Johanna never did *savasana* at all, so she got up and left the room because she knew that in the silence, the voices would come, first one, then the other, telling her the truth about herself.

She entered the changing room to pick up her sweatshirt and yoga mat bag. She stopped. A woman crouched in the corner startled her. The woman had a haunted look in her eyes. At first, with her hair pulled back and up, as if she, too, had been about to do a yoga class, Johanna didn't recognize her. Then she realized it was the shiny-haired woman from the first night, Shell Williams.

Johanna approached. Shell stared ahead, unseeing. She was trembling and there were tears on her cheeks. Instinctively, Johanna looked her over for marks and for bruises. She crouched down and looked into her eyes. Small pupils, a bit glossy.

"Shell?" The woman didn't move. "Are you all right?"

Shell's eyes came into focus. "Oh," she said, looking around the dim changing room. "I'm fine," she said, touching her cheeks, as if surprised to find them wet.

"You're not," Johanna said. "Can I help you to the bench?"

Shell let Johanna guide her to sit. She sat with her shoulders slumped. She didn't speak.

"What's going on?" Johanna asked.

Silence. Then Shell's brittle voice. "You don't want to know."

"I asked. I do want to know." Johanna was reminded of the way she had felt some days at work, like she was involved in an elaborate dance with a person who had so much to say, so much buried inside, so much help they needed to ask for but couldn't. Grace probably felt that way every day. And she did such a good job of getting people to talk. Every moment, she realized, Grace was in her head. But this was not the time to be thinking about that.

Shell said, "You're the social worker."

"That's me," Johanna said. "*Was* a social worker."

"Really? You let that maniac ruin your career, too?" That stung.

Johanna tried not to show it. She recalled those moments in the anger management group when she had spilled out her story.

"It's complicated. I shouldn't have unloaded on all of you like that."

"No. It was very brave. And you have enough problems. You don't need to hear about mine."

Johanna leaned against the wall behind them. She tilted her head up and looked at the ceiling. There was a water stain. "What if I said hearing about someone else's problems would distract me from mine and I might even like it?" She laughed softly. "Sorry, is that mean? I've been called jaded before."

Shell laughed for a fraction of a moment, too. "I'm supposed to be in that stupid anger management group right now," she said. "I had no intention of going to yoga at all. I put on the clothes and found a mat, but I was never going to go. My plan was to hide in a changing room. It seemed like such a *good* plan—"

"Can I ask you a question? Did you take something?"

No answer. But Johanna knew there was a larger picture she wasn't seeing. The silence continued until she decided it was more important to let it go and keep Shell talking to her. "I don't blame you for not going to anger management," she said. "Anger management group is terrible. And that Ruth . . ."

"She's a little nuts."

"Agreed."

"Anyway, I'm not angry."

"Me neither."

"I'm sad."

"Me, too."

"And I think—"

Two women walked into the changing room.

"Let's go outside," Johanna said.

Outside, a hot wind smacked their faces but the rain had stopped.

They fell into step and headed for the beach with its now dull gray sky and strangely morose surf, flat as slate. So much for paradise. The weather just kept getting worse. They both paused to take off their shoes when they reached the damp sand, then moved toward the water and let the surf touch their toes.

Shell bent, picked up a rock, looked at it for a moment, then tossed it. "I've always wished I could skip rocks," she said as the stone sank.

Johanna picked one up, too, a smooth flat rock the color of a terra-cotta roof. "It's all in the wrist," she said, flicking hers and sending the rock hopping. "My dad taught me. He taught me to pitch baseballs, too, but he said skipping rocks was way different. Be gentle, he always told me. Here, try this one." Now Johanna picked up a skinny flat rock. "This one is perfect. It has a little chip. You can grip it better." Johanna thought of her father, who had taught her to do this in the big lake they lived near, on a gray afternoon when she had been starting to realize he wasn't going to be there with her for too much longer, that advanced pancreatic cancer was not something you recovered from, that there were going to be a lot of things left unsaid between them because he was running out of time. "You have to put your index finger around it. It's the kind of thing that seems impossible until you do it, and then you wonder how you ever doubted yourself." Johanna realized she was repeating the exact words her father had said to her. She found herself wishing she had listened to everything he had ever said more closely. Maybe he had always been trying to tell her some-thing about her life.

Shell didn't throw the rock, just looked at it. "He separated us," she said. "Things are so bad between us that we aren't even in the same villa."

"You and your husband?" Johanna asked.

Shell nodded.

"Who separated you?"

"Miles."

Johanna's eyebrows raised. "Really?" she said. "I didn't know they did that."

"It's not what we need," she said. "And I don't know how to explain that. No one is listening."

"I am."

Shell threw the rock. It didn't even reach the ocean, just hit the sand and rolled into the water. "No one knows why we're here," she said.

Johanna focused on a faraway wave, tried to follow it with her eyes as it crashed toward shore, but lost it eventually; it blended in and disappeared.

"Our daughter died," Shell said. "She was three. Our only. Our baby."

"I'm so sorry."

"Thank you. It's awful. Do you know you're the first person I've said that to, that she died? The only person here, other than Colin, who knows?" Shell bent down and picked up another rock. "What's the trick, I just . . . ?" She flicked her wrist but held on to the rock, didn't let it fly.

"Hold the stone like this," Johanna said, putting her fingers over hers and showing her how. "Try not to think about it too much."

Shell turned it over and held it the way Johanna showed her. "I thought it would be a lot harder to say that, to talk about it. I thought I'd fall apart."

"You're very strong."

"That's what he keeps saying." A pause. "I've heard half of couples don't survive the death of a child. I don't want that for us, but I don't know how to fix things."

Shell released the rock. This one sank, too.

Johanna was embarrassed by how badly she had wanted that rock to skip for Shell. The world was not a perfect place. It wasn't even close. Shell bent down and picked up another rock. She threw it hard. It splashed into the water. And she grinned for a moment. "Sometimes, it just feels good to throw things," she said.

Johanna whipped a rock, too, pretended she was throwing a baseball.

"Whoa, you must have been some pitcher."

Johanna smiled. "I wasn't bad."

"You know, I feel like I can barely make it through another day, let alone the rest of my life. It was just over a year ago, her death. I feel like I should be letting go, but I don't want to let her go, ever. I even feel her with me sometimes." Shell trailed off. "And when I don't, I drink. Another thing I find it hard to talk about. Should you be charging me by the hour?"

"No one could blame you for drinking, for caving under the pressure of all the grief you must feel. It's normal."

"I blame myself, though. For all of it. No wonder my husband can't look at me. We're finished. We're for sure finished. And this is just an incredibly painful, embarrassing end to it. Probably what I deserve. I don't know. It's all so murky, but it must be what I deserve."

"You really shouldn't do that. People do, all people do that when something bad happens. They blame themselves—but you're being way too hard on yourself."

Shell turned to her. "You know, when you were telling that story the other day, about that man and the gun, I just kept thinking that I would have begged him to kill me."

"No. Trust me, you wouldn't have."

"How do you know?"

"Because I was there. I know what a person feels when something like that happens. You want to live. Even if you think you don't. You understand what your life is worth. You see the light you couldn't see before. Maybe just for a minute, but you do."

Shell picked up another rock and heaved it. "Thank you," she said.

"For what?"

"I needed someone like you. And you were there. It feels like a miracle."

"I can listen more. There's nowhere I need to be."

"It's okay. I should probably get back. I feel really tired." Her voice was weakening.

"Listen, we're in Bungalow Seventeen," Johanna said before Shell walked away. "If you need anything, anything at all, even if you just want to talk again, come by."

"Sure," said Shell. Johanna watched her walk away. The wind picked up and, with it, her sense of foreboding. She almost followed, but she couldn't think of any more to say.

race was surprised to see Colin Williams, rain in his hair, distress in his eyes, standing at her office door.

"Should I have called?" he asked. "I'm sorry. I know I haven't come to my appointments for the past few days, and now I'm just showing up, and it's just about dinner. But I really need to talk to someone."

She tried to smile. "Of course." She could not allow it to show, how badly she had wanted the next hour to herself. Just to think. And to take a Tylenol for the searing pain in her wrist. "Come on in."

His face was too young for his silver hair, and there were circles under his eyes and a tired defeat in them. She thought about his wife and she thought about Miles and found herself looking away from him as a sword of guilt stabbed at her heart. *You could put a stop to this. You never have. It's on you, too.*

"I'm sorry I haven't been coming," he said. "You probably think I've been working, but I haven't. I lost my phone chargers." Grace felt a prickle of alarm. "It's so stupid—both of them, gone. Like they've disappeared into thin air. So, I haven't been in touch with anyone. And I started doing some soul-searching about all that—about exactly why it was so important. And then I started looking for my wife. I need to see her. I need to talk to her. Where the hell is she? No one at the front desk would tell me. They looked *scared* when I asked. I've started to consider knocking on bungalow doors, until she opens one of them. Can you help me? Do you know where she is?"

"I'm sorry—what do you mean, *where* is she?"

"We've been separated. You must have known that."

"Oh. Yes." She swallowed and picked up her notebook so she'd have something to do with her hands. She disagreed with separations, and strongly. She had told Miles this, but it didn't matter. He prescribed them anyway. This time, without mentioning it to her. She thought of Colin's missing phone chargers, Shell's confiscated vodka bottles, the safe in one of the boardrooms where Ruth kept the sleeping pills and valium and anything else she decided could potentially stand in the way of the work they were trying to do. They were playing God, all of them. They were a trifecta, Miles, Ruth, Grace. The father. The child. And Grace, the spirit, hanging in the background, standing by and doing nothing. Some argued that was where the real power lay. Grace didn't feel so sure. All she knew was that she needed it to stop.

"I know, I know, it's against the protocol to know where she is," he said, mistaking the blank look on her face for something else. "But this so-called protocol is killing me. I need to talk to my wife."

"Why don't *we* talk for a while? And then—the truth is I actually don't have her bungalow number with me right now, but I'll get it to you. I promise. Okay?" He allowed her to deflect his other question. He was a good man, she could tell. Lost, broken, confused—something there inside him, something really bad that had happened between him and his wife, but a good man, ultimately. Gentle. Sad. Now the stab of guilt inside her turned to something else: an ache of empathy. This was a man who was suffering deeply. She could feel it in the room. But instead of feeling ignited by the possibility of helping him, she felt tired.

This is your job, she reminded herself. *You always have to be ready.*

"Have a seat," she said.

"I've made a mess of this. I should have said no when Miles suggested this ridiculous separation thing. But I was so angry with her. We've been through so damn much. And, to be honest, I did need a break. I needed to think. And I have been doing that."

"What have you been thinking, exactly?" She tried to focus just on him. But, instead, she saw Johanna, there beside him on the couch, and then she saw Ruth, and then her sixteen-year-old self, Grace Tyler, the person she had been once. And she saw Shell Williams, with her sad, defeated eyes. She recognized that sadness and defeat. She blinked her eyes rapidly, making them all disappear.

"Shell's anger is one real issue," he said. "And my workaholism is the other. It's not just that, though. There's more. So much more."

She didn't feel strong enough for it, but there was no other choice. "Tell me what happened to you two." She closed her eyes for a moment and pictured their home, Colin and Shell's. It would be big, airy—maybe a bit too airy. Empty. A lake. Trees. A view they probably stopped noticing. There would be the issue of Shell's drinking to contend with. Grace wondered how that fit into their lives. But she also knew there was something worse they were dealing with. Something big and dark and all-consuming. *So much more,* Colin had said. She braced herself.

Colin looked up at the ceiling of her office and rubbed his neck, as if priming himself. "Okay," he said. Eyes closed, eyes open. "Our little daughter was killed in a car accident. A drunk driver." His voice, calm and smooth a moment before, sounded like it had been pressed against a metal rasp and grated into the room. And her heart felt shredded, too, as she watched him lower his head into his hands the way he probably had the moment he heard his child was gone.

"Oh, no. I'm so sorry, Colin. Was it—Shell? Was she behind the wheel?"

He looked up. "What? *No.* Shell would never have done that. She only started drinking again after. Shell's mother was driving. She was up for a visit from Toronto. Shell and I wanted a night off, just the two of us, so we sent them into town to watch a movie at the Heritage Centre. But Pamela got lost, and they ended up on a back road. And—"

He started to cry now. "Zoey," she heard him say, anguish in his voice. She pictured a little girl with her father's eyes and her mother's steady gaze. Moments passed, and she held out the tissue box uselessly, but he didn't take it. Finally, he looked up and wiped his eyes.

"It was my idea. I told Shell we needed some time alone. I was going to cook her dinner, we were going to relax. Because Zoey, she was a real handful." Now, he was smiling and wistful.

The little girl Grace saw had shiny dark hair, like her mother's. Her footsteps through the house were light and constant.

"I mean, she was wonderful, but a fairly typical three-year-old, you know? It was nonstop. I just—I thought since Shell's mom was visiting, we could take advantage of it. Just for one night. We'd been living in the middle of nowhere for a year, the mine was just breaking ground and I was working nonstop, and she was taking care of Zoey all day, and at night she was exhausted. We were losing our connection." A pause. "You have no idea what I would give if I could go back and do that night over. Because now? We have all the nights alone we want. And they're awful."

Grace nodded. Anger, and grief, and confusion. She understood. The bottles of vodka not hidden, but out. Broken glass on a floor. Shouting, with no one to listen. Grief like a broken bottle, spilling fumes and scattering shards of broken glass. You wouldn't have been able to breathe in that house, you wouldn't have known where it was safe to step. And she could see that this was not the way it had been in that house before Zoey died. Lonely, maybe—but not desolate, no. Love and laughter. She could see the loss of that in his eyes, hear it in his voice. He had loved his wife and daughter, and he still did. But the place where he had loved them, that was gone.

"They took a wrong turn, that's all. If I'd given Pam better directions, if I'd warned her about the roads near the mine, and maybe how you never knew—but I should have known. What some of those guys are like."

Grace saw the late evening summer sunlight on the brown corduroy road, like a song she had heard once, something about weeds standing shoulder high. She saw those, too. A forest of them on either side of that road, and light filtering through pine needles. Bugs hitting the windshield. The grandmother making a joke. The little girl in the back seat, in a hastily installed car seat. Back at home, bags under a mother's eyes and a mother's love; a father's distraction and a father's adoration. A husband and wife, alone for the first time in a while. Maybe a little shy of one another. Or, maybe, finding their rhythm again easily.

"They were near one of the mines, and one of the guys who was working there—he had a problem. I'd heard about him, you hear these things in a small town. I'd talked to his boss about it. They were supposed to do something. I thought maybe fire him, but he was a good worker, apparently. Efficient. Even while high." Bitterness in his voice now. Grace didn't ask if the man had died. She cared as little as he did. What did it matter? "That's the kind of thing—you check for, you know? All kinds of safety checks are important, at a mine. That's *my* job. That's what *I* do." He sighed and looked out the window. The little glass clock ticked. "Employee wellness program," he finally managed, as if these things mattered now.

"Colin?" She'd seen it: when he talked about his work, he went on autopilot. He didn't have to feel and so he didn't.

"Yes, sorry, I was just—"

"Distracted."

Their eyes met. "Come back," she said.

"It's so hard."

"I know."

"We hadn't even started to worry, when the police came to the door." A lengthy pause, with a lot inside it. Panic, a drive in the darkness, maybe he almost forgot to put the headlights on, maybe she hastily turned off the radio because she couldn't stand the sound of music, or hearing what the weather might be like tomorrow. "And the hospital— they did everything they could, but it was just a cottage hospital. They didn't have the resources. They tried to MedEvac them to Winnipeg, but it was just too late. Halfway there . . ." Tears, again. This time he took a tissue. Grace could see it, feel it, smell it. Blood and antiseptic and a low-level building with only a few beds. A curtain around one of them. Someone crying. Shell. The doctors unable to conceal the distress. The helicopters, the pointless flight. A little angel girl dying up there in the clouds. A mother, too, the pillar Shell would have needed to help her through this. Grace understood what this scene would look like, and later, what the silence would feel like when there was nothing left to say. When hope had flown.

Her scalp was tingling. She felt a dampness, just below her eyes. She wiped the tears away, fast. He couldn't see it. This had to be his pain, not hers. She could not allow transference. She had worked so hard to be stronger than this.

He had his eyes closed. He hadn't seen her misplaced sorrow yet. The expression on his face was pure agony and there was nothing she could do for him but wait. While she did, she couldn't help it: she saw herself in a hospital room, too, an infant in her arms, hers. Baby Boy Markell. His body was perfectly still and peaceful while her own body shook with the sorrow and rage and the pain of life. With the wrenching loss of the joy that could have been him. With all of the emotions he would never get to feel.

And Miles, entering the room. Miles with anger in his eyes. *This was because of you*, he had whispered, and the nurse had surely thought he was offering whispered words of comfort to his wife because she left Grace alone with him. *Because your womb is filthy*, he whispered. *Because you are a traitor.* She had believed him, of course. She had blamed herself. *If only I had been someone different, my baby would be alive.* You believed anything, in those hellish moments. And what you believed was almost never true.

Paul. Writer of gospels. That's what Miles named their dead child, that's what he told the reverend who came to baptize him the name was. A cross of water on his perfectly still, blue-tinged forehead. It hadn't been the right name for him, though. Grace had known this even though she had barely known her son in this world—but she had *known* him. In the world of her body: that's where they had met, a place where flutter-kicks and rolls just below her skin were a secret language. Her womb hadn't felt filthy or traitorous when her child had made it his home. And his name hadn't been Paul, she'd known. His name had been Sol: a name that meant peace, sun, wonderer. Grace had wanted her son to find the love of God, but she had also wanted him to be able to seek that path on his own.

Who knows what Miles would have done to him in the end? Maybe Sol would have healed her husband, eased his mind. They never got the chance to find out.

Which is why she understood the man before her. Which was why, as exhausted as she had been, moments before, she was glad Colin had come. She knew she could help him, and that helping him would help her, too. This was the way it had always been. Why she did it, year after year.

She waited for his sobs to subside, for him to sit upright again. Nothing to do but wait, she knew, for time to do its job.

"Take a breath," she said. "It's all right now. Breathe. Just breathe."

He did, long and deep. "When you go through something like that . . . I think some couples come together, but we fell apart. Shell did what you're supposed to do when you're grieving, at least at first. She moved through all the phases, while I stayed stuck in one. Denial. She was alone, completely. I just stood by and said nothing. Because it was *my* fault that we lived out there. *My* job that had brought us somewhere no one could save Zoey when she was hurt. Damn it, it's no wonder she started to drink. No *wonder* she started to try to numb herself against all that. That night, the night she died, I was so hasty. Practically pushing Pam and Zoey out the door. I didn't take enough care. I just wanted to be alone with Shell. What were my last words to them? I don't even remember. Shell lost her daughter and mother, everything in one moment. And all I probably said was, 'Have fun, you two.' "

"Does Shell tell you that? That it was because of you?"

"She doesn't have to say it. It's just the truth. But no. She would never say that."

"She loves you."

"She did, once. I don't know how she feels anymore."

Only the sound of the ocean and the rain outside the window. She wished for sunlight for him, though she knew it wouldn't help.

"Are you angry with her ever? Do you ever get angry about the drinking?"

"Yeah. Sometimes. But it's not all that mystifying that she would choose that poison, of all things, even if it's what killed our daughter and her mother. Shell stopped drinking, years ago, when we were in school. She knew it was a problem. She conquered it. The condition was that I was supposed to stand by her. We didn't say it. We didn't have to. It was just us—who we were. Stronger together. But I abandoned her. It turns out I don't know how to take care of her when she's weak, only when she's strong. I'm a terrible husband."

"You can't take all of this on yourself."

"I can't put it on her, either."

"Don't you think she does the exact same thing? Do you really think she sits there alone, blaming you? No. She sits there alone trying to think of all the things she could have done differently, too." *Or, she sits there with my husband, while he tricks her, in her weakened state, turns her mind into something she no longer recognizes. We have to do something, Colin. I* have *to.*

"What she could have done differently is not marry me."

"But then you wouldn't have Zoey."

"We don't have her. She's gone."

Grace leaned in. She put her hand on his arm and made him look at her. "She's not," Grace said. "She's with you. All the time." She felt something in the room with them as she spoke those words. Maybe it was a little girl with shimmery hair and blue eyes, maybe it was a father's love. It's not what Miles would have said to him. Miles would have talked about heaven and being together again someday—but Grace knew how long a lifetime could be, waiting for that. She knew what people needed to get through every day.

Colin was crying again, silent tears. Grace saw Shell alone in that house, saw Colin asleep at a desk in a portable, beside a gaping hole in the ground that reminded him, every time he looked at it, of the grave he had left his daughter in. She understood the depths of that hole.

Grace saw Colin standing at the edge of the mine, saw the landscape of it, a stark, empty cavern, full of such potential, but only if you managed it properly. A place to escape to. To disappear into. A well of grief. She understood this so well—that you could believe that, with enough searching, with enough mining, you could bring your child back. Time did not heal that. You had to step away from the ledge.

And he did. She saw it. He shook his head, came away. He could see her again. "I had a dream once that Shell was drowning. And I tried to save her. And she pulled me under and we both sank. I'm afraid of her grief. It's bottomless. That dream had me convinced that we have no future. Don't all couples who lose a child break up eventually? I came here with hope, but there's no hope, is there? I think she suggested it because she wanted to prove that we were finished. So we could say we'd tried it all."

"That's a myth. More often, it's not true. Couples often get stronger after a loss like yours."

"What's wrong with us, then?"

"Nothing is wrong with you. You just need to find your way back to each other."

"And in order to get us to do that, you separate us?"

"That wasn't my choice."

"It wasn't?" A flicker of surprise.

Oh, but she was so, so tired. She shouldn't have said that. Grace turned and picked up the phone, using her good hand, as she had been all day. Trying to hide how much her wrist hurt. She called the front desk. "Yes, I *am* authorized to be given such information," she said, and she worked hard to keep the frustration out of her voice so he wouldn't see through it to the rot and ugliness and betrayal she was trying to cover up. "Thank you." She hung up and turned to Colin again.

"Your wife is in Bungalow Four. It's closest to the ocean. Beside—" she swallowed hard "—Miles's office. Go to her. Hold a hand out to her. I think you'll see that she doesn't pull you under, Colin. But you have to reach out first, because someone always has to be first. Okay?"

"Yes."

"And stay with her. Bring her with you for your session with me tomorrow. It's very important that you do that. Don't leave her side."

———

Grace said goodbye to Colin, then waited a moment before closing and locking her office door. She couldn't go to dinner. Not now. She was too exhausted. And she didn't feel like herself. She felt like Grace Tyler. The veil was so thin. She couldn't go out.

She took a ring of keys from her desk drawer and walked to her bookshelf. She unlocked the bottom cabinet and ran her finger along the spines of the books that were inside. *Reparative Therapy*. *Shame and Attachment Loss*. She opened the first book, but instead of reading the words, she ripped out a page, crumpled it in her hand, and tossed it on the floor. Soon, she was surrounded by balls of paper. Now she sat, curled up, held her knees tight to her chest and pressed herself against a wall.

Hello, Grace. We're glad you're here. We praise the Lord that you have decided to wrest your soul away from the devil. This is Miles Markell, our new youth minister. We thought you might be more comfortable with him here.

She stood and crossed the room to the hidden bookshelf again. There was a photo in there of Grace and Miles at their wedding. She kept it in here, made sure there were no wedding photos on display in their home or throughout the resort because she had been so young, too young, a child. Married at seventeen. It embarrassed her now.

Lord, help us exorcise this demon from this child's body.

There she was: her seventeen-year-old self, a child in a wedding dress, a look on her face that was full of naïveté and hope, instead of grief. Her brother was dead. Miles had convinced her he was a sinner, had encouraged her to pray on it over and over. *You won't ever see him again*, Miles had said to her. *He won't be waiting for you in heaven. Forget him. It's too late.* Who knew you could do that? Forget someone. She had, for a while. That had been the true sin. The wedding had been strange, like Sunday morning church but with the focus entirely on the two of them. It had almost felt like sacrilege, to be so shining and perfect and deity-like, in a church. Whispers as she walked down the aisle, but not the ones she had grown used to. It just took a few minutes, a practiced series of *I dos* and *I wills*, and then Grace Markell was as whole and pure as Grace Tyler had been broken and sullied. When they became famous, there had been a few headlines. Grace Markell, child bride? Did Miles take advantage of one of his flock? But none of it stuck, because look at them: the perfect couple! Who could find fault?

Except that their entire lives had been built on a fault line.

In the photo, Grace was looking up at Miles like he was a savior. And he was looking at her like he believed he was exactly that. *You make me feel perfect*, he used to say to her. *You make me feel like I can do anything.* She had given him too much power by letting him believe he had healed her. She had turned him into a monster. *She* had.

Outside, the wind blew. She put the photo back, stood, and walked to the huge window, where she had a panoramic view of the furious sea, the suffocating blanket of clouds, the darkness rolling in. The stars were coming out in patches where the clouds parted to allow it. She watched them out the window and wondered, as she often did, what else was out there. Miles would tell her nothing, that they were the only ones—but on nights like this she knew, just as she knew many other things, that this could not possibly be true. And she liked to think this: that there were other planets just like earth. Making herself and her kind matter less made her problems seem less huge. She had learned this from a client, actually, from a conversation in her office, a client confiding in her about the relief he sometimes felt when contemplating his own potential insignificance.

She learned so much from them. She was going to miss that more than anything, when it was all over. Because it had to be over. Today, this week, had made her see that. She could not do this anymore. She could not live this lie. The work wasn't saving her anymore. It might kill her if she wasn't careful, might make her want to die again. For years, it had felt like having a creature inside the walls of a house. She had heard it scrabbling in there, trying to get her attention. It had been much easier to ignore—but now the creature had died. The death and the rot and smell and the presence of it couldn't be ignored any longer. It couldn't. The way she was feeling about Johanna Haines—it was wrong. It was simply wrong. And the way she had been standing by and letting Miles wreak havoc on women's lives was wrong, too. Let him make his own bed. She couldn't do it anymore.

She was not Grace Markell. She was beginning to feel there was no way back. She was Grace Tyler, broken, bruised—but real. She was going to have to find a way to live with that.

"I'm leaving," she said to the stars out the window, but they disappeared as soon as she said it.

When?

Soon.

It broke her heart, but it also made her feel like there could be a chance, someday, that she actually *would* be healed.

She went to her desk and opened a notebook. She started a list.

Passport.
Cash.
Plan.
When?
?
?
Laptop/Phone
?

She stopped. She knew she was going to have to go into Miles's office. It had the information about her secret bank account in an encrypted file, and that bank account contained the money from her inheritance.

She could do this. She would pick the right moment. She would get the laptop and the information, and then she would slip away one night, unnoticed, and by the time dawn broke, she would be gone.

But not yet. She had to help Colin Williams and she had to help Johanna Haines—

Help Johanna Haines. That was all. And then never see her again.

She picked the books up off the floor and put them on her desk, turned them spine in and placed her clipboard on top, ready for the next day. She cleared the floor of the crumpled pages. But when she made it to the door of her office, she found she couldn't bring herself to open it. She was safe in here. Out there, she was not. The exhaustion overtook her, and so did the fear. The throbbing in her wrist. If Miles broke her any more, she would not have the strength to escape when the right time came. And she would certainly not have the strength to help anyone.

So she did something she had never done before. She stayed where she was, even though she knew her husband was waiting for her to join him and spend the night pretending to be different people than they were. She had granola bars in her desk drawer. She had water. She had her couch, and a sweater to cover herself if she got cold. She'd survive. And he wouldn't come for her, not here. He might tap at the door softly and call her bad names in a whisper, tell her stories about her special place in hell, but he would not bang at this door or break it down because her office was in among all the other bungalows. Everyone would hear him and understand what and who he really was. A man too damaged to help any of them. A man who, more and more, wanted only to help himself. She closed her eyes. It was such a relief.

*I*t was dark outside when Shell woke up. No clock in her room. She ordered dry toast and tea from room service. "No. Thank you, that's all," she had to say twice. Then a knock at her door. She expected the room service attendant, but instead it was Miles, holding a plate domed with metal flat-palmed in one hand and a bottle of sparkling water in the other.

"What are you—"

He stepped past her into the room, and turned. "Room service," he said with a lupine smile. "Close the door, please."

She did, but at the last minute left the door very slightly ajar. "What are you doing here?" A frown passed over his face but he replaced it with the smile again.

"Bringing you dinner."

He put the plate down on the small table by the window and lifted the metal dome with a flourish to reveal a plate filled with yellow rice and big chunks of chicken smothered in a deep brown sauce. She put a hand to her mouth to stifle a gag.

"That's not what I ordered. I ordered dry toast," she said.

"This is my favorite. You have to try it. Come. Sit."

She did sit, but mostly because her legs felt weak. This was not normal. She knew this should not be happening. It had been a slow dawning, as the effects of the pill wore off. But she knew that what was happening, it was not right.

"Do you hand deliver meals to all your clients?"

"Only the ones who need it. Man cannot live on bread alone.

Woman, either." He smiled wider at his own attempt at a joke. His accent twanged at her. It didn't sound so warm anymore. The smell of the chicken and spices continued to turn her stomach. He was pouring the sparkling water into two champagne glasses. When he put the water in front of her, she sipped it, grateful for that, at least.

"I'm really not feeling well. That pill—"

"This is our chef's specialty." He picked up a fork and cut a piece of chicken with the side of it, then sat and held the fork up to her.

"Please . . . I really can't."

He held the fork there for another moment, then put it down with a sigh.

"What were you doing, just now?" he asked.

"Thinking."

"About?"

"Home."

"Do you miss it?"

"I miss the way it used to be," she said cautiously. "I don't think I have anything to go back to."

He pushed the plate aside and leaned toward her, eyes alight with intensity.

"Maybe you don't have to go back," he said.

"What do you mean?" Her heart had started to beat rapidly.

"Let's test it. Let's do some more EMDR. Right now. Please?"

She felt a chill, as if the air conditioner had suddenly been cranked up. "I don't want to."

Another sigh. "Do you know how close you are? To feeling better, to feeling whole again? You are so, so close. And you keep fighting me. Do you really want to live like this?"

She realized he expected her to answer. "No."

"Do you know what your husband has been doing these past two days? He's been on his phone, taking calls and meetings. He hasn't attended a single counseling session. He is completely out of touch with his emotions, and with you. More than ever. But I am here. I *see* you.

Your beauty, your strength, your great potential. To be whole. Isn't that what you want?"

"Yes." Her voice was small.

He stood and put the dome back on the chicken. "I'm sorry," he said. "I'll go back and get you some toast after this. And some tea with honey. Maybe a little cinnamon, too. That always helps me when I'm feeling under the weather." His voice was gentle. "But let's—can we sit on the bed where it's more comfortable?"

"I don't want to."

"Shell." The sharpness was back. "You're being a bit ridiculous, don't you think?"

She followed him slowly. He was already sitting, and when she sat beside him, he held out a palm. A pill.

No. Not this time. "This is not right. You need to leave." She was about to stand but he put his hand on her arm and held it, hard. It scared her, his strength. She tried to stand again and couldn't.

"Was I wrong about you, Shell?"

"Stop it. Let go. I can't get up." She struggled and he held tighter. "That *hurts*."

"Tell me, was I wrong? I thought I saw something in you, but I don't see it now. I thought you had nothing left to lose. I wanted to give you everything. I'm trying to build something here and I thought you might want to be a part of it. You could join us. I could make you great."

"I have no idea what you're talking about."

"You said yes, you said it was what you wanted—"

She thought back to that afternoon. His face, too close to hers. Her lips were swollen after their session, a strange taste in her mouth, an extra button on her blouse undone. "You drugged me," she said. "You did it on purpose!"

"What are you talking about? You drugged yourself."

"Why are you doing this?"

"Why am I doing what?"

"Lying."

"You called me, just now. You begged me to come."

"No, that's not true!"

"You were threatening your own life. I was so worried. I brought you food. It went against my professional sensibilities, perhaps, to come here alone, but I came because I care about all my clients. But your behavior when I got here, it was so wildly inappropriate, it was embarrassing. Is this really what you want, Shell? It doesn't have to be like this."

"This is not what I want, not at all."

"My recommendation for you is rehab. I was coming in here to tell you that, but I wanted you to have something in your stomach first. Come on. Is this what you *really* want, Shell? Because it could be so different. Let me show you how different it could be. I don't want to give up on you."

"You're a—monster?" It came out like a question. Because could this be true? Could this really be happening?

"I'm really quite gentle, once you stop fighting." He leaned in and put his mouth on hers, and he was so casual about it, like a man at a buffet, sampling because he could. There was an antiseptic and familiar taste on his lips. She tried to pull away but he had his hands on her, holding her tighter and tighter.

The door swung open.

Colin.

He backed out of the room, and before she could scream, Miles covered her mouth with his hand. *Colin.* Why hadn't he stayed? Hadn't he seen how scared she was?

"No one will believe you. Not even him." Finally, he let her go.

She gasped for air, then slapped him as hard as she could.

"Jezebel," he hissed, jumping to his feet. And for a moment she was sure he was going to hit her back, right in the face, too. It seemed like a reflex for him. But he didn't. He opened his mouth. She braced herself for the awful things he might say. But he didn't say anything.

He spat. It landed on her chest. "Apparently, I *was* wrong about you," he said, in a cold, controlled voice. "And now, after I've come to your room to help you, you've thrown yourself at me, which your husband just witnessed, and you've physically attacked me, which my bruised cheek will attest to. I hope you're as ashamed of yourself as you should be." He started to walk toward the door, then turned back. "You chose this, you know—this life you have now. You focused on working, on being a 'career woman.'" His voice had a mocking tone now. "And then, when it was almost too late, you had a baby. One baby. And you lost her, probably because you could hardly focus on her."

He left her there, slamming the door behind him. She managed to stand and lock it. Then she went into the bathroom and, hands shaking, she took off her clothes. She stuffed them into the garbage can. She stood in the shower until her skin was pink and tender, but she could still feel the way he had soiled her with his saliva and she was sure she would feel it forever. She stood in the shower so long her legs began to tremble. She stood in the shower until her grief turned to anger, and it started to burn, red hot. She slid down the smooth wall and sat on the floor of the tub. Since the moment Zoey had died, she had had so many regrets, about the moments leading up to it and all the moments after. She had blamed herself for so much—but those things Miles had said, she knew they weren't true. It was not her fault. It was not because of the choices she had made. She hadn't known this for sure before, but she knew it now. The anger and grief began to feel like a volcano. She clenched her fists at her sides, opened her mouth and screamed.

Everyone heard it. The word *No* echoed over the bungalows, over the ocean, into the waves. Later, they would all remember pausing. Later, they would know they should have seen it coming.

Day Six

Him: You keep saying you loved him. But he was violent
     with you.

Her: Yes. All the time. I deserved it. I wasn't worthy. My
     womb was an abomination.

Him: Do you really feel that way?

Her: What does it matter, how I feel? It's just the way
     things are. It always amazed me that *she* didn't feel
     that way, considering what she was. Who she *is*.

Him: [Shuffling papers.] It was later revealed in the
     media that Miles had a genetic variant that caused
     stillbirth. Two other women came forward with the
     same story. From the group he was trying to start.
     He would say he had business meetings and go back to
     Texas. He impregnated two of the women during those
     meetings. We've talked about this. He had invited
     them to come back with him, when his wife was—taken
     care of, he would tell them.

Her: [A sharp intake of breath.] I don't believe those
     women. Those horrible, horrible women. And that's not
     true, the part about the genes. It wasn't *his* fault.

Him: So, it was yours? Does that really make sense to you?
     Are you going to let him keep punishing you, even
     from beyond the grave?

Her: You don't understand.

orning. A tap on Grace's office door. Johanna. Grace felt relief. She stood to welcome her. Despite her mental exhaustion, despite sleeping on her office couch the night before, despite the fact that for the first time in years her clothes were slightly wrinkled and her hair was unwashed and pulled back in a ponytail, she felt prepared.

But it was Miles at the door, his expression angry. "Please," she began, her heart plummeting. "I have clients coming. Johanna, and then Shell and Colin. You can't be here." He stood in the frame, looking into her eyes for too long, his eyes changing. She had seen this before.

"Grace," he said in a soft voice. "Why didn't you come home last night?"

She lifted her chin and met his strangely blank eyes. "You hurt me," she said.

"I'm so, so sorry."

"Don't do this. Not right now. I have clients coming, I told you."

"Shell and Colin won't be coming, you know." He sidled past her, into her office and closed the door. "They're probably never going to have another counseling session again. They're hopeless. We'd probably have to give them their money back, but they never signed the contract." He shrugged and looked around the room. "You know, it's been so long since I've been in here."

A wave of desperate nausea. "What did you do to Shell? Why aren't they coming to counseling?"

"What a question. Can't a husband come by to say good morning to his wife? It's not like you have anything else to do. They're not coming, I told you."

"What. Did. You. Do?"

"What did *I* do? It's more like what did she do. Shell has come unhinged. It's such a disappointment. And he's not so balanced, either. I understand they lost a child. Sad story. Sometimes that does something to you—something unfixable. Not everyone can be as strong as we were about it, Gracie." She found she couldn't speak. She felt paralyzed as he roamed her small office. He touched the lava rock she now kept close, on the table, and she wished he wouldn't. He picked up her little glass clock. "That's lovely," he said. "Where did you get it?"

"From—" She swallowed hard. "The market I go to," she said.

He turned. "Ben Reid mentioned, in one of our sessions, that his wife visited a market, too." He stepped closer. "Johanna. Did you see her on Sunday?"

A roar in her ears. She heard the word *No* coming out of her mouth, as if from a distance. She remembered the woman at the market, the fear in her eyes, telling her a man had been on the path. She remembered the dark sedan. She watched as he tried to open a drawer. What was he looking for?

"Stop it," she said.

He turned back to her. "What are you hiding?"

It was such a ludicrous question. It was not a question they asked one another. *Nothing. Everything. What are* you *hiding?*

"Wives shouldn't have secrets from their husbands," he said. "Wives shouldn't hide in their offices at night, away from their husbands." She held her breath, waited for it—but there was no rage in his voice.

Still, she felt her legs go weak.

"Oh, Grace. It is sad, isn't it? The two of us. You're not a wife. I'm not a husband. Not to *you*." Now his hand was on top of her notebook. She forced herself to step forward, but he was too fast. He opened it, flipped a few pages. She tried to snatch the book away, but he was

181

stronger. He was reading her list. "Passport? Cash? You're feeling as I do, I see." She started to walk toward the door. She didn't have to stay in here with him, she told herself. She could make her own choices. There were people around. They'd hear her if she had to scream. But then his voice, a gentle hum. Cajoling, unnerving. "You've reached your breaking point, haven't you? You're ready to run, aren't you? Me, too. It's all becoming so—monotonous, isn't it? So *boring*. But we can't *both* leave."

She stopped walking. She bit down on her cheek, tasted blood, metallic and harsh. She turned. "You followed me. Didn't you?"

A small smile. "To the market that day? Of course I did. I have several times. I figured out your little secret, the way you like to hide from me. But you can't. You should know that by now." A pause. "Interesting, though, isn't it? That *she* found you, too. I mean, we never knew you had a type, did we? I've always had mine, but you—"

Her cheeks were burning with remembered shame. "I don't know what you're talking about."

"She hasn't told you yet. She hasn't told you everything. She will." As if he knew more than he should. As if he had somehow been listening to their sessions and knew how close they were to a breakthrough. He looked back down at the notebook and flipped through a few more pages. "Maybe today." She could see he had reached the final blank page. "It's quite the story. I've been enjoying my sessions with Ben. He knows things about her no one knows. He knows things she doesn't *know* he knows. A fascinating relationship, that one. He's desperate for her love, and she's desperate for—" He put down the notebook. "Well, *you* know what she's desperate for, don't you? You're desperate for the same thing. You must be able to smell it. You must be able to almost taste it."

"Don't. She's my client. And it's not like that."

"I know exactly what it's like."

"How?" And she thought she saw it, his eyes flick toward one corner of the room. She spun around. "Where is it?" she said.

"Where's what?" His voice was calm and infuriating.

"The camera, the bug, whatever it is. I can't hide from you—but not because you're some kind of god. It's because you're spying on me. In every way. Aren't you?"

"That's just ridiculous. Anyway, no matter what happens, I'm sure you and Johanna will have some . . . lovely moments. Professional boundaries don't bother her. Trust me. Now, if you're planning to leave—" He closed the distance she had opened between them and she thought she might finally scream, thought she might finally alert everyone to the truth of him, the truth of *them*, but when she opened her mouth, no sound came out. It was a secret hidden for so long it had rusted, it wanted to stay put. "I don't think I can let you do that, Grace."

She thought of all the times he had told her she would be nothing without him, the threats he had made. The night, after a guest had brought scotch in his bags and Miles had "confiscated" it and downed an entire bottle, he had said to her, *I'll kill you if you leave, Jezebel. And then you'll burn in hell.*

"But you and Ruth," she said. "You could be here with her. Just let me go, and find your love for her again. You can say I left you. You can play up a broken heart. And then, when the time is right, you two can marry. For real this time."

He laughed. "Marry, for real this time." His tone was mocking. "I only did *that* to keep the two of you happy, that little sham of a ceremony. Did you really think she would ever be enough? That this would be enough? Look at me—angry, unhappy, just *look at me*, Grace. What is it you think I've wanted, all these years? You haven't been able to give it to me, and neither can she." He shook his head. "But you can't leave. No. You need to just stay right here where you are. And wait."

"For what?" she whispered.

"Look at me," he commanded again. *Look at me*, he always said. She'd been looking at him for years. Everyone had. But she knew him better than they did, the people who came here, who traveled in and out. "What is it I want?"

"More," she answered, because she knew him so well. "It's been growing in you for years."

He had his hand on her shoulder now. He was rubbing it gently, but still, it caused her pain, burning her from the inside out. "Yes. Good. That's right." He was speaking to her as if she were one of the guests. As if she were in one of his counseling sessions. "More of what I deserve. But, what is it *you* want, Gracie?" His voice cajoling, and it was a Pavlovian response to feel abruptly comforted by it, the way she had when she was so young, too young, scared and broken.

"I've always wanted to help people. Instead . . ." *Instead, I've put them in your path.*

"No. That's not exactly it."

"I want—I *don't* want to live like this anymore."

"Exactly," he said, smiling that smile of his, the one that some people thought was movie star handsome but made her feel like he was so hungry he was going to eat her up.

"Where is it? Just tell me. The camera. The bug. Just tell me."

He had no reaction to her words. Instead, "Wait," he commanded. "You'll get what you want."

Then he turned and glided from the room. She could picture him, in the silence that followed, like a snake, moving down her hallway and out the door. But where was his venom, where was his rage? A venomous snake like him didn't just change his mind about striking. He didn't just suddenly lose his taste for the kill, for the feeling of power over another being.

She walked to her desk and opened the notebook. Her words seemed almost childish now, her little list so hopeful. She saw it as he would have seen it. She saw how weak she looked. Running away, with Miles's blessing, would not be running away at all. She squeezed her eyes shut but a teardrop still made its way down her cheek.

What do you want?

He knew. And he wanted to make sure she'd never get it.

The walls were closing in. She walked slowly around the room, touching the walls as she went, but she felt nothing. She climbed up on the couch and looked up at the ceiling. Nothing. Nothing that she could see, at least. She closed her eyes. He was gone, but she could still feel it, what she knew he had really wanted to do: put his hands on her neck, block her air passage until she had to beg. The smell of his cologne in the room started to choke her, and she stumbled off the couch and toward the door, holding back her sobs so no one who shouldn't be listening would hear them. *I need to get out. Help me. Someone. Please.* But who was going to hear her if she didn't have the courage to scream? Who was going to help her if she didn't ask?

"Sorry," Ruth said to Shell, barring the door to her office. "The internet's down right now. And I have a meeting. You can't be in here."

"But I want to email my daughter," Shell said.

"A lot of people want to email their kids, be in touch with their families. You aren't the only one. The internet is down today because of the wind. And I have a meeting to get to now, with Miles." Just the mention of his name was enough to make Shell want to run. But she didn't. She stood her ground, tried to appear calm.

"Okay," she said. "Maybe later?"

Ruth shrugged. "Maybe." Ruth turned and locked the door. Then Shell followed her down the stairs.

"See you later, Ruth," Shell said. She veered into a bathroom.

Inside, she stared at herself in the mirror. Her hair was tied back in a bun. She started pulling hairpins out of it, one after the other, until there were ten in her hand. She slid the pins into her pocket. She went out into the hall, looked both ways, then headed toward the stairs that led to the tower, and Ruth's office, once more.

She'd learned how to pick locks from one of her brothers. The eldest. They had been teenagers, out past their curfew. She'd had too much to drink—it had already started, although she hadn't realized at the time. And it had just been a few coolers. She remembered it all clearly, despite the drinking. Somehow, drinking had always provided her with razor-sharp clarity, and never, ever, the oblivion she wanted. She knew she remembered how to do this because the year before, she'd left her purse at a store, and when she got back to the house,

Zoey was crying for her milk and she couldn't get inside to get it for her. She'd pulled a pin out of her hair and picked the lock from memory. She had laughed about it when she told Colin later.

She tried and failed with four different pins before, finally, the satisfying click. She was back in Ruth's office. Shell sat down in the now-familiar chair and looked out at the now-familiar view, which was windswept and gray, like a watercolor almost completely washed out by a glass of water, accidentally spilled. Heart pounding, she hit the browser button. As she had suspected, Ruth was lying about the internet being down. But why? She didn't stop to think about it. She had already decided what she was going to do. It had come to her during a long sleepless night. She wasn't alone. She couldn't be. There had to be other women Miles had done this to. And she wanted to find them, although she couldn't quite explain why. She was angry and she was afraid—but she wanted to know she wasn't alone. She had thought of it in the shower, a way to reach out. Maybe if she knew there were others, she'd find the strength to figure out what to do next.

She created a Twitter account. She named herself Zoey W., left her profile photo the little white egg. It made her sad, the lonely little egg, but this was not about Zoey—or, if it was, it was about creating the world she would have wanted her Zoey to live in.

She wrote about Miles, one tweet, another, another, all with the same hashtag so many other women had used, to tell secrets like this, to try to move past *What if no one believes me?* and into *What if there are others?* Soon, she forgot about the why. She lost herself in the comfort she found in sharing her story with these other women, even if they were far away, even if she didn't know them. Of telling them it had happened to her, too. Of telling them that no, they weren't crazy if it had happened to them. She had heard people say, "This has gone too far." But she knew exactly what too far really meant.

Are there others? she wrote. *Has Miles Markell done this to other women? I need to know.* #MeToo

She was about to log out and attempt to cover her tracks when she noticed something in the margin of the page.

Trending:

#HurricaneChristineMayanRiviera

#PrayForMexico

Then a voice. *"What are you doing?"*

"Where are you off to this morning?" Ben said to Johanna. He was smiling and tender. She tried to be the same.

"I have a session with Grace. You?"

"Miles," he said.

"How's that going?"

Ben was shaving. He rinsed the razor and set it at the side of the sink and Johanna noticed he wasn't quite meeting her eyes now. "Good," he said. "Intense, you know?"

"I do," Johanna said, and couldn't explain why her breath hitched and she walked into the other room and stared out the window at the ocean, feeling nothing but panic. Ben left first, kissing her too deeply and possessively, and Johanna stayed behind, brushing her tangled hair, then abandoning the task, half-finished. There was only one direction her session with Grace could go. She had started her story, and it was time to finish it. Outside, the air was muggy and heavy, full of rain. It felt like a struggle to get enough oxygen. Her chest felt heavy, her body not quite hers. She headed down the path toward Grace's office, but then she stopped and turned away. She walked toward the ocean instead. The sound of her flip-flops on the brick beat a pattern. *I can't say it. I can't say it. I can't say it. I can't.*

The surf pounded, loud and hard, but it didn't silence the voices in her head calling her names. In the distance, she could still see Grace's office window—and two shadowy figures facing one another.

The panic intensified, but it wasn't just herself she was afraid for now. Suddenly, she felt frightened for Grace, too. She moved away from the beach and back the way she had come. With each step, she became brave. With each step, she realized how close she had come to missing her chance, skipping her session, forgoing her time with Grace when they had so little time left.

She was on the path again, in front of Grace's office, when Grace herself burst from the door, gasping for breath, the way Johanna had been just moments before.

She didn't see Johanna at first. She charged forward toward the beach path, and Johanna didn't know what to do but hold out her arms. When Grace stumbled into her, she gasped and recoiled and it seemed to take a moment for her clouded eyes to understand it was Johanna. Her hands were in fists. She was holding the lava rock, Johanna realized.

"Grace, are you all right? You weren't at dinner last night . . ."

"Oh. I'm fine," Grace said. "I think I ate some bad ceviche, is all." They stood staring at one another. Johanna knew she was lying.

"So—should we?"

"Yes. Our session. I have an idea. What if we had an outdoor session today? Let's walk." She didn't wait for Johanna to answer. She seemed to want to get as far away from her office as possible. Johanna followed. They didn't speak, but that was okay. Johanna heard Grace's breathing become more even and knew hers was becoming that way, too. Soon, the resort was far behind them.

"Up there," Grace said. "See those rocks up ahead? Why don't we sit there?" The rock was like a bench, and faced the sea. After they sat, Johanna glanced down at the rock Grace was still holding tight. *Who was in your office with you*, she wanted to ask. *Why did you seem so scared?* Then, Grace handed her the rock. "Ready?"

Johanna felt happy they were outside. She could get more air into her lungs and the space felt big enough, the sky and ocean limitless enough, to contain everything she needed to say to Grace. But, still, she felt unsettled. Johanna remembered how Miles had left the restaurant the night before with a domed platter in hand she had presumed was for Grace. She thought of how uncomfortable he always made her feel, even though everyone else seemed to think he was some kind of saint. Or a god. Had he been the figure in the window with Grace? Had they argued? Johanna thought of the man coming down the path to meet Grace in the cenote. Had Miles found out that Grace had a lover? Even the thought, the word, did something to Johanna's heart. An ache. One that didn't belong. *Lover. Grace.*

She watched Grace fiddle with the long-sleeved tunic top she was wearing—long-sleeved despite the heat. Grace saw her watching. She said, "Johanna, I'm really fine. It's not me we're here to discuss. We had started talking about some big issues in your last session. You need to work through those things. We might be running out of time."

Those words echoed her own thoughts. *Out of time.* Johanna tried to imagine the day that would come, and soon, when she would not be able to come and sit near Grace and talk. "I'm scared," she said.

"You're safe here."

"Are *you*?" It was a whisper, and Grace must not have heard. She was silent, watching the sea. What if it rained again, Johanna wondered, would they run back to the resort together, or stay where they were and let it soak through them both? She would do either. She would do whatever Grace thought was best.

"Did you know that the average person is keeping thirteen secrets, five of which they've never told another person?" Grace said, breaking their silence. "Ruth told me that. She's always doing great research for us. But the worst thing about keeping those secrets is the mental toll of it. Secrets are difficult little beasts to conquer. You bash them down, but they keep popping up their heads when your mind wanders. Sound familiar? And headaches—headaches that feel like migraines—those might be symptomatic of you trying to keep tamping down the truth." She paused. "I once asked you when you got your first migraine, but you didn't say. Is it because you don't remember—or is it one of the secrets you keep, one you're afraid to tell me?"

"That's an easy one. On our wedding night. That's when the migraines started. But that's not really my most important secret."

"What *is* your most important secret? Last session, you were so open and brave. You can do that again, I know you can."

Johanna looked down at her hands. "Those pills," she began. "The ones that were found in my stuff. Did anyone look at them? The name on them?"

"I didn't," Grace said, and something in her tone made Johanna wonder who had.

"The name was Cleo. Cleo Von Hahn." Johanna looked at Grace, waited for name recognition, but her expression was neutral. "Chad Von Hahn's wife."

"She was your friend?"

"She was my client. And—my lover." That word again, now said out loud. Johanna watched Grace closely but she could see only her profile.

"Tell me about her," she finally said.

"She was a beautiful mess. I met her at the gym, five years ago. A cliché, I know. It wasn't a cliché at all, though. Cleo was like a rainbow, and she was also like a storm. She made me feel like myself, finally. But it didn't last. She had secrets, addictions—and a violent husband. We broke up—I just couldn't deal with how unpredictable she was, and how I never knew who she would be from day to day. She ended up going back to him. I didn't see that coming. I blamed myself. Then I made a huge mistake."

"What was that mistake?"

"I was so worried for her, I got her on my client roster. We were still friends, we'd promised to always be friends, and I told her I wanted to help her get away from him for good. It worked for a while. I was her social worker, and I was able to get her into a women's shelter with her kids, and then an apartment. She was working, she was thinking of going back to school. But *he* always seemed to surface. Chad was a habit she just could not break." Johanna shook her head, but it didn't go away, that feeling of frustrated mystification followed by an utter sense of loss every time she thought of Cleo now. "I think I wanted to help her so badly because I never helped my mom. I never even thought to *ask* if she needed help, just wrapped myself up in my bitterness, my anger at her for being what I saw as weak, for being with Ivan at all after my dad died. He wrecked my life, he wrecked *me*, and she didn't even seem to notice. Cleo wasn't weak, though. There was never any stopping her."

"What did you want to stop her from doing?"

"Making mistakes. But it turned into the biggest mistake I could possibly make." A pause. All she could see was Grace's profile. She had no way of knowing how she was reacting to her words. "When I met Ben, I was with Cleo, in court. He said he had never seen a social worker so passionate about a client. He said it's why he fell in love with me at first sight. And when I met him, I was getting so tired. I was getting so worried I'd never be happy. He said he wanted to make me happy. He said he'd make my life perfect. And I knew it couldn't really be true—but I wanted to believe it. I wanted someone to save *me*. Because I felt like all I ever did was try to save other people. I wish I had waited."

"Waited for what?"

"Just—maybe Cleo wasn't all there was. Maybe I would have found something else. Someone who wasn't—" But she couldn't, not yet. Rain was falling now, but it was a gentle mist. Neither of them moved.

"Can you continue?"

"Those pills," Johanna said over the lump that had formed in her throat. "I know what it sounds like, but they were a gift from her. They were all I had of her after she was gone. I don't know how she got them, Cleo was always getting things she shouldn't have from who knows where. I don't even really know what's in them—she said they were from some kind of drug trial. Ketamine, I think? But I know they worked. They made my headaches go away. I have a feeling they would have made me pretty high if I took enough of them, but I never did. I didn't want to be like her. But it made her happy, to be able to help me. So I let her do that. I took her gift. It was just a few weeks later that—" Johanna swallowed hard. "This isn't easy," she said.

Now, Grace turned to her. "I know it isn't. But you need to go on."

"I don't know what more I can say. He found out we had been lovers. I have no idea how. Maybe she told him. She must have, right? But I have no way of knowing. I can't ask her." She put her face in her hands. "He killed her. She died because of me."

"How was it because of you?"

"How is it not obvious? It made him so mad, finding out that we were once together. Maybe he thought we still were. Maybe it pushed him over the edge. He killed her, and he killed himself, because of that. Because of me."

"You tried to help her."

"And she died."

"It was Chad who killed her. A person like him, abusive and violent and manipulative—he was always going to kill her. There was nothing you could do about it. No matter how hard you tried. That's a difficult truth about the world. Something that needs to change—but blaming yourself isn't going to make any difference."

There was sharp pain in her eyes, her nose, the back of her throat, a stabbing ache as if crying wouldn't be enough—and then the secret had coursed through her body, and out, and she was sobbing. The realization of what she had revealed, and what she really wanted to reveal, was a wave that crashed into her. She had lost her footing. But then Grace had her hand.

"It's okay," she said. "Shhh. You're going to be fine."

"I don't want to hate myself anymore. Please, can you help me?"

"Of course." As if it were the simplest thing in the world. Grace's palm was smooth and cool, her grip firm but gentle. The way Johanna remembered it feeling, the first time they met. Grace's hand made her feel strong. Grace's hand did for her what she imagined the lava rock was supposed to do, what she had always imagined keeping Cleo's vial of pills as a memento would do. Courage. But still, she couldn't stop crying.

"Johanna? You need to go on. You said earlier, you wished you had waited. Waited for what?"

"There have been other women I've had feelings for, crushes on, over the years. Nothing else that I've acted on, but it's always been there." She closed her eyes, but that didn't make it easier, so she opened them and looked at Grace's face, open and expectant, no judgment there. She let go of her hand and said, "I've always been convinced this can't be my life. It's so frustrating. Instead of making it easier for myself I've just made it harder and harder. Buried myself, tied myself up. Why?"

"Do you think you can answer that question yourself?"

Johanna thought for a moment. "I've always heard Ivan's voice, or Marybeth's voice, or any number of voices saying it can't be what I am. But it *is* what I am. Why am I so scared?"

"Maybe it's because you've never actually said it. Maybe that's the first step for you. Saying it and knowing that the person you're telling understands."

Everyone has secrets. They take a mental toll. "I do not love my husband. I can't love him because . . . I'm gay."

Johanna thought something would happen, maybe an earthquake or a sudden storm, and she felt foolish when nothing did. She understood how big the secret had seemed, and how it didn't seem that way anymore, now that it was out.

"Good," Grace said, businesslike but warm. "Now you're finally being honest with yourself."

"I've made such a mess. My job—I pretended I couldn't go back, but really, my relationship with Cleo came out during the investigation and I got fired. My husband has no idea. I kept it from him. And I thought it would be as simple as just walking away from him and never having to tell him. But no. I got scared and kept saying yes to whatever he wanted, instead. I told myself that Cleo's death would make me really live, and instead, I feel I've been dying a little more each day. What was I doing, coming here, as if there could ever be a chance this could be fixed? I'm going to hurt him, too, and I'm just delaying it. More collateral damage."

"Are you sure Ben doesn't know?" Grace's voice was soft. "Even if there's not enough love there, or the right kind of love, he must know you better than anyone else."

Johanna shook her head. "No way. I've hidden from him the most."

"You're sure?"

"Positive. Why do you keep asking?"

"I just—" A shadow across her eyes. "I just know that it can be impossible to hide from the person you live with."

"I don't want to talk about Ben," Johanna said.

"All right. We're going to have to, but this has been a lot for today."

"What's next? What should I do?" As she said the words, she turned to Grace and watched as she lifted her hand to tuck some damp hair behind her ear. Her sleeve slid down her wrist. Time stopped.

Johanna had seen bruises like that, so many times. Still, when she saw these bruises on Grace, she forgot about everything else, even the intensity of the previous moments. She saw bloodred in her vision. "Who did this to you?" She reached out and held Grace's arm carefully, above the bruises, but still, Grace winced. Finger marks. Unmistakable. Moments before, her secret had seemed like the most important thing in the world. But now she understood there were things that mattered more.

"Johanna, *please*." Fear in her voice, the fear from before. "You can't save everyone."

"Tell me, exactly why not?"

"I'm fine—it was . . . I bumped it."

"Grace."

"Don't." Grace pulled her hand away and stood. "We need to get back. I have another client."

Johanna looked up at her. "Please," she said. But Grace just shook her head.

They started to walk back the way they had come, silent again, as if none of it had happened. But they dawdled and strayed toward the ocean. When the salt water hit her ankle, Johanna felt it sting. She leaned down.

Grace did, too. Her cool fingers were on the inflamed skin of Johanna's ankle, her touch whispered across the painful heat of the rash and Johanna wanted to cry out, but not from pain. Grace straightened.

"Did you go to the nurse about that rash?"

"Yesterday. She gave me something, but it didn't help. Cortisone, I think."

"I have something I think will work. I can give it to you later." She thought for a long moment and seemed to come to a decision. "It's in my house. I'm finished with clients at five. Come back then, and we can go to my villa together. I'll get it for you."

Johanna understood. "I'll stay while you get whatever you need," she said.

"Please don't say anything," Grace said, her tone suddenly urgent. "To anyone. About any of this. The only person you can trust here is me. You can tell your secrets to me, but you can't tell them to anyone else. Do you understand? And we can't talk about anything in my office. Not anymore."

Up ahead, the resort, a scattering of buildings that had seemed like diamonds and garnets and beautiful jewels, looked dull and ominous. There were clouds gathering behind everything, and Johanna and Grace walked straight toward them.

*W*hat are you doing?"

Shell looked up from the computer screen. She fought for control. "Did you know about this storm, Ruth?"

"Miles has it under control."

Shell stared at her in disbelief. "You understand he can't control a storm, right? Especially not a category four." As she said it, Shell's voice rose in fear. She couldn't help it now. The articles she had just read said all flights had already been canceled. There was no way out, not now. Maybe yesterday, but not today. She stood. "Where is my husband?"

Ruth didn't reply. She walked over to the computer. She reached forward. She was wiggling the mouse and hitting the back button. "What is all this?" She read for a few minutes, then turned to Shell. "Lies," she said simply. "No one will believe you."

"I think we both know that's not true," Shell said, but already, she didn't believe herself.

"I think a lot of people in your life probably know you're a lush." A cruel laugh. "I think I'll tell anyone who asks that you snuck several bottles of vodka here and drank every single one—"

"That's not true!"

"I'll dump them, say you drank them—no one will believe you."

"You're crazy, too. You're just as bad as he is. Does he pay you to keep his secrets? Pay you extra?"

Ruth narrowed her eyes. For a moment, she seemed to be in pain. "It's not like that at all," she said.

"Well, what does it matter, anyway? A huge storm is coming. And you've hidden it from everyone. You, and Miles, and Grace, too."

"We've hidden nothing. The internet was down. It must have just started working when you broke into my office." She raised her heavily penciled brows. "We had no idea."

"I don't believe you."

"Oh, grow up a little. You're acting like a child. So dramatic. You're safe here. It's a big storm, sure, but this building is perfectly safe. It's survived many hurricanes. You have nothing to be afraid of. Now, could you please leave my office? I need to make some phone calls. You should go back to your bungalow and wait for instructions. Do what you're told for once."

"No," Shell said, willing the waver out of her voice. She had to be strong. She reached forward and opened another article on the screen. "*Look*. This thing has been building for days. It's the strongest storm ever to hit the region."

"It's going to be fine, I said."

"How can you be so calm? How can you be so *evil*? No one is allowed phones here, or access to the outside world! No one but you, and Miles, and Grace, I'm sure. This is monstrous. It's purposeful."

"We didn't plan the storm, Shell. That's just ridiculous."

"I didn't say that. But you knew. I can tell."

"You can't!" Her voice was sharp. "You know nothing! Go! You've done enough!"

"You know about what he does. Don't say you don't."

"He's great at what he does."

"He's a predator."

Ruth stared at her for a long time. "You wanted it," she finally whispered.

Shell picked up the phone beside the computer. "I'm calling the police," she said, suddenly certain it was the only solution. She dialed 911. A voice answered her in Spanish. "I need help," she said, and felt immediately foolish. "Does anyone speak English?"

A torrent of Spanish in response. She heard the word *hurricane*. "No, no," she said, "it's not about the hurricane. Not yet, at least. It's about

Miles Markell." She glared at Ruth, who didn't appear at all concerned. Her heavily made-up face was as still as a stone.

"¿Cuál es el problema?"

"Someone needs to come out here."

"¿Hay alguien herido?"

Ruth took the phone from her hand, her grip surprisingly strong as she pushed Shell's arm down. "Hey!" Shell shouted.

She began speaking, her voice low, her words fast. "Sí. Sí. Lo siento. Sí sabemos sobre el huracán. Nos estamos preparando. Gracias. Adiós." Then she hung up.

"You can't do this," Shell said.

"I am doing this. And you need to leave this room now, or I am going to call security and tell them that the woman with all the vodka has broken into my office, for the purposes of getting her hands back on her alcohol." She slid open a drawer and Shell saw them in there, two of the bottles she had brought with her. But one of them was gone. She remembered that familiar taste on Miles's lips and felt sick. Ruth took one out of the drawer and placed it on the desk in front of Shell. Shell tried not to look at it. Not now. She couldn't falter now. But just the sight of it had caused her to shake.

Ruth leaned against the desk, as if they were having a casual conversation. "We get women like you every year or so. Desperate for affection, neglected by their husbands. Miles is handsome and charismatic. He can't help the way he is. They fall for him. Like you have. And they'll sacrifice anything, even their own dignity, even the truth, to get him. It never works. It's certainly not going to work now. No one is going to believe you. You think you have more power than you do."

"But I'm sure there are others." Shell had to pry her eyes away from the vodka. Ruth saw, and smiled.

"You made your own choices. Don't ever forget that. Like this." She reached for the bottle. She held it aloft. "Maybe you want to take this with you. Just take it, and drown your sorrows. Make things a little easier on yourself. Make that choice."

All at once, Shell didn't even have to think about it. All at once, the longing was gone. She *had* made her choice, she realized, when she sat down at that computer earlier. She had chosen to be the kind of person who was believed—and she would now tell her story to the person who mattered most. And he would believe her, too.

The sound of her feet was loud on the stairs as she fled. She half expected Ruth to follow, but she didn't.

*I*t had rained all day as Johanna had waited, telling Ben first that she was going to a yoga class, and then something vague about a group enrichment session. But now the rain had stopped. The ocean was dark blue, the sky deep into the gloaming. There was a line of dusky peach fading to pale yellow right along the horizon of the ocean. Dark clouds were above that, but they were distant. And she was finally with Grace again, walking toward her house. "It reminds me of an Astro Pop," Johanna said, trying to make Grace smile, pointing at the horizon as they walked. The wind was strong and blew her hair out behind her.

"I haven't thought about those for a long time. My brother and I used to love those. My father didn't allow sweets except on special occasions but sometimes we'd sneak to the general store and buy them." It was the first time Grace had mentioned anything about herself, Johanna observed, about her life outside of this place. It was as if she could do that now that they were outside of the confines of her office.

"Wow, no sweets, what kind of childhood was that?" Johanna said, but something about the look on Grace's face when she said that made her regret it. "I'm sorry," she said quickly.

"No, no, don't be," Grace said. "My family was very religious. That was just the way it was." She looked toward the ocean for a moment and Johanna got the feeling that, normally, this time of day was sacred for Grace. Her alone time. She would walk by herself and think about the things she had heard all day. The secrets, the lies, the truths. *She* was the helper. Johanna understood this. No matter what else was going on with Grace, she understood this. So she stopped trying to make small, anxious chatter and walked beside her in silence until she reached the steps leading up to their front door. Johanna paused at the bottom of the stairs.

"Is he in there?"

"I'm not sure. We'll see."

The villa was boxy and modern on the outside, and airy and light on the inside, completely open concept with a wall of glass at the back leading to a private swimming pool. "It's gorgeous," Johanna said.

"Thank you. We designed it ourselves. We lived in the main villa at first, but it just didn't feel right. We needed somewhere separate. A little more privacy." She led Johanna toward the kitchen area while Johanna wished she could just stop and look around, take it all in, every little thing, the place Grace Markell called home. Now, Grace paused and lifted the hem of her harem pants, revealing a hint of redness at her ankles. "My rash looks a lot like yours, see? And I have some ointment I think will work. I get it at a market near here." Now their eyes met, and Johanna opened her mouth to speak.

A male voice startled them both, and Johanna's hand reached, for just a second, toward the kitchen knives on the wall.

"Hello," Miles said to Johanna, a quizzical expression on his handsome face. He approached his wife, bent down and kissed her on the lips, lingering for a moment too long while Grace stood motionless and so did Johanna. "I missed you," he said. "It's been a long day."

"Honey, you're home," Grace said.

"Anything in the fridge? I can't wait for dinner. I'm starved." They were like a couple on a fifties sitcom. Except something wasn't right, and Johanna knew it now.

Grace pulled out of his embrace and reached into a cupboard to retrieve a small mason-style jar with a lid. As she unscrewed the cap she said, "I'm not sure. Why don't you have a look. Johanna has a terrible rash, so I offered her some of my ointment."

Now Miles stood between them. "Grace gets that at a market in Akumal," he said, and Johanna couldn't read the look that passed between them as he spoke. "Your husband mentioned you're a fan of jungle markets, too, Johanna."

"Yes," she forced herself to say, hoping her voice sounded normal.

"Maybe you picked up the rash there?" A raise of the eyebrow, a signature smile. "I hear the jungle is full of mysterious plants. Mysteries in general. Hey—" He paused and tilted his head like an actor playing a role, and badly. "Do you think it's possible the two of you were at the same market?"

Johanna's gaze flitted to Grace and then back to Miles. She didn't like the sound of his voice, or what was behind it. She didn't like that he was trying to intimidate her. She knew he wanted her to be afraid. And she knew she needed to try not to be. She owed that to Grace. "Maybe," she said, and this time her voice was stronger. She looked at Grace. "The market I went to was in Puerto Morelos. There was this amazing cenote and I want to get a closer look. I wish I could go back. It looks like the perfect place to swim."

Grace dropped the jar. It hit the counter, not the floor. There was a clatter but it didn't break. "You all right, Grace?" he asked, but kept his eyes on Johanna.

"I am," Grace said quietly, picking up the jar again.

"I've heard of that cenote," Miles said. "But it's not open anymore. Something about a crocodile. At least that's the rumor I heard. But people still swim in it, I hear. Who knows why people take the risks they do, right? Anyway, Grace tells me the market she goes to is in Akumal. So you couldn't have been in the same place after all."

Grace tells me. Grace's hand was frozen in midair. Then Johanna watched as she recovered and continued to spoon the ointment out, focused and determined. "I warn you, this is strong stuff," she said. "Miles thinks it stinks. I kind of like it." The smell was so familiar to Johanna.

"That stuff *does* stink," Miles said, his mouth now curled in a repulsed sneer.

Grace shrugged and smiled. "What can I say? I need it. So, what's the plan for tonight?"

"Oh, yes, tonight!" Now he was smiling. And the lid was back on the jar. "We're going to play a favorite game of mine."

"What's the game?"

"It's called Do You Trust Your Wife? It's based on a game show my father used to watch when I was very, very young. Dick Van Dyke was the host. Not many people remember it."

"I've never heard of it." Johanna didn't want to hold his gaze, so she looked at the knives. There was a big one, closest at hand. She could reach it if she had to, she could reach it fast. "How does the game work, exactly?"

"It's a lot of fun," he said. "Three couples are the contestants. The husband is asked a question and he has to decide whether to answer it himself or trust his wife to answer it."

"Why is it the husband deciding whether to trust the wife? Why isn't it the other way around?"

"It doesn't have to be the husband," Grace said. "The couples choose who gets to be the question answerer. Remember, Miles?"

"Right," Miles said, finally taking his eyes off Johanna. "It can go either way. All right, I'm hitting the showers. See you tonight, Johanna. And you'll be there, too, won't you, Grace? You're feeling better, aren't you?" Questions, orders, commands.

"See you later," Grace said. Miles walked up the stairs slowly. They both watched. When he was gone, Johanna moved closer to Grace.

Johanna put a hand on her arm gently and moved in close to Grace's ear. "You are never trapped," she whispered. "You are never trapped until he kills you." She had said this once to Cleo. And it had been true.

Grace moved away from her, silent. She picked up the jar she had filled, reached out to hand it to Johanna. Their hands touched and they stayed like that for a long moment. "I know," Grace whispered.

They could hear the shower upstairs. Grace stepped closer to her again.

"It was you," Grace said. "Right? I saw you, at the edge of the cenote. The one in Puerto Morelos."

Johanna nodded again. She couldn't have spoken if she wanted to.

"It's not safe to talk about it now. But we will, later. I promise."

Finally, Johanna found her voice. It was the words, *it's not safe*, that did it. "You need to go up and get some things. You need to stay somewhere else tonight. Somewhere you can be safe."

Grace nodded. "My office. I stayed there last night."

"We'll think of something. We'll come up with a plan." *We.* It was effortless. It was terrifying. But the idea of Miles upstairs was even more terrifying. "I'll wait at the bottom of the stairs." Johanna looked to the knife rack, indicated a small paring knife. "Take that with you," she said. "Hold it in your hand."

Grace held the knife pointed downward as she walked up the stairs. It was almost completely hidden. Just a small glint of metal before she disappeared. She was fast. She came down only a moment later carrying a garment bag and a duffel bag, as if she had had them packed already, ready and waiting. They walked to the door together.

"I'll shower at the yoga studio," Grace said. "I'll see you at dinner, and for the game. But there's something I need to do first, so I may be a little late. Remember what I told you before, okay? You need to be careful. Don't tell anyone anything."

"I know. So do you."

They parted near the villas. The clouds were thick again. Johanna stood and watched as Grace was swallowed by the night.

Up ahead, closer to the bungalows, Johanna thought she heard a banging sound, over and over. Like someone knocking on doors, endlessly. She stopped to listen, but it was gone. Just the wind and the waves, the gathering dark. And Grace, somewhere out there, alone.

*S*hell knocked on door after door. Her knocks got louder, more insistent. If Ruth wanted corroborators on her story of an unhinged woman, she had them now, but Shell didn't care. She needed to find Colin. She needed to explain what had happened. The next few villas were empty. She came to the one she remembered Johanna saying was hers. She would tell Johanna first, if she had to. But when Johanna's husband answered the door, Shell lost her nerve.

Ben appeared bemused to see her. "Hi?"

"I was just—could you tell Johanna I stopped by, please?"

"She should be back soon," Ben said. "If you want to wait."

"It's fine, really." She had fled, moved on to the next villa as fast as she could, then the next and the next. Either a stranger answered, frowning and confused, or no one at all.

And then, finally, him. Colin flung the door open almost the moment she started to knock.

"Colin. Please. You have to listen to me."

His expression was guarded, but still he said, "I'm glad it's you. I was going to leave, I've been intending to book a flight—but I thought we should talk first. That I should at least say goodbye. It's gone too far, hasn't it, Shell? There's nothing to save of our marriage, is there?"

"No. I swear to you, it was not what it looked like. What you think you saw with Miles, it wasn't real." She started to sob, then forced it back in. What she needed to be now was strong. Stronger, perhaps, than she had ever been. "Please, please, you have to believe me. You of all people. We've been through too much for you to stop listening to me now."

He let her in. She had known he would. She had known when she finally found him, he would let her in, out of the coming storm. Because he was Colin, and he had made promises to her that he was always going to keep, no matter how far into hell they went.

*T*he yoga studio was empty. Grace was alone. She waited. She checked her watch. Miles could potentially be expected to miss dinner, but he would never miss his favorite game. Not even on account of her. But still, she waited even longer. Eventually, she went outside again and she walked back toward their villa. All the lights were out.

She fumbled in the darkness, but didn't turn on any lights until she reached Miles's room. Even then, she only turned on a table lamp. She moved quickly in a room that was increasingly unfamiliar to her, but a room she knew the secrets of no less. Where he kept his extra keys, for example. Yes, they were still at the back of his sock drawer. That had never changed, not in all the years they'd been together and all the homes they'd lived in. She took out the keys and replaced them all, one by one, with extra keys of her own. Decoys so he wouldn't know, unless he tried the keys in locks, that she had his extra key. The key to his office. The key to his desk. The key, she hoped, to finding out where her laptop and phone were.

Outside again, it was dark except for the solar-powered lanterns along the path. It was windier than it had been earlier. Her hair lifted behind her. Miles's office was in a small bungalow, just like hers. She climbed the stairs and tried two of the keys, then found the right one—the third. The door opened. Inside, it smelled like his cologne and the essential oil diffuser he kept running at all times. Even now, it was chugging away in the corner. They spent unfathomable sums on oils, bought from someone back home, a friend from the church.

She turned on his desk lamp. She tried all the small keys she had, in his desk drawers and filing cabinets. None of them worked. She tried them again. She was running out of time. She stood in the center of the room, helpless and confused, a sheen of sweat on her brow. She glanced at his laptop, sitting on his desk. Then she walked over and opened it. It was password locked, of course. She tried a few combinations: his birthdate, her birthdate, Ruth's. No luck. She bit back her tears and stood still. *Think, Grace, think.*

His favorite Bible verse. Philippians 4:13. It didn't work with no caps, it didn't work with all caps. She tried one more combination, just a capital at the beginning and no colon—and she was in. But she paused when she saw a flashing notification at the bottom of the screen. Miles's cell phone was linked to his laptop and a text was coming in.

> L: Miles, are you there?

Grace stared down at the screen, wondering who *L* was. She scrolled backward in the stream of messages. There were hundreds of them.

> Miles: How is recruitment going?

> L: We have two more prospects. I'll email you their profiles.
> They have money. They gave us all their banking info. How are
> things going there? Any updates?

A few days later:

> Miles: I was there today. I watched her swim. I
> wore socks so I wouldn't get that silly rash she
> always gets. I know she does it on purpose, but
> she's not fooling me. She never has. Anyway,
> it's perfect. I just need to find the right time.

> L: It will take great courage. But you're a courageous man.
> That's why we follow you. Now keep following her.

> Miles: Thank you, darling. And you are a courageous
> woman. All of you are. We'll be here together, soon. I'm
> working as hard as I can. I'm looking for someone who
> can help you lead. It's going to be big. You'll need help.

Grace's palms had started to sweat. She had to wipe them on her skirt so she could continue to read back through the messages.

> . . . Make it look like an accident.

> . . . Accidental drowning.

> . . . I followed her to the cenote. It's perfect. But I need to wait
> for the right time.

> I have her laptop but need to find someone who can help
> me hack into her encrypted files. I know she has money
> somewhere. I know she lied when she said her mother left all
> her money to her childhood church . . .

> . . . . When she's gone, I'll be free. I can end all this and start
> doing what I really want to do.

> Our organization will be strong, it will be formidable. Together,
> we will embrace our destiny.

Absurd, nervous laughter bubbled up in Grace's throat. He had started a fucking cult. He was planning to kill her. She put her hand over her mouth, and the laughter turned into a terrified sob as she saw a message from Miles come up on the screen.

> Miles: I'm busy now. We have an activity going. But,
> our prayers have been answered. Our prayers for

> guidance and clarity in how to cleanse my life of
> abomination and sin. God has sent us a storm. There
> will be no question it's an accident. The storm is how
> she will die. Leave it with me. And more tomorrow.

As if to punctuate his words, the wind outside increased its strength and a gust of it caused the bungalow walls to creak. The power flickered and she stayed where she was. Then she opened the internet browser and searched in the news for "Mexico storm."

"You monster," she said.

Later, when she had read all she could, she went into her own room. She turned in a circle, wondering what she would take, if she could take only one thing. She opened one of her drawers and reached to the back of it. She found the letter she had taken from her mother's home after she had died. *Dear Garrett, I'll get right to the point, I am the son you and a woman named Barbara Moore gave up when you were teenagers.* She folded it small and put it in her pocket. Somewhere, a part of her brother walked this earth. Somehow, knowing that made her feel less afraid. But only a little.

iles had the microphone. Ruth stood in the shadows behind him. Grace wasn't there yet. Johanna felt uneasy as she sat with her husband in front of a makeshift stage: just a platform with a curtain, dark red and billowing in the wind that was blowing into the open air restaurant, a wind that had picked up as the evening progressed. The tablecloths were weighted down, but a glass blew off a table and shattered. There was only one waitress, an older woman. She eventually brought over a broom. She looked worried, maybe even afraid. Miles stood over her as she cleaned up the mess.

Then, "We should get started," Miles said. Johanna's sense of unease increased. Still no Grace. She could feel the soothing balm on her ankle. Grace had been right, it had worked almost immediately. But where was she?

"This is my favorite night." Delight in his voice, eyes behind his glasses dancing. "Our entertainment team . . . has taken the night off," he said, curving his head toward the stage behind him. "But that's okay, because I have a game planned. First, I need three couples to volunteer. The word of the night is *trust*. You have to trust me. Just raise your hands, then come to the front."

No one moved, and as the moment dragged out, Miles's smile faltered. Then Grace appeared. She was wearing a royal blue dress. It had long sleeves and flowed down past her ankles but there was a slit up one side and it flared out as she passed Johanna and Ben's table. Johanna saw the golden skin of her leg, the redness at the ankle, and her polished toes in golden sandals. She felt a yearning so deep inside her that she almost rose from her seat.

213

"You okay?" Ben asked from across the table. "You're not getting another headache, are you?"

"Maybe," she lied, and touched her hand to her forehead as Grace passed.

"Have some water," Ben said, pressing a frosty glass in her hand. She held it but didn't drink. Ben kept watching her.

Grace was standing beside Miles now. Her easy smile, the one she had flashed at them all so often, was gone. She was holding herself stiffly. And Miles didn't acknowledge her as he usually did.

"Three volunteer couples, please," he repeated, and still, no one moved. In the flicker of candles in hurricane vases, Johanna could see that there was fear in Grace's eyes. Even more than there had been earlier, when they had been in the kitchen with Miles.

"We should volunteer," Johanna said, and Ben looked surprised. "Come on, let's go up there."

The stage was set up close to the edge of the restaurant, next to the sheer drop and those hammocks she and Ben had lounged on their first morning. It felt like a long time ago. Johanna looked to her left and to her right. At those sharp rocks at the bottom, lit by lanterns on stakes driven into the rocks. She looked at Miles, and she thought of the bruises. And now that familiar voice. *You should be dead. I should kill you, like I killed her.* She wished that voice would go away forever. She imagined herself pushing Miles over the edge, and had to battle that thought away. It wouldn't help to hurt in return.

"All right, stand here," Miles said, pointing to the front of the stage. Ben was beside her and Grace was at her other side, standing, looking out at the crowd. "Two more couples," Grace said, and just as she did, the lights flickered, on, then off, on—and then silence and darkness and a collective gasp of surprise filled the room.

Who reached for whom? Johanna would wonder this later, over and over, how it came to pass that the smooth, recognizable palm of Grace's hand pressed against hers in the darkness. The wind blew and she felt Grace's dress dance across her calf. Grace's voice, in her ear. "We need to meet. Come to my office after this. There's something I have to tell you. I need help. We *all* need help." They both squeezed and then let go, all in one moment, as a distant generator kicked in and the lights came back. In the light, they were standing apart, as if they had never touched.

The power cut out again. But this time Johanna didn't move. The waitress was shining a flashlight, talking to Miles animatedly. Another staff member had come out of the kitchen. He had found a flashlight, too, and a lantern, which he placed on a table. Miles was shaking his head, and his voice was rising. Johanna knew some Spanish, but it was rusty. *Yo lo hago. Es mi trabajo.* "I'll do it. It's my job," is what Miles was saying. While Johanna watched, the man from the kitchen threw up his hands, then untied his apron and tossed it on the ground in front of Miles's feet. Miles smiled benignly as the man walked away, as if this sort of thing happened all the time with the staff.

Then he turned to the small crowd. "We're having some issues with power. It happens sometimes," Miles said reassuringly, his voice loud over the rain outside. "We can't run the power up here, apparently. Something is wrong with the generator. So tonight's event is canceled. Everyone should go back to their villas, where, rest assured, the generators are working and you do all still have power. The path-side lanterns are still lit. Look down, you can see them, can't you? We'll try again tomorrow. Get into your robes, and have a cozy night. Meet back here in the morning. We might have a little tropical storm blowing in that we need to discuss, but nothing to be worried about at the moment."

All at once, a commotion at the entrance of the restaurant. The voice of Colin, Shell's husband. Shell was standing beside him. "You're not going to say anything, Miles?" Colin shouted. "You're not going to tell anyone about the hurricane you've probably known about for days?"

Johanna heard a sharp intake of breath from Grace, who was still nearby.

The smile didn't leave Miles's face. But she saw him turn and mouth the words "Get security" to Ruth, who had been hovering behind him.

She saw Ruth mouth back, "No one is left."

Johanna began to feel afraid. She began to understand that, as terrified as she had been before, it hadn't been enough.

Someone in the crowd shouted, "What storm?"

"What the heck," Ben, beside her, muttered.

"It's really no big deal," Miles said smoothly. "Just a little weather." But Johanna didn't believe him. It had happened right in front of her, in front of all of them, and they'd been too trusting to notice. Or, perhaps in her case, too distracted. She looked at Grace. But Grace was staring straight ahead. The idea that maybe she had known about what Colin was accusing was deeply unsettling. "Alongside our clients, Grace and I stay off the internet when we're in session and only read the news on weekends, when we have a little time off. If there really is a storm, as you say, I had no idea. I just thought we were having a bit of weather. That a tropical storm might be blowing in, and that's nothing we can't handle. Now, please, can we get a security guard here? I'm sorry you all had to see this. Sometimes, clients get a little—"

"But Ruth had internet," someone said. "I was emailing my kids."

"She said it's been out for a few days—"

"Exactly. How could she have known?"

"It's all lies!" Colin shouted. He grabbed Miles by the collar and held his fist aloft while Shell, behind him, said, "Please, Colin, don't, he's not worth it."

Johanna saw Miles's eyes shift briefly to Shell, as if just noticing her there, but then they moved away. He looked up at Colin's fist, his expression still impassive. "Take your hands off me," he said.

"Wasn't that the crazy lady banging on everyone's doors tonight?" Johanna heard someone murmur.

"Oh, I forgot to tell you," said Ben to Johanna. "She was at our door, looking for you. She seemed really off. Do you think what they're saying could be true?"

"Look around you, Ben. We should have seen it."

"Miles would tell us. I trust him. He's my therapist. He wouldn't hide something like this."

Now two of the guests, the big man from anger management and another, were behind Colin, wrestling him away from Miles.

"Don't you see?" Colin was still shouting. "Miles is a liar! He's insane!"

"You're the one who seems insane, bro," said one of the men.

"Jo, this whole thing is nuts," said Ben. "They need to get that guy Colin away from him. And we should just go. Back to our room, like Miles said. We don't need to see this."

"Ben, come on—"

"But what's going on?" someone else called out. "*Is* there a storm, or isn't there? Is this guy just crazy? It does seem awfully windy. And the power . . ."

"I'm going to make a call," Miles said, now that Colin had been pulled back. "How about that? Why don't you all just hang tight, and I'll be back in a few minutes with some news." He was pulling a phone out of his pocket.

"Hey wait," someone else said. "*He* has a smartphone. So how could he not have any access to the internet . . . ?"

"The internet wasn't working," someone else hissed.

Voices rose around Johanna again but she heard only Miles as he said, "Grace," his tone sharp, the phone still in his hand. "Could you come with me, please? And Ruth. My office. Now." Grace stood still, staring at her husband. She shook her head. Johanna saw her mouth the word *No*. Then she turned and walked away from him.

Johanna waited only a moment before she followed Grace, without saying a word to her husband, knowing that if he followed, she would say no, too.

*S*ixteen-year-old Grace sits silent, unsure of what to say or if she can trust herself to speak. But she takes the pill and drinks the water because her throat was raw and sore for days after the last time, her esophagus felt like it was coated in battery acid; by the end of it, she was throwing up bile, and she can't do that again.

"We spoke to your brother," Pastor Kesey says.

Grace closes her eyes. "I know," she whispers. "He was really upset. I didn't mean any of it. He didn't hurt me. It's just that you asked me and I said the first thing that—"

"We spoke with your parents. And they're on board with us having separate sessions with Garrett, to get to the bottom of exactly what happened. He needs to be held accountable."

"He hit me with a toy truck. We were kids. It was a stupid thing to tell you."

"But you did tell us. And we can't ignore it."

"What do you know about my brother? You know nothing! He has his own problems, he's struggling with his own stuff, he and Barbara gave the baby up for adoption, and my dad is really—he's been hitting him a lot—and dealing with this has just thrown him—"

"Are you saying your brother is mentally unstable?"

"No! That's not what I'm saying. I'm saying this has nothing to do with Garry, and that you need to leave him alone because he's struggling!"

"Grace, leave this to us. We're experts."

"Are you really? Have you done this before?" She sensed the same feeling rise up inside her that she had felt sometimes in church during Sacred Music Night, a feeling so intense it was almost rage. She had gone home and written in her diary, "I think I felt the Spirit move within me tonight," but now she *realized it was just raw human emotion, it was just passion, and you could feel it about anything, good or bad.* "You are all sick. Something is wrong with all of you, not with my brother!"

"Shut your mouth, child. The demon is coming through you. I've seen it in you before and it's here again."

Grace is scared. Grace believes in heaven and she believes in hell and she's scared. She wishes for simpler days. Days when her questions didn't contain such fear. Sometimes, when she was younger, she would look down at her hand and try to envision it, and all of humankind, all the way back to the Garden of Eden. Naked Eve and her temptress ways. But back to even before that, when there was only a great Nothing. She asked her mother so many questions that her mother finally made her an appointment with the pastor. He was kindly and patient, but not enlightening at all. "When there was nothing, where was God?" *she had asked him.*

"God was everywhere and everything," *the pastor had said, sounding a little tired.*

"And now? Where is he now?"

"He's everywhere and everything now, too."

God is in the church basement now. She knows this. And he's judging her. And she's so scared. So she doesn't say anything more. She lets them chase the demon away—and it chases a part of her away, too. The part of her that her brother had known. Perhaps she was his only true friend in the world.

What did they say to him, what did they do to him? She'll never know. She never asked. *He is mentally unstable, he is a sinner.* So many labels, after the fact. And it's true, a mentally sound person would not have done what Garrett eventually did: walked into the ocean in the middle of a storm, for the purposes of ending his own life. But Grace in the church basement, in that moment, didn't know the storm was coming. Not yet. She had no idea what her brother was going to do, in just a few more months. Had no idea that she was going to lose him.

"Ah, here he is. You remember Miles Markell, don't you, Grace? Our new youth minister? He's going to help us again today, too. I think the two of you have a real connection."

She relaxed when she saw Miles. The only face that didn't scare her. She turned toward him and he smiled. "Hello, Grace."

——

A knock at Grace's office door. She was leaning against it, her duffel bag in one hand, the knife in the other. If it was Miles, what would she do? Did she have the courage, did she have the strength, to defend herself? She gripped the knife tighter.

"Grace, are you in there? Please, open the door. It's me."

Johanna.

She stood, slid the knife back in her bag, zipped it shut and opened the door. Johanna's hair was windblown, her expression was tense. "Did you know?" she said in an anguished tone.

Grace put a hand to her lips. "Shhh," she said. "We have to whisper." She pulled her inside. "About the storm? Of course not. I would have told you. I would have told everyone. I only found out a few minutes before I got to the restaurant. I don't know what to do or how to get help, either. I have a laptop and a phone, but Miles has hidden both." She had to put her mouth close to Johanna's ear to be sure she could hear her. "And we won't have any connection to the outside world soon. This storm is going to be bad. I can feel it."

The wind howled. Grace pulled herself away from Johanna. She moved across the room toward her desk. She wanted to show Johanna something. She moved aside books until she found the ones that she had hidden, spine in. She handed one over. "Reparative therapy?" Johanna whispered, an agonized expression on her face. The lights flickered again. Grace started looking for the flashlight she hadn't used since the last storm—and that had been just a tropical storm. *A little weather*, as Miles had said, but it had still terrified her, had still brought it all back, as all storms did. Garrett—*he* was in the storm. And all of her mistakes, all of her lies, and all of her shame.

No more.

"This is me," she said softly, stepping close to Johanna again and bringing her lips to her ear once more. "I understand you as well as I understand myself."

"What do you mean?"

"Those books were given to me by my church. Those methods of 'curing' homosexuality are what I had done to me, the kind of so-called treatment I received, starting when I was sixteen years old. Miles believed for a while that he had healed me. And that made him feel so great, so powerful. But it was all a lie. *This* is the way I am." So quiet she almost wasn't saying the words aloud, but she did: "I'm gay. I always have been. And when I was a teenager, around the time you figured it out for yourself, the ministers and elders at my church were attempting to purge it out of me. Miles among them. That's how we met. He 'fixed' me. Except there was nothing to fix. They broke me. And now, here I am. A person who has always been as afraid as you, and maybe more."

"Grace," Johanna breathed, but she didn't say anything more. Grace felt grateful for that: that Johanna kept still and waited for her, just as she had done for her, day after day. No other words were needed.

"When you spoke about feeling responsible for Cleo's death because you were too afraid? I knew how you felt. Because my brother Garrett, my *best friend*, died for the same reason. He killed himself because the church accused him of doing terrible things to me. And I never spoke up. I was too afraid to stand up and be who I was. He paid the price, for me. He was the collateral damage in my denial. But I was never going to change. And yet, there have been moments this week when, for the first time in decades, I felt whole again. And all of those moments revolved around you. I know how wrong that is. I know I shouldn't say it. But something changed, the first moment I saw you. I stopped being a therapist. I became myself."

Darkness, sudden and insistent. The power, gone again. Grace turned on the flashlight she had found. She could see the shadowy edges of Johanna's perfect face now. "When you came, when you stood at the edge of the pool—tell me again. It *was* you, wasn't it? That day at the cenote, wasn't it?"

"Yes," Johanna whispered.

Relief flooded through her. "I felt like what I had dreamed of and asked for, what I had truly wanted my entire life, had come to me fully formed. And it was you. I knew then that God didn't hate me. You came. You saved me."

"You saved me, too," Johanna said, so close to her now their lips were almost touching. It was as if Grace had breathed all these words into her mouth, all her secrets that would always be kept safe and maybe even turn into something beautiful. "I felt the same thing, when I saw you. I knew it was impossible, an impossible dream, but I still felt it. Like you were my destiny." She squeezed her hand tight, but then pulled it away. "But, Grace? There was a man. I thought he was going down the path to meet you. I thought he was your lover. I realize now—"

"Yes. It was him. Miles. He followed me there. Johanna, he's planning to kill me. I was in his office earlier, and I saw messages on his laptop. He has a group, back in Texas. A group of women who believe his lies. I should have known something like this was coming. He wants more. He told me that. But I didn't know what he meant, exactly. Now I see. He wants total devotion. To be worshiped. I don't do that. I haven't given him that. And I haven't given him children, either. That's something else that Ruth and I weren't able to give."

"You *and Ruth*?"

"Shhhh. Be quiet, okay? I think he's spying on me. We have to whisper." Johanna's eyes widened. "I thought maybe Ruth was a solution, a long time ago. She fell in love with him and I know he cared for her, that he at least enjoyed the adoration, so I made a deal. If he left me alone he could take a second wife."

"But he's so religious. Why would he do that?"

"Miles? He's not religious. Not exactly. He hides behind religion, he bends it to suit him. But Miles doesn't believe in anyone but himself. I'm so ashamed."

"Why are *you* ashamed?"

"There are so many things I could have done. Should have done. I stood by and let him hurt people."

"I don't see what you could have done. It's like what you said to me about Chad. Miles was always going to be this person."

"No. Maybe not. Maybe I gave him too much power. Maybe I should have left a long time ago, at the very least. Been true to myself, if nothing else. I never could, though. I was too scared. Not just of what he'd do but who I'd be without all this." She gestured toward the room, the couch, the table, the desk, and the light from the flashlight bounced like a ball. "I love this part. I love talking to people. Helping them. I love being a therapist. It's the only time I feel whole, the only time I can forget about everything I hide, everything I am."

"We should run away. Together. You can be who you are with me. And I can be who I am with you. I *know* that. You can be whole again."

A strong gust of wind outside. "I know that, too," Grace said. "But we can't go anywhere. Not with this storm rolling in. We won't be safe anywhere but here." Then she covered her face with her hands and the flashlight dropped to the ground. "But here—I'm not safe. Miles thinks the storm has been sent by God. He wants to use it as a cover to kill me. I'm terrified."

"No," Johanna said, bending to pick it up. "It's okay. We can stop him. We can go to the police." She was close to her again.

Grace put her arms around Johanna's waist and spoke into her hair, as quietly as she could. "The police aren't going to come out here. Trust me, they're already busy dealing with other things."

"But if we get his laptop," Johanna whispered back. "If we bring it to the police. If we show them the messages."

A banging at the door caused them both to jump apart. Johanna clicked off the flashlight. They stood in the darkness. Miles's voice: "Grace, are you in there?" Another knock, softer. Then Ben's voice. "Johanna?"

Grace grabbed her, pulled her back. The couch was angled against the wall. They crouched behind it in the darkness.

"I was sure I saw a light in here when we were walking up," Ben said.

"Sometimes the mind plays tricks," Miles said, his voice soothing. "They must be somewhere else. We'll keep looking." A pause. "We'll find them." And Grace knew. She knew that Miles was well aware that she and Johanna were hiding from him, just a few feet away. That he was enjoying their fear. Controlling it. "Grace and I always find each other. It's what good couples do."

The door closed. Their voices faded away.

And for just a moment, Grace forgot her fear. She reached up in the darkness and touched the silk of Johanna's cheek. Johanna lifted her hand and touched hers, too. Their lips met, for just a moment. Then Grace pulled away and whispered, "I have an idea."

I'm scared," Shell said.

"Don't be," Colin replied. "We'll get through this. The phone at the front desk was still working. I called the Canadian consulate. They transferred me to the Emergency Watch and Response Centre in Ottawa. They've got their hands full right now, but someone is going to get back to me."

"We have to get home."

"We *will* get home. I promise you."

But then they both stood still and watched the moving waves, and she knew what they were both thinking: that the word *home* didn't mean the same thing anymore. What did they have to go back to? He took her hand, like perhaps he was going to show her.

His bungalow was the same as the one she had been staying in, and the one they had been staying in before, but there was one major difference: it smelled like him. It smelled familiar. It smelled like home.

"I'm so sorry," she said when they were inside. "For everything. For even *letting* him—"

"He took advantage of you. He should go to jail. He *will* go to jail. I'm the one who's sorry. I shouldn't have let this happen." They had changed out of their rain-soaked clothes. She was wearing one of his T-shirts and he was barefoot and shirtless in pajama pants she hardly recognized anymore, soft flannel ones he used to wear and—oh, it hurt her heart to think about it—playing with Zoey on a blanket Shell would put on the floor for tummy time. She remembered him on the floor, too, lying on his stomach in front of the baby, making funny faces while Zoey lifted her head and grinned her gummy grin at him.

Meanwhile, Shell had sat in a chair in the living room, tired, changed, not the woman she had been before Zoey had come along. Blurred at the edges, softer. She hadn't known how lucky she was. She should have been paying attention.

All at once, she felt something break that had already broken, so many times, and she felt the sadness spilling out and she was helpless, chagrined, *not now, not now, he doesn't like it when you do this*—but the tears fell down her cheeks anyway and all she could do was stand still and let them. She was prepared for him to look away from her now, she even turned her head away in preparation for it. But instead, he reached for her. He looked into her eyes. It must have been awful, what he saw there, but still he stared into it.

"Oh, my darling. I am so, so sorry." He was crying, too, the tears that slid down his cheeks mirrored her own.

She reached for him. There was nothing to say.

Outside, the rain fell and the wind pummeled the windows. But they paid no attention. Silent, bottomless grief. But this time, finally, it was shared. They moved through it together.

He kissed her and sobbed. It had been so long that he felt new. She said, "I want—" but she didn't need to finish. He had lifted her up and was carrying her to the bed already and everything changed. They were given a reprieve, and who knew how long it would last? She seized the moment. She threw her head back and he kissed her neck. Hot breath, his lips and tongue, they were two broken pieces fitting together and finding when they did they weren't as broken anymore.

"Whatever happens next," he began, moving inside her.

"I'm with you," she finished. "We're together."

And suddenly, the word *home* had meaning again.

Day Seven

Morning

Dear Guests,

As we are all now aware, a hurricane is heading our way: Hurricane Christine, Category 4, with sustained wind speeds of nearly 150 mph. Traveling at 250 mph, the full force of the storm will make landfall late this evening—but there is nothing to fear, as long as you follow our directions carefully. We understand that many of you are hoping to find flights out, but there are no longer any flights leaving this area. We will assist you in arranging for transportation once the storm is over.

You may sleep in your bungalows tonight, but first thing tomorrow morning, please report to the main villa with all of your bags packed. Please also bring your bedding and pillows, and any water bottles remaining in your room. Remember: anything you leave behind may not survive the storm. And once you have arrived at the villa tomorrow morning, there is no leaving to retrieve anything from the bungalows.

The villa is a strong building that has weathered many storms, some of them worse than this one. It is very likely that the safest place to be in this entire region tomorrow night is our spacious basement. We have plenty of food, water and supplies; you will be safe and cared for. All we ask is that you have faith in us and follow these simple rules:

—Stay in the basement of the villa.

—Move to the center of the basement in the afternoon and evening, when the storm will get stronger, and do not leave that area until you receive the all clear. Ruth will be giving the instructions. Do not do anything without her go-ahead.

—Do not, under any circumstances, go outside at any point during the storm. There will come a time tomorrow night when all will be quiet and you may think the storm is over. That is the eye

229

of the storm—and with a fast-moving system like this just making landfall, it will only last a few minutes. The safest thing to do once the eye arrives is stay in the basement, as close to the ground as possible, and wait for further instruction.

But please, don't be alarmed! Have faith that you are safe and cared for. Remember: a crisis can be a great opportunity to show love and care to your partner. Let's all use this opportunity to show our strength, and fight for what we love and want the most.

Sincerely,
Miles Markell and your
Harmony Resort Team

ONLINE UPROAR ABOUT BEHAVIOR OF CELEBRITY MARRIAGE COUNSELOR MILES MARKELL—"He didn't fix my marriage, he broke it," says sexual assault victim.

Hurricane Christine is heading to Mexico, but that may be the least of the worries for celebrity marriage counselor Miles Markell, who is one half of a marriage-fixing power couple who may be living a lie. Comments about Markell sexually harassing, drugging and even assaulting clients began surfacing on social media yesterday when a woman known only as Zoey W. posted detailed accusations. Click here for the details. Now as many as a dozen women have shared portions of their stories and indicated they want to share more—but they also want the man himself to respond to them.

So far today, he has ignored all social media comments (which is unusual because he's normally quite active on social media) and has not taken calls from CELEBRITYSCOOP or, according to other news outlets now picking up the story, anyone else. His wife has also failed to comment thus far. And people with loved ones at the resort are getting very worried. "I've been trying to contact my sister for days," said a woman who does not want to be named. "I've been quite concerned. We talk or text daily, but since she got to that resort, it's been total silence. Now I think she should know that the man who is counseling her on the state of her marriage could be a sexual predator. But she hasn't replied to any of my calls, texts or emails. And when I call the resort itself, I only get voicemail."

Could it be the resort staff are simply preparing for the coming storm, or is something more sinister going on? Watch for developments on this story.

231

Him: Did you know about the storm?

Her: That was a surprise. Storms are always a surprise.

Him: You knew before everyone else did, though.

Her: Yes. And it brought us even closer together, or so
I thought. Commiserating on what we would do. How we
would keep everyone safe. We were a team. He put me
in charge. I was quite pleased.

Him: Why would you not just tell the guests right up front
that a storm was coming?

Her: [A pause.] He said high-pressure situations brought
people closer together. He said if it was going to
be his last session, if we were going to run away
together as I had suggested, he wanted it to be a
huge success. It was bad enough that Colin and Shell
Williams were so broken, were so hopeless. He didn't
want any of the other couples to fail. He wanted to
go out with a triumph. That's what he told me. And
also—

Him: Yes?

Her: He told me Grace was very afraid of storms because
of something that had happened in her past. He was
concerned for her. He said she had been behaving
erratically, and that the best thing to do for all of
us would be to keep her in the dark for as long as
possible.

Him: Do you think there's another possibility? That he
just wanted to be in control? That he wanted to play
God? That it was one of his games?

Her: Doctor, in my world, he *was* God.

orning had come. And so had more wind, a steady barrage of it now. Grace crept out of her office. After Johanna had returned to her bungalow, Grace hadn't slept; she had just sat on the heather-purple couch, staring at the locked door she had dragged a filing cabinet in front of until the light started to change and then it was morning.

Outside, she leaned into the wind and walked toward the main villa. All she had was the small duffel bag she had packed the day before. And the letter from Garrett's son, tucked up small inside her pocket, her secret talisman. She let herself into the villa through a side door she had to battle to open. All was quiet inside the building. It was early; none of the guests had begun to arrive from their bungalows yet.

She stopped and listened, just to be sure. Then she headed down a dim hallway, and into the boardroom with the safe hidden in a closet. This safe was where Ruth locked the smaller contraband items she took from the guests' bags. The narcotics, to be specific—and there was always a surprising amount of them. Grace punched in the safe's combination and felt relief that it had not been changed. This sort of thing needed to be locked away from Miles, not her, not Ruth. He had never been told the combination, although he had begged and raged numerous times. It was the one area in which she had never seen Ruth relent. It was the one reason she knew Ruth was not as weak as Miles made her seem.

She slid her hand inside the dark space—she hadn't turned the lights on in the boardroom—and felt half a dozen smooth pill canisters there. She pulled out two, but then put them back because they weren't what she wanted. Xanax, Ativan, nothing that was strong enough. But the next one was: Shell Williams's sleeping pill prescription. Zopiclone 7.5 mg. She opened the canister and tapped out five of them and put them in her right pocket. She replaced the lid and put it back in the safe. But she hesitated. She plunged her hand into the safe once more. Now in her hand was the canister that bore the name Cleo Van Hahn.

She put the pill bottle down on the boardroom table in front of her and stared at it in the dim light. Nothing special. Just plastic, just a pile of chemicals inside. But a gift, a strange gift, given in love. She couldn't picture Cleo, she hadn't wanted to, but now she tried. Slim, tattoos like Johanna, but more of them. Strange and alluring pictures on her muscled back and arms. Dark hair and high cheekbones. Eyes that gleamed with mischief, glittered with despair. Grace opened her eyes again. And, without really knowing why, she opened the canister and shook out five of those pills, too. This hadn't been part of the plan, but she still slid them into her other pocket.

Then she put everything back in the safe and locked it again. A sound in a hallway, footsteps growing louder. She pressed herself against a wall in the corner of the room and waited until the footsteps faded away.

*T*he atmosphere in the basement was oddly festive. There were a few couples sitting in foursomes in the main room, on blankets laid out like they were at a picnic; some of them had food on the blankets, plates of fruit, crackers and cheese. "There's plenty to go around," Ruth had told everyone on one of her rounds. "And we should eat what could spoil when the fridges lose their power."

One woman popped a bottle of nonalcoholic champagne and laughed. Shell could smell cooking from somewhere down the hall. But she couldn't shake the sense of foreboding, the need to hide away from everyone. And even though she felt closer to Colin than she had in so long, she couldn't shake the creeping sense of guilt, the shame she was sure she was now going to have to live with. She kept hearing Ruth's words: *You wanted it.* There were moments when she felt even the storm was her fault. Her shoulders slumped under the weight of all this anguish, guilt and worry. And she didn't quite know how to talk to her husband about it. They had torn down the barriers between them, yes—but some burdens were just too hard to share, even with the person you loved most.

She said to Colin, "Maybe we could find somewhere more private to wait out the storm? There are a bunch of boardrooms and smaller rooms down that way." She indicated the hallway where the anger management group had taken place.

"Sure." He started to gather up their blankets and pillows. He paused and looked down at her. "You're okay?"

"Really, I'm fine," she lied. "I'll meet you in there. Try the second door down the left hallway. I just want to get us some water."

She headed toward the room with the makeshift sign that said CANTEEN. There was a woman in there, one of the only two staff members left, making sandwiches and doling out the water, the stores of which seemed alarmingly low to Shell.

After Shell had what she needed, she turned down a hall and froze, realizing two things far too late: one, that she had taken a wrong turn and two, that Miles was walking toward her. It was reflexive; her heart started to pound. She wanted to run. She couldn't move. She had never known fear in her life, not really. Not until she met Miles Markell.

But, she understood as she cowered, something else was overtaking her. She wanted to stand her ground and say something to him that would make him see how wrong he had been about her. She wanted to spit words at him the way he had spit at her.

He was drawing closer. His face came into focus. When he spotted her he stared with cool, expressionless eyes and said, "Good morning." Then he just kept walking. If he'd been wearing a hat, he would have tipped it. An established gentleman, nothing to be afraid of. But she knew what he was capable of.

Did anyone else?

He was gone, but she still couldn't move.

She had no words for what he had done to her, how he had made her feel. She wanted to hurt him. Pull off his glasses and grind them under her heel. Scratch at his eyes. Leave marks on his face.

She was shaking now. Colin's sandwich had fallen to the floor. She bent to pick it up and when she rose, she saw another figure walking down the hall. Grace.

This time, Shell was ready. She rushed toward her. "How could you do this?" she hissed when Grace was close enough to hear. "How could you keep the fact that a hurricane was coming from all of us? We're in danger now! We should have been evacuated! This is insane, and I think you know it."

Grace looked startled. She opened her mouth and closed it several times, as if trying out and discarding different combinations of things to say.

"I'm sorry," Grace finally said. "I really am. You're right. Proper steps weren't taken. I truly believe we'll all be safe here, but still. You shouldn't have to go through this, none of you." Now she stepped closer to Shell and looked into Shell's eyes. "*You* shouldn't have had to go through any of it, Shell. Maybe, someday, I can find a way to make all this up to you. I hope so."

Just then, the wind shrieked outside, so loud they could hear it through the walls. Grace's eyes grew wider. She shrank away from the sound, and Shell saw how afraid she was. Grace lowered her head. Her voice was a whisper, and Shell had to lean in to hear her. "You need to be very careful," she said. "You need to stay close to your husband tonight until the storm is over. Promise me?"

All Shell could do was nod.

Day Seven

Afternoon

Him: They were probably quite frightened, those people.

Her: They were. I know they were.

Him: And you?

Her: Of course I was. But I tried to have faith that it would all be okay. And truly, I was finally happy again. We had a plan. We were going to run away together. That was what I thought.

Him: But really . . .

Her: [Rustling. A sigh.] Really, he had his own plan. You read about it all, in the media. That group he had started. All that mess. When what *I* wanted was so simple. I had been funneling money out of accounts for months, the way he had asked me to. We both had access to those accounts. It would have been so easy for us to just walk away. Except he was using the money for something else, wasn't he? He was literally hemorrhaging money into the most horrible of causes. [Pause.] Now that was an interesting word choice, wasn't it?

Him: You shouldn't relive this. This is all in the past. It just upsets you. We need to start moving forward.

Her: It's not in the past for me. I relive it every single day. Where I went wrong, what I could have done differently. All I wanted was for us to wait until the storm was over and then just . . . drive away. But he had made it so complicated, and I didn't even know. Those women he was gathering up—oh, it was horrible, wasn't it? He banned the internet, at the resort—but oh, how he *loved* it. Oh, how it *tempted* him. It was his apple in the garden, and once he had his first taste, he could never stop eating.

Him: Perhaps a glass of water. You're growing agitated.

Her: No. I'm fine. I don't want anything. Please, let

241

me continue. It was easy enough for him to gather
followers, but those women he chose— Women in prison?
Addicts? Alcoholics? And they were so willing to give
him everything. I suppose he didn't see anything
wrong with it. He would have fought all those
charges, if he had lived. I know him. He thought
he was going to be their messiah. But they weren't
worthy of him. [Another sigh.] It was such a mess
in the end, wasn't it? If he had asked me to be the
leader, I would have made everything so different.
But he never had any faith in me, none at all. He
wanted *her*.

Him: Situations like this don't tend to end well.
Narcissists—

Her: He wasn't a narcissist!

Him: You really don't think so? You're so well educated,
you were an assistant psychologist, and you didn't
recognize narcissistic personality disorder?

Her: I loved him.

Him. Ah. Yes. We're back to that. Love is blind. The best
therapists, they know that. And so do you.

iles walked into the meeting room. He had found her. Grace had known he would and she had wanted him to but still, she had to hold her trembling hands in her lap under the table. Two cups of coffee sat in front of her, still steaming. One of them, the one on the left, was for him—and *only* for him. Inside it, she had dissolved some of the sleeping pills she had taken from the safe, crushing and stirring until they were gone. She waited until she was sure her hands wouldn't betray her and then put her hand around the cup.

He stood in the doorframe. "Grace. Good morning, darling." He was speaking in his stage voice. A couple passed and she could hear their murmured greetings. Then he stepped inside, and she braced herself. He was holding a small bag. "I was worried about you last night. When you didn't come home. I'm not used to it. I gathered up a few things for you. Things I know you'll need." He put the bag down in front of her. She saw her ointment on top of a few folded items of clothing. "You'll go crazy without that ointment. Won't you?"

"Thank you," she managed. "Thank you so much." This was the type of kindness others would find touching, but it only alarmed her. She inclined her head toward the coffee machine in the corner of the room. "I just finished making us coffees. I was going to go find you. Because who knows how long we'll have electricity to do things like make coffee, right?" She tried to smile. "And I know how you feel about your morning Americano."

Miles didn't say anything. He didn't move. His expression remained still, unreadable. Grace picked up her own cup and took a sip. When she replaced the cup on the saucer, there was a loud rattle.

Her hand was still shaking. Damn it. She hadn't been able to hide it. She had been thinking of how still he was but how quickly he moved, sometimes. The way he would lunge when she least expected it. One minute, she'd be drinking a coffee; the next, screaming in pain.

"I've been up for hours," he said. "I've already had two cups. But thank you."

"You're certain?"

"I'm always certain, Grace."

When he left the room, Grace closed her eyes and allowed her body to slump for a moment, defeated. She resisted the urge to throw the cup across the room. But, no. This wasn't her only chance. She still had pills in her pocket. She would just have to try again.

She had a bottle of water in a bag at her feet. She took it out and set it on the table. Then she reached into her pocket. Footsteps in the hallway. She had to hurry. She unscrewed the cap and crushed three more pills over the mouth of the bottle. She closed the lid and shook the bottle. She was putting it back down on the table when Ruth came into the room.

I'm always certain, Miles had said to her. She didn't want him to be the only one anymore.

"Ruth, hi. I'm glad you're here. This is one of the last bottles of alkaline water we have," she said, holding it up. "You know how Miles loves this water. You should take it to him. Give it to him to drink. He'll be so happy. It will help him relax." Not a lie, not exactly, but Grace still felt a brief moment of guilt as she saw the gratitude on Ruth's face. A way to make Miles happy—it was all Ruth ever wanted.

"Thank you," Ruth said, taking the bottle from her and holding it tight.

en was hardly speaking to Johanna—which seemed ridiculous to her, given the circumstances. She thought of the letter that had been slid under their bungalow door the night before, pushed by an unseen hand. *Remember: a crisis can be a great opportunity to show your love and care to your partner. Let's all use this opportunity to show our strength, and fight for what we love and want the most.*

Ben was not what she loved and wanted most, and she knew this. Perhaps he was starting to understand it, too.

"Where the hell were you?" he had said the night before, sitting upright when she had finally returned to their bungalow, after leaving Grace's office. She had marveled for a moment that he had still fallen asleep, not knowing where she was.

"Grace was upset." Johanna had struggled to keep her voice calm. "This is a crazy situation. A major storm blowing in that no one knew about? I think we all should be taking this as seriously as she is. It's shaken her."

"Sure, we're all scared. That's no excuse to take off like you did. You can't just disappear. I was so worried. I looked all over for you!"

I know, she could have said. *And we hid from you, we hid from Miles.* "I'm sorry," she had said instead, and there had been nothing else, after that. Just resentful silence lasting through the night and into the morning.

Now, they were off in a corner of the common area. Johanna was fidgeting, biting her nails.

"You okay?" Ben asked, but he barely looked at her. He was reading a book, his back against a wall.

"Not really," she said.

"Miles assured us that we're all going to be safe here. This villa has weathered many hurricanes over the years. I'm not nervous at all. I believe in what Miles says."

"Jesus, Ben!" She couldn't help herself, especially knowing what she knew about Miles. "How much of the purple Kool-Aid have you had to drink?"

"How much have *you*?" Ben snapped back, dropping his book to his knees. "Taking off like that, Johanna? You and Grace running off together like . . ."

"Are we still on that?" But she knew it wasn't fair. Ben hadn't done anything wrong. "She was upset," Johanna said, lowering her voice. "I told you. She needed to talk to someone. She's my—"

"She's your therapist," Ben interrupted, while Johanna wondered what word she had been intending to use, and how Ben had known she'd been about to say something else, something she shouldn't. "And you're not being appropriate."

Johanna looked at him for a long moment. There had been a point when she had considered asking Ben for help, even though Grace had implored her not to talk to anyone but her. And she still wondered. It was Ben. He was a good person. He would want to help, no matter what—wouldn't he?

The wind howled again. "Ben," Johanna began.

"It's okay," he said, mistaking the look on her face for fear of the storm, or maybe remorse about their fight. "It's going to be okay—really." Then he bent his head and started to read again.

The burden stayed with her as day began to turn to night; the only way she could tell in the windowless room was because her watch told her so. The secret felt heavier with each second that passed. It would have been so easy, to just blurt it out to Ben. *Miles has been abusing Grace. He wants to kill her. He's a monster. He needs to be stopped. She gave him sleeping pills so he won't be able to hurt her the way he wants to. And as soon as the storm is over, we're taking off, and I don't know what our plan is, but I know we have to get away from here. I know that as long as we're together, all will be well. I'm afraid of what will happen if we're not.*

He wouldn't understand. How could he? She felt like she was on a precipice, wondering what it might be like to jump, to fall, to ruin everything. Maybe she would fly, that was the thing. Maybe, this time.

She didn't even look up when Grace passed by every little while. This was a very difficult thing to resist, but Johanna did. The secret felt lighter when she smelled Grace's shampoo as she passed, heard the rustle of her clothes. Then hours passed, and no Grace. Johanna started to worry.

Eventually, Ben said, "You know what, I think I'm going to be able to fall asleep." And he promptly did so. This had always made Johanna crazy, the ease with which he moved from being awake to asleep, no transitioning. It always took Johanna time—and she knew that on a night like this, no sleep would come. How was he so peaceful, how was he so unaware, not just of what was going on outside, but of what was going on inside of her, inside of their relationship?

You never tell him anything. How's he supposed to know? You never say anything, and you do everything he asks. And tomorrow, you're just going to get up and walk away and he's never going to know why. Do you think that's right?

She lay awake, her thoughts an endless barrage. She kept hearing Miles's voice, she was sure of it. Once, she thought she heard him shouting down a hallway. And outside, the ocean pounded and the wind gathered more power—she could feel it. As the voices in the room turned to murmurs, then whispers, then near silence, her thoughts began to roar like that wind. Was it really going to be so simple? Or were they living out some sort of twisted fairy tale that couldn't possibly have a happy ending?

She waited, listened to Ben's breathing, waited some more.

Then she stood up.

She needed to find Grace. She needed to make sure she was okay, that it had all gone according to the plan Grace had told her about when they were hiding together in her office. She needed to find out if the monster was harmless, fast asleep—or gathering strength, the way the storm was.

Getting stronger instead of weaker.

Getting ready to strike.

If he was, Johanna was going to have to do something about it.

Her: She did something. She poisoned him. And I think
that's why he was acting that way. Because it wasn't
like him.

Him: It wasn't like Miles to behave erratically, as
everyone in the villa that night reported? It
wasn't like Miles to threaten people, to foster an
environment of tyranny, to manipulate?

Her: You don't know him! You don't know him the way I do.
[A sob.] *Did* know him. And to think that I warned
her! To think I tried to help her! I told her to hide
because I wanted her to be safe. I knew if he hurt
her, our entire future could be put into jeopardy.
And she'd drugged him! It was her fault he was so
volatile that night! Or mine, for being so foolish.
For trusting someone like her, even for one minute.

Him: What exactly are you saying?

Her: She gave me a water bottle. She suggested I give it
to Miles. *It's his favorite*, she reminded me. The
alkaline water, and it was the last bottle left. I
was touched. It gave me pause. I thought maybe she
did care for him after all, and I admired her for it.
But I also thought of all the times she took credit
for things. I wanted the credit for this, so when I
gave it to him I didn't say it was from her. I realize
now he never would have drunk it if he'd known it
came from her. I was so desperate for his attention I
became blind to everything else. But he knew exactly
what she was up to, because there was never any way
for her to hide from him, no matter how hard she
tried. He drank that water because he trusted *me*. And
that's the moment everything changed. [A long pause.]
But that's not what killed him. Whatever she put in
that water didn't kill him. It made him stronger.

Day Seven

Night

A tap at the door of the small office Grace was sitting in, alone, watchful, waiting, unsure of what to do or where to go. It hadn't worked. That much was clear. No, Miles was wide awake, roaming the halls, talking to himself and to others. Grace wasn't sure what he was saying but had seen the strange looks on some of the guests' faces. "Maybe he's really freaked out," one of them had said. "Best to just check in with Ruth. Let him alone."

He hadn't found her yet. But Grace knew he was looking.

"Grace?"

She looked up, startled. Just Ruth. Her face was pale under the makeup, and her eyes were afraid. "Something is very wrong with Miles."

A surge of relief. It *had* worked. Finally. One of the wonders of the human body was that your heart could be pounding, your blood flowing through your veins like rushing whitewater—but on the outside, you could remain completely composed. Miles had been doing it for years. They both had.

"I'm sure it's all right, Ruth. Let him sleep. He's probably just exhausted. This is a stressful situation. It's getting late. Maybe he just needs to rest."

Ruth stepped closer. They'd lost power a few hours before, and the generator hadn't lasted very long. Now their only light came from lanterns in the hurricane kits, which the two women had placed in as many areas in the basement of the main villa as possible. As they had worked so silently and efficiently together, Grace had thought about how different things could have been.

The light gave Ruth's face an eerie glow. "No," she said. "He's not tired. He's not calm. He's not asleep. He's scaring me."

"What do you mean?"

"I'm trying to get him to stay in one of the boardrooms because he's been scaring the others, too, saying strange things to guests when he passes them. About serpent and apples, about heaven and hell. His eyes are wild. Like he—like maybe he took something?" Now Grace stared down at the table, thinking about what she may have done, in-advertently. The wrong pills. Damn it. "We both know he's had his problems in the past and I forgive him, *I forgive him*, Grace, because if he faltered now, who could blame him? But he's saying things. Talking about—well, he's talking about killing people. I don't know who, he just keeps using the name *Jezebel*."

Grace's legs had started to go numb. She thought she might be sick. She gripped the table.

"I think it's you," Ruth said. "I think *you're* Jezebel, aren't you?" But for once, there was no judgment in her voice. "I came here to tell you to hide. Now. If he does anything to you, it will ruin everything. We'll never be able to . . ." But then, she shook her head. "Just hide. Please. Go up to my quarters. I don't think he'll look up there."

Grace's heart was still racing: she felt pulled along, powerless. She had made a mistake. A terrible one. She had been so nervous when she was mixing the pills into the water that she had reached into the wrong pocket, chosen the wrong pills—she must have. What had she been thinking, taking some of Cleo's pills, anyway? She'd had it in her head that they could be a gift for Johanna. When everything was over, maybe they could have some kind of memorial, bury those pills and Cleo along with them.

Admit it. You're jealous. You wanted to find a way to bury Cleo's memory, make Johanna forget about her. And now look what you've done. Not sleeping pills, no. You gave him something else. Something that isn't going to make him tired. Something that's making him worse.

"Up in your quarters?" she said. "But—we're supposed to stay down here. Where it's safe."

"You're not safe down here, Grace. I think you know that." Just as Ruth said that, there was a commotion in the hallway. "I'll distract him." Ruth moved toward the door. "Count to ten, and then, *run.*"

"Colin?" Shell said.

But he was breathing slowly and deeply. He had been asleep for a little while, like a child beside her on the blanket on the floor of the office they had closed themselves within. She felt such tenderness toward him. She touched his forehead, his cheek. He made her feel safe.

But she needed to use the washroom. She had delayed it as long as she could. She didn't want to go alone—she had heard Miles's voice a little while earlier, and she couldn't risk running into him again—but she also didn't want to wake Colin. He needed his rest. She thought of Grace Markell, who had warned her to be careful. But she'd be all right. There were so many people around, asleep in the common area or lounging in hallways. She'd be fine. Miles couldn't hurt her. He wouldn't dare, not with all these people around.

She stood. She left the room and walked down the hall. Aside from the continuous howl of the wind, which had become like white noise to her now, it was quieter than she had anticipated. She was alone.

But then, shadows and sound up ahead; she froze and pulled herself into the darkness. She heard Miles's voice, loud, angry, strange—was he slurring? And Ruth, her tone gentle and afraid and angry, too. She pressed herself against the wall and tried to make herself disappear into the darkness.

"Please," she heard Ruth say, her voice rising. "Don't hit me. Not tonight." Miles had his hand raised above her face. Shell moved forward. She imagined pulling his arm down and away, saw herself stopping Miles from hurting someone else. She would do it this time.

But she lost her nerve, she faltered. She fell back into the shadows as Ruth cried out, *"No, stop it, you're hurting me!"* Then Miles was gone, moving quickly in the other direction. Ruth slumped against the wall and sobbed quietly, her shoulders shaking like the wings of a wounded bird.

race had been sitting on Ruth's bed, lost in her thoughts, when she heard the pounding footsteps on the stairs—she hadn't been paying attention. *No, no, please, no.* She slid to the floor, panicked and rolled under the bed as the door to the room burst open. She had the small paring knife in her hand. She pressed her body back into the shadows. There was no bed skirt. It was a terrible hiding place. It reminded her of the times she would play hide-and-seek with her brother and her hiding spot would be so weak that he'd walk into a room and see her immediately. And they'd start to laugh.

But there would be no laughing with Miles.

Right now, all she could see were his feet.

"Are you in here, Jezebel? Do you think you can hide from me?"

His voice was thick. "Hell-oo-oo?" he wheedled, and she watched his feet and the bottom of his legs as he turned in a slow circle. Had she left an imprint on the duvet when she was sitting on the bed? Would he be able to see it in the dim light of the battery-powered lantern in the room? She tried not to breathe, then found herself needing to gasp for air. She opened her mouth and released the air as slowly as she could. The wind screeched above and she felt grateful for it, instead of afraid of it. *Imagine being less afraid of a hurricane than you are of your own husband.*

"Oh, darling," he said, his voice gentler now. "I wish you'd just come out of your hiding place." She heard him open a closet, riffle through hangers. "You'd make this so much easier. All I want is to talk to you. It shouldn't have to be like this. What went wrong with us? We could have had it all." She was reminded of those first moments in the church basement, when he was the only person she had been sure she could trust. It didn't matter that she'd been so mistaken; her body and soul always had this reaction to him. Like a curse, like a spell, cast on her decades ago.

But it didn't last. She thought of Johanna. She heard her voice. The adrenaline flooded her body again.

"I don't want to hurt you. I just want to talk to you."

His feet in his polished leather lace-ups were right in front of the bed. She could see across the room, to the oval standing mirror Ruth had in one corner. It was tilted down slightly—and, she realized with alarm, she could see herself in it, could see her own terrified face pressed against the floor under the bed. *No. No. No.* He was holding a bottle of vodka, almost empty. A sloshing sound as he took a swig. And she saw it in her mind's eye: Cleo's pill bottle, and the bold letters that had been on it. WARNING. DO NOT CONSUME WITH ALCOHOL. MAY CAUSE HALLUCINATIONS.

If he looked in the mirror, he was going to see her. It was just a matter of time before he did. When it happened, she had to be ready.

But he didn't look, not yet. He walked into the other room in Ruth's suite, the room she used as an office. Through the shouts of the wind she could hear him opening and closing doors and muttering to himself. The door to the staircase was ajar. She could run, now. But what if he caught her on the stairs, or worse, just as she was coming out from under the bed?

It was too late, anyway; he was back in the room already. She kept her eyes on the mirror, her hand wrapped around the paring knife. Finally, he approached the glass and gazed into it. She waited for him to see her.

But he was looking only at himself. He took another swig of vodka, then let the bottle drop to the floor. She could smell the alcohol as it spilled, close to where she hid. If he bent down to pick it up, he'd see her for sure.

He reached up one hand, as if he could caress his own skin through the mirror. "You're a good boy, Miles," he said in a strange voice, touching the glass with his fingertips. It was almost feminine, and so unlike him. She felt the bile rising in her throat, and fought back a scream. She didn't want to be watching this. No one needed to see this. "I love you, Miles," he said. "You're a good, good boy."

His left arm was dangling down at his side. She saw it now, what he had in his hand. His hunting knife. It was the only thing of his father's he had. It was old and battered and normally sheathed in leather, but not at this moment. Now it was out of its sheath and glinting at her in the light of the lantern reflecting off the mirror.

She felt an awful twinge of empathy for a damaged, abused, un-loved boy. But she stayed still. He lifted the hand with the knife. As if in a trance, he made a cut. Blood dripped down onto the carpet. She watched it drip, slowly and steadily. It smelled like rust. It smelled like death. "This is my blood, shed for you," he said. The sound of his voice, delirious, deranged, whatever had been in those pills stripping him of any last vestiges of sanity, like a sheath removed from a knife reveal-ing nothing but cold and unreasonable deadliness. And the vodka—the vodka was like gas poured on a flame.

His voice had changed. He turned. "If you're in here, my Jezebel, I want you to come out, and I want you to come downstairs because it's not safe up here. It's not safe," he repeated. He moved toward the door. "The strongest part of the storm will reach us in a few hours and then, you never know, this tower might just get ripped right off the build-ing." A pause, a soft chuckle. "It might, you know. And if you're still up here, you might be making it very easy for me. Less messy. Freeing me up to deal with . . . other things." She could see him in the mirror, put-ting the sheath back on the knife and sliding it down into his pocket. It still stuck out. He turned away. This could have been her moment. She could have found the strength, the speed, the agility, the bravery, to roll out from under the bed and stab him in the back with the little knife she held in her own hand.

But her fear, as it had for so many years, held her captive. She couldn't have moved if she wanted to.

He closed the door behind him, and he was gone.

Shell stepped out of the shadows. "Ruth?" she said softly. "Ruth? Are you all right?"

Ruth looked up. Her face was tearstained. Shell could see bruises, even in the poor lighting. Poor thing. She needed help.

But she didn't want help. Not from Shell. "*You*. Get away from me. This is *your* fault, all of it! And hers! All of you! I *hate* you!" Ruth turned but then stopped. She faced Shell again. "You deserved it," she whispered. "Everything bad that has ever happened to you. You deserved it. And you deserve everything that will." Ruth walked away from Shell, her footsteps echoing and receding down the hallway. Shell couldn't move.

She didn't know how long she stood there.

The wind was so loud she didn't hear him coming.

eet pounding down a staircase. Shouting in the hallway. A scuffle. A woman's voice, and then him.

Miles. His voice reminded Johanna of Ivan's, when he'd had too much of everything. She felt a chill move through her veins, but the cold quickly turned to hot anger as she imagined the bruises on her mother. The bruises on Cleo. The Möbius strip of women with bruises like that, inflicted by people like Ivan, like Chad Von Hahn, like Miles. By people who had been hurt and so they hurt others, in return.

Johanna had to do something. The storm outside was becoming a storm inside of her. She slid her hand into her pocket and felt the lava rock there. She had kept it after she and Grace had talked out on the beach, that last time, when she had told her everything. It was smooth in some areas, sharp in others. She heard Grace's voice, the first time they talked. *It's supposed to give anyone who holds it courage.*

Johanna stood up and opened the door. She started to walk toward the sound of his voice. She wasn't out looking for Miles, she told herself. She had promised Grace she'd stay as far away from him as possible. All she wanted was to maybe catch a glimpse of Grace, whom she hadn't seen in too many hours now. Make sure she was okay. As she walked, she held the rock tight in her fist.

Was that a scream, from up ahead? Was it the sound of Miles's voice, saying to *shut up, be quiet, just shut the fuck up*? She didn't want it to be, but she knew what she was hearing. She clicked off her flashlight and listened. It was Ivan all over again and Chad, too, it was that awful afternoon in her office, it was the cold of the gun against her neck and the words, "You fucking dyke, you should be dead," banging into one another inside her head.

You're right, you're right, you've always been right.

But then, a new voice in her head: *No. No. No.* It almost seemed to be coming from above. The next day, when she was gone, when she and Grace were gone together—because she had to believe they were all going to get through this—what would become of Miles? Would he just get to stay here, having this life, hurting more women, yelling at them the way he was yelling at someone now? Hurting and hitting when he didn't get his way, or simply when he felt like it? Weren't there ever consequences for men like this? Because she knew Grace would bear the consequence of him, wear it like a mantle, no matter how far she ran. And she also knew that she couldn't sit still anymore. Their plan hadn't worked. Miles *wasn't* asleep. He was roaring around the villa, and he was going to hurt someone—and Grace was going to end up in his path, Johanna knew it. If he hadn't already, he would hunt her down. Maybe he already had her.

Johanna followed the sound of Miles's voice, and the sound of a scream. She rushed ahead and pushed open the door. She remembered the missive, under the door. *Do not go outside during the storm, under any circumstances.*

But he had led her here. She had had no choice but to follow.

———

Miles was dragging a woman through the wind and rain, toward the restaurant stairs. Johanna imagined the sharp drop, the rocks that would await anyone flung down there, and she felt the panic in her veins. *Grace.* It had to be. He had her—but Johanna wasn't going to let him hurt her. She felt strength flow through her body—strength, anger, love. She started to run. She wasn't going to let anything stop her.

But then she did stop. Because Miles was holding a knife against the woman's throat.

And it wasn't Grace he was dragging away. It was Shell.

*S*he had been so stupid, so careless, so foolish. So cowardly. She had crept away from the scene between Miles and Ruth instead of stepping in. She had let Ruth's cruel words paralyze her. And now she was getting what she deserved. Ruth had been right about that, at least. Such an easy place for Shell to default to: *Your fault, your fault.* But it was. Everything was. He had grabbed her and dragged her down the hallways and outside. And she hadn't been able to do anything to stop him.

The raging wind, his arms around her, hard as the steel of his knife pressed against her throat. How stupid she had been to imagine he would not be able to find more ways to hurt her. And how truly surprising it was, to find out how badly she wanted to live, when just days before she had been sure she wanted to die.

She thought of Johanna's words, that afternoon on the beach, when they had been skipping rocks and Shell had told Johanna she would have wished to die, had she been in her shoes when the man had walked into her office with a gun. *I know what you feel when something like that happens to you,* Johanna had said to her. *You want to live. Even if you think you don't. You understand what your life is worth. You see the light you couldn't see before.*

"You still have a chance, you know," Miles shouted. "I can really see you, I can see who you really are! I've always been able to! You could still join me, and none of this would happen to you! It doesn't have to be this way!"

"What do you mean, *join you*?" she screamed, and felt her words get lost in the storm. She could shout for Colin but he would never hear her. He was probably still sleeping, unaware she was even gone. What a fool she was. She could still be in there, safe with her husband. She struggled, but it was no use. Too late.

"I am the leader!" Miles screamed. "Let me be yours!"

She tried to jerk away. "Let go of me!"

He was very still for a moment, holding her in a vise grip. "No," he said. "I won't." And then he was pulling her up the outdoor restaurant stairs and her legs were bumping along uselessly. She knew this was the very last place they should be right now. When the most powerful part of the storm arrived, she imagined this restaurant detaching itself from the side of the cliff and tumbling away into the waves. She knew Miles wouldn't care what happened to her.

But up at the top of the stairs in the main part of the restaurant they were slightly sheltered from the wind. Miles lowered his head, touched his lips to her ear. "You are a sinner," he said. "You are a worthless sinner." She struggled against him, but it was no use. He held the knife against her neck and she felt the sting of a shallow cut, felt blood dripping down her chest, just like she had felt his saliva there, the day before. He was intent on marking her, this man. He was not going to stop until he had ruined her.

Movement. She saw someone at the top of the stairs leading to the restaurant. She thought it was Colin but then she realized it was Johanna. And that she was advancing toward them, her hand held high. Shell remembered their moments together on the beach again. She saw Johanna throwing rocks into the water, showing her what to do. But this was not a skipping stone. Johanna held a rock the size of her fist. Shell wanted to shout *He has a knife*, but she didn't get the chance. Johanna unleashed the rock. *My dad taught me to pitch baseballs*, Johanna had told Shell that afternoon on the beach. And: *You want to live*, she had told her. And: *It's so easy*, Johanna had said. *Once you stop thinking about what you're doing. Just throw.* Shell closed her eyes and whispered, *Please*—to whom, she did not know. *Please, let her aim be true. Please, save me.*

A thud. Then Miles fell backward, pulling her with him. But she was able to pull away just before he hit the floor with a sickening thud. She stumble-ran away from him and slid over the wet tile floor toward Johanna. "Thank you," she was going to say. But as she got closer to her, she saw that there was no triumph on her face. Only terror.

Shell turned around.

Miles was up already. His head was bleeding, but he was moving forward, roaring like a demon. She barely heard his words, only the ugly sound of his voice, not that different from the banshee shriek of the wind.

"Jezebels!" That horrible, cajoling, wheedling shout. "Slatterns!"

He was coming closer. "You filthy whores. You evil snakes. I will fucking kill you. I *will*."

She had always told herself, after Zoey was born, that she would try to make the world a place worthy of her beautiful daughter. And, she realized, even though she was gone, she felt the same. She knew it was magical thinking, but she couldn't help but believe it in that moment: that if she could make it a world worthy of her daughter, maybe Zoey would come back to her.

And a world worthy of her daughter could not possibly contain a man like Miles Markell.

Shell took three steps forward, arms outstretched. Three more. She was pushing him backward, pushing him away from them, pushing with the strength of everything she had lost.

He had been right. She really was powerful. She knew he saw this as his body flew over the ledge and down.

Johanna locked the door of the main villa behind them. She and Shell gazed at one another wordlessly. Rain dripped from their bodies to the floor. "I need to go to Colin," Shell whispered. Johanna put her hand on her arm, but she didn't know what to say to her. Shell just shook her head, then disappeared into the darkness.

Johanna checked inside every room, opened every door she passed. Finally, she found a door that led to a staircase. She hesitated, thinking that *up* would be the last place Grace should go during a storm—but something told her she may have had no choice. That she may have needed to go to the last place she thought he was going to look.

Soon she was at the top of the building, and the wind was howling louder. A door, a suite of rooms: someone lived up here.

She opened the door and saw skittering movement, someone retreating into the shadows. *"Grace?"*

Grace stepped forward. "I thought you were him," she said, and she was crying, too, shaking almost in unison with Johanna. "He's going to come for me. I'm so scared. He's going to come for both of us, now that you're here. He has a knife."

"You don't have to worry. He's not going to come."

"How do you know that? How?"

How could she tell her what she had done? What they had done, together? And yet, how could she not? Miles was either dead, or seriously hurt. Not telling anyone, leaving him out there, was murder. But telling Grace, making her the one to choose—Johanna knew what would happen. She knew Grace would do what she thought was right. And, remembering the maniacal, murderous look in Miles's eyes, she knew that in this case there was more than one right decision. That if there was any chance Miles was just injured and not dead yet, she needed to take the choice away from Grace so that Grace would be safe.

Miles wasn't the only one who could play God.

"I just—I saw him sleeping," she said. It wasn't quite a lie, not entirely. Maybe he *was* sleeping. Sleeping forever.

Grace sagged with relief, sagged into Johanna's arms and put her head on her shoulder. "I thought I messed it up. I tried to give him the Zopiclone in coffee so he wouldn't taste the bitterness, but he wouldn't drink it. So I dissolved more pills in water, but I was rushing. I—I had Cleo's pills there with me, too, from the safe. And, the way he was acting, I started to think I accidentally gave him those instead of the sleeping pills." She looked up. "What did you say was in them?"

"Cleo's pills?" A slow dawning, a prickle of dread as she considered what might be found in his system, and the possibility that it could be traced back to her. "Ketamine, I think. You—you put them in water? The pills Miles ultimately took?" He would have tasted the sleeping pills in water. But Cleo had once told her the pills she had given her had no taste, that Johanna could dissolve them in any liquid if she was having trouble swallowing them because of their size.

"How did they make you feel, when you took them?"

"I never took a whole one. I only cut them in half, if the migraines got really bad. They took the pain away, but I didn't like the way they made me feel. Jumpy. Jittery. I hallucinated once, and it was scary."

"I'm so glad that's not what I gave him."

It explained so much—but she couldn't tell that to Grace. Not now. She needed to offer her comfort. "There's nothing to worry about. And now that he's asleep, I think it might be best for us to go downstairs." The lantern burned out as she said that. She waited for her eyes to adjust in the dark.

But all she could see was Miles, first toppling like Goliath, then flying over the edge of those rocks like a fallen angel. "Come on," Johanna said. "Take my hand. We'll find the door. We'll get out of here."

$\mathcal{S}$hell pushed open the door of the office she and Colin had been resting in earlier. Colin was awake. She saw his worried, frightened face in the dimming light of the flashlight he was holding. He walked toward her. "Where were you? Why are you soaked?"

"I needed the bathroom, I didn't want to wake you."

"Did you go outside?"

"I took a wrong turn, I went out the wrong door."

"Shell."

She was shaking. He could see it all, could see right through her.

"Oh, Colin," she whispered, accepting his embrace. "I didn't know what else to do." Then she began to whisper it in his ear, the awful story. He kept her in his arms, but she could feel him stiffen.

"Why did you go alone?" he moaned. "Why didn't you wake me?"

"I'm sorry. I'm *so* sorry."

Now he pulled away and looked down at her. "He's still out there?"

"Yes."

"If we leave him out there, it will be—"

"Please, don't say it."

"I should go out there. I should see if I can—"

A groaning sound outside interrupted him. Shell knew it was the wind, but still, she imagined it was Miles, grown larger than life and coming for her, for both of them, all of them. The wind was so strong for a few minutes she didn't know if they were inside or out. And then, all at once, an eerie silence. Colin reached for her hand, Miles forgotten. "It's getting stronger. We need to get to the middle of the building," he said. "Come on, let's go."

They closed the door behind them, and in the slam of it she heard so much more: a crushing secret, a horrible act, one she knew she wouldn't be able to keep behind a closed door forever. But for now, she clung to Colin's hand and tried to imagine that none of it had happened, that it was just a bad dream.

As they moved down the hallway, she saw someone running toward them. It was Johanna's husband, Ben. He was soaked through, too, as soaked as if he'd been swimming in the ocean. As soaked as she was. "Have you seen Johanna?" he said through chattering teeth. Shell didn't know how to answer him. "Please, have you seen her? I'm afraid she might be outside!"

"She's not out there," Shell finally said. "I know Johanna isn't outside."

"We'll run, tomorrow," Grace said to Johanna. A reminder, as she followed her through the room, that there had to be a light at the end of this tunnel.

"Tomorrow, when this is over." Johanna's voice, ahead of her in the dark. "Yes. We will."

"No matter what." But it was in Grace's head, that pounding refrain: *No. No. No.* She could feel it growing louder. It had started when Johanna had come into the room. When Johanna had told her not to worry, that Miles wasn't going to come for her. Just before the lantern went out she had seen it in her eyes. A terrible knowledge, and a change in her. Something awful was happening. Somehow, Miles was going to take all this away from her. She knew this the way she knew things about her clients, when all she had to do was close her eyes and let herself feel—and there it was: the secret and the truth.

Grace paused. The cacophony of her thoughts had distracted her from the fact that everything else had gone silent, all at once. The storm noises had stopped completely—no wind, no rain. The world was a vacuum.

Johanna stopped feeling her way through the dark, but she had kept hold of Grace's hand. "What's going on?" she asked in the stillness. It felt like a miracle, but Grace knew it wasn't.

"It's the eye of the storm," she said. "It's here. And I don't know if we have time to get downstairs now. We can't be on the stairs when the other eyewall hits. The walls are thin. They could be torn right off, and us along with them." She squeezed Johanna's hand. "Follow me, now." She felt her away along the wall, back the way they'd come.

*T*here was a drop in pressure so sudden Johanna's head began to pound. It was as if all the air was being sucked from the room. Grace tugged her hand harder and they stumbled across the room, blind in the dark. A door, and Johanna had to shove it open, hard. It slammed behind them. Was there any air left in this tiny room? Yes. Yes, she could breathe. "The tub! Come on!" Grace pulled Johanna down into the tub. They lay side by side, bodies pressed together. "It's hitting us now. The other side of the storm."

"But Miles," Johanna said. It had seemed so right, earlier, to do nothing. But now Johanna felt panicked. Now, she knew beyond any doubt there would be no going back. What was done was done. And she hadn't been able to keep it inside her. "He's still out there. I left him out there. I'm so sorry. It's true, what you suspected: he ingested the wrong drugs. He was violent. And then—"

The sound of glass breaking. There was no time for Grace to respond to what Johanna had said. Maybe she hadn't even heard her. "Close your eyes, squeeze them shut."

Johanna did as Grace had told her to do, burying her head in Grace's hair as glass rained down on them both. The wind screeched above them, and Johanna thought maybe the roof had been pulled off the building. *If I die now*—but there was no way to finish that thought. There were noises all around: bangs, shatters, crashes, groans of walls and beams. Johanna knew she should be more frightened than she was. But she was in Grace's arms, and there was no fear there. She put her lips on Grace's, because wasn't that what you did when there was a storm? You sought shelter. You found safety.

What would you do if it was your last night on earth? Had anyone ever asked her that? The answer was this: She would kiss Grace Markell's soft, beautiful lips and she would hold her face in her hands. She would say, "You are perfect. I'm so glad we met. No matter what. I'm so glad." And Grace would say, "Me, too, you saved my life." She would hear Grace's voice above all else, even the wind.

Hours or minutes, she didn't know. But the wind died down and the world came back into focus. When Johanna finally moved, her entire body was cramped. The dull ache from the pressure drop was still in her head, but otherwise she was fine. She moved her head slightly away from Grace and looked into her eyes in the dim morning light, now flowing in through the broken window. Johanna's body flooded with relief and she kissed her again.

The door flung open suddenly, just as they stopped. It was Ben. He took them in, huddled in the tub, saw Johanna's hand tangled in Grace's hair, saw their closeness because there was no way not to see it. Johanna opened her mouth, but closed it when she realized what she had been about to say: *Nothing happened.* A reflex, to deny. But saying nothing had happened would have been the biggest lie of her life. The storm had come and washed her away. It had made her new. She had to be true to this new person she had become. "Come on."

Yet, somehow, Ben seemed to see none of it. Maybe he saw only what he wanted to see. Maybe he always had. "You both need to get downstairs, now. We have a serious problem. Hurry. Before anyone sees us."

Johanna was afraid, but still found herself marveling at the fact that they had survived.

But not everyone had. She knew that, perhaps more than anyone.

And she also knew that what was to come next would take even more bravery.

Day Eight

Dawn

Her: This is what really happened. This is what no one
      knows. I went outside looking for Miles. And I saw
      every single thing that happened. And then—well,
      you can be the judge. [A pause.] Please. Judge me.
      Someone needs to, now that he's gone. I tried to give
      him one last chance, in my own defense. I gave him
      the chance to say he was sorry. He wouldn't. He said
      terrible things instead. He hurt me again. And so I
      was the one who killed him. I loved him, but he had
      hurt me so badly. I just couldn't take it anymore.
      All of a sudden, I needed to end it. So he would stop
      hurting people. So he would stop hurting me.

*T*he five of them walked toward the restaurant in the strange silence of the aftermath of the storm. They were on high ground, and Grace could see some of the damage to the property: the bungalows were slumped, some of them roofless and filled with sand. Most of the palm trees had snapped in two. The roof of her house was gone. To Grace, it looked like the wreck of a property she and Miles had bought more than a decade before, after Hurricane Wilma. It was like none of it had ever happened, like she was getting a chance to start over.

Except.

"What's going on?" she asked Ben. "Why are we out here?"

"Miles," he said. "Ruth." That was all he said, but the way he said it brought back all the fear from the night before. They were not safe. Not yet. He kept walking, Johanna behind him, then Grace, then Shell, and Colin at the end. A macabre parade.

Grace's throat was dry. It felt like it was on fire. She had picked up a water bottle as they had passed one of the supply tables inside. She took a deep drink, but it did nothing to put out the fire inside her.

They got to the stairs of the restaurant, somehow still intact. Storms were so indiscriminate—she had seen this. What they chose to destroy, what they left alone. They walked up the stairs. "Oh, my god," Shell murmured.

Grace saw. Miles was on the floor, his legs bent at unnatural angles, blood dribbling from the corner of his mouth, from his eyes, from one of his ears. His face was impossibly pale. Ruth was there, cradling his head in her lap. They were whispering to one another. They looked like two lovers bidding one another a gentle goodbye. But Grace knew better. She knew it wasn't right, what he was saying to her. Ruth's face was anguished, and not because he appeared to be dying. It was because of his words, whatever ugliness was still streaming from his mouth, even as he lost his strength by the second. Ruth bent in close and shook her head. *No, please*, she mouthed. Was he smiling, was he laughing? How was that possible?

It didn't look right and this was why: Ruth was cradling Miles, yes, but she was also holding a knife to his neck. As Grace saw this, Ruth looked up and saw the five of them.

"Get back!" she called. "Get back, now, or I swear I'll kill him."

"He looks like he's already dying," Colin said, stepping forward.

"Get back, I said!" Now Ruth's voice was a scream. A hesitation and then they all retreated at once, to stand on the staircase landing. If they stood on tiptoes, they could still see her. Grace did, and she watched as Ruth leaned down her head again. "Please," Grace thought she heard her repeat. Then, "No, no, please, no, stop saying that!" Her voice was growing louder. "No!" A shout with surprising depth and power. "Stop! No more! You've ruined me! I won't let you anymore!"

Ruth lifted the knife, and they could all see it now. They fell back in a wave, toward the stairs. Grace moved forward to stop her, because surely someone needed to—but a hand pulled her back. Warm fingertips, a touch she knew. She let Johanna pull her away and stood still, her body touching Johanna's, all of them frozen in time as Ruth lifted the knife with both hands, then plunged it into Miles's chest.

She did it again.

Again.

Again.

Again.

No one moved, except for Ruth. Except for the knife. Miles wasn't moving anymore, but Ruth still wouldn't stop. She stabbed him over and over—and Grace imagined she was doing it for every time he had hurt her, every single time, maybe even for the times he had hurt anyone else. They could all be standing there forever, watching her kill an already dead man. It felt like they were. It felt, in that moment, like they were all one person, like they were all Ruth. Like they were making sure he was really dead. Because with a man like Miles, you wanted to be sure.

Finally, Ruth stood. She dropped the knife and started to shake. "I killed him," she said, her voice surprisingly calm. "I did it. He's dead. I killed him. It's over. Call the police." Ruth was looking at Grace, and Grace had to look away. Grace felt Johanna move away from her. She didn't want her to.

"No," Johanna said. "It wasn't you. I started all this. I'm the reason he was injured in the first place. This is my fault. I don't want you to be punished for this, Ruth."

After Johanna spoke, there was no sound in the restaurant but the chastened ocean, the calm wind and a seabird overhead, above the damaged roof, testing out its wings in the brand-new world. Then Grace's voice. "Johanna, please don't."

*T*he truth is a strange thing. You can mold it sometimes, and bend it to your will. But there are some things that are beyond anyone's control. Shell was certain everyone who was there that morning saw it in Grace's eyes, heard it in her voice. And she felt brief comfort because she knew that what they saw in that moment was love—and if, later, they decided it was not that, if they decided it was anything but that between these two women, then that was their own fault, because it had been shown to them, clearer than anything. So many things in the world are complicated, but love is really quite simple.

Shell walked toward Johanna and turned. Now she was standing facing all of them, her back to the cliff and ocean and sky. "That knife Ruth has, it belongs to Miles. Earlier, I left the room Colin and I were in to go to the washroom. Miles was in the hallway, and he grabbed me and dragged me outside. And then I—"

Colin's voice. "No. Stop. I can't lose you because of him."

Shell just shook her head. She tried to tune out the voice of her husband. She needed to take responsibility for her actions, no matter what the consequences. She needed to be strong. For Zoey. For all of them. Maybe if she did what was right she wouldn't feel so scared anymore. Because all around her, she could still see Miles. She could still feel his grip. She turned her head and looked at him lying there dead on the ground—and knew that she had wanted him to be dead more than anyone. And he *was*. He was gone. Which meant someone was going to have to endure the consequences. "He held the knife to my throat and he said he would kill me." Shell noticed Grace was fiddling with something in her pocket, panic in her eyes. Shell could make that panic go away. But—something white, in Grace's hands. What was she doing? Were those pills? Shell struggled for focus. Grace was unscrewing the cap of her water bottle. She looked away. "I pushed him over the edge of the rocks and I left him there to die. But he must have landed on the net and climbed back up. And then—Ruth. Yes, she stabbed him, but it wasn't her fault. You all saw it. He was going to die anyway, I'm sure of it. She just finished something that I had already started. I pushed him."

"I won't let you take this on alone," Johanna said fiercely. "I was with you. I hurt him, too."

Colin moved forward, too. "This can't be happening," he said. More movement in a corner of Shell's vision: Grace was shaking the water bottle she held in her hand, up and down, over and over. The water was cloudy, and then it wasn't. Shell felt a slow dawning. She blinked and all certainty was gone.

"Ruth." Grace's voice was firm, strong, different. "Listen to me." The power in her voice: for a frightening moment, it reminded Shell of Miles. She glanced down at him again, at his lifeless form. Just to make sure. One last time. "Ruth," Grace said again. She was holding up the water bottle. "Come away from there. Drink this water. You need it. Drink."

"We have to think of something," Colin was saying. But Shell had a feeling Grace already had.

*I*t was no good. Grace was not Miles. Ruth was not going to listen to her. She had never taken orders from Grace, and she was not going to start now. "You need some water, you need to sit," Grace persisted. Ruth's wide and scared eyes were staring into Grace's, but she didn't obey.

"No," she said, and Grace felt herself start to panic. *She's going to go inside, covered with his blood, and she's going to start screaming about what she did, and it's going to be too late. Or, the guests are going to come outside and see us all standing here. See the wounds Johanna inflicted, Shell inflicted, Ruth inflicted—and then what? And an autopsy will show that I drugged him. Will we all go to jail? I did the only thing I could do, the only thing left. But I've failed so many times. It isn't going to work.*

"Ruth." Another voice now: Ben's. "I'm a lawyer. I can help you. But you really should have something to drink. Try to calm down." He was beside Grace now. "Give me the bottle," he said under his breath.

Ruth turned to look at Ben. "I *am* very calm," she said, but her entire body was still trembling. "I don't need a lawyer. It's very simple. I'm guilty." Light in her eyes. Hope. *Oh, child*, Grace thought. *You poor, poor child. Thinking your only hope lies in judgment.*

"I'll help you," Ben said. "I'll help you tell your story. I'll help you with whatever you need. Just have a little water and we'll go inside." He was holding the bottle up to her and Grace was wondering what he knew, what he had seen, what all of them knew. Ruth hesitated, but then she lifted her mouth to him, like a baby bird—like a woman so used to doing a man's bidding it was the most natural thing for her to do so now.

283

Ruth drank. She winced for a moment, perhaps at the bitter taste of the doctored water. But she kept drinking. She was so far gone perhaps she thought the taste was Miles's blood. "You're right," she said to Ben, grateful. "This does feel better." She drank more. She finished the entire bottle.

Ben said, "Come. Sit at this table. Let's be sure we have your story straight." She followed him.

Eventually, Ruth was swaying, her head was nodding forward. This was what Grace had meant to happen to Miles. If she had done it right, everything would be different. Ruth was slumping now. Ben had her. "I need help," he said, and Colin advanced. They lifted her in their arms. Everyone understood now. They were working as one. Solidarity.

"Where?" They looked to Grace. She looked at Johanna, then at Shell. She knew it was a lot to ask.

"Could the two of you stay here? With . . . him? We'll be back soon."

At least she knew they were safe. At least she knew this: that Miles was not going to be able to hurt any of them again.

Him: Maybe it's time for us to take a break. You seem
     quite upset.

Her: I told you, I'm fine. It feels good to have the
     truth out. I think this confession might mean that,
     finally, I'm free. After all these years. Not
     physically, but from these chains inside me. They
     keep getting tighter. It's hard to breathe. I need
     to be judged. In fact, I'm desperate to be judged.
     Please, don't make me wait anymore.

While Ben and Colin put Ruth on the floor in the room where Colin and Shell had been sleeping earlier, Grace went upstairs to Ruth's quarters to find a fresh white lab coat to replace the one Ruth had been wearing, which was now spattered with Miles's blood. She found the packaged cloths Ruth used to wash her face and took both downstairs with her. Back in the room, Ben and Colin looked away while Grace changed the coat and wiped the spots of blood that had landed on Ruth's face, then carefully cleaned the blood from Ruth's hands with the cloths. She felt like she was tending to a child. This was not a sensation she had ever experienced.

Soon, it was done. They all stood and looked at Ruth's peaceful, innocent, sleeping form. Her eyes fluttered, she murmured something. Then she was still.

"Let's go," Grace said. "There's still more to do."

"Grace," Ben said "I need to talk to you. Colin, could we have a minute?"

"I'll go check on Shell and Johanna." He closed the door behind him.

Grace braced herself for what Ben was going to say to her, for the accusations he would fling. "This is not the time," she began. "There's too much we have to deal with."

But his expression was anguished, not angry. He put his face in his hands. "Please, I need help. What have I done?"

Him: Ruth—

Her: Please. Let me this time. It's so strange, you know.
I woke up inside the villa, and all of this seemed
like a bad dream. Like it had never even happened.
But I know it happened. I know the story. And you
need to let me tell it.

I love my wife." Ben's voice caught, over that word, *wife*. He clenched both fists. "But I know—I *know* she doesn't love me. And I felt so angry about that last night. When she was gone, when I woke up alone, and she wasn't beside me, I was so angry. That may have been what started it. I started walking through the halls, looking all over for her. But I didn't find her. Then I saw water, wet footprints leading from one of the doors. I thought maybe she had gone outside. I was so worried." Water dripped from the ceiling. There was a smell of damp rot in the room already. "I opened the door and called her name, and I heard something, but it wasn't her."

"You shouldn't tell anyone this," Grace began.

"No. You don't understand. No one else should take the fall for what I did. I found Miles in the restaurant. He was spitting up water and vomit. He smelled horrible, like he was already dead. Johanna hit him with the rock, okay, and Shell pushed him, yes, but he landed on that net, I guess. Shell's right about that. That hammock Jo and I were in on our first morning here must have saved him. And he climbed back up. He was still alive. Very much so. He saw me, and he started saying such horrible, ugly things. He said you were a Jezebel. He said you were all whores. He said I was a sinner for having Johanna in my bed in the first place. He said he was going to kill you, and kill Johanna, and Shell, and Ruth, because you were all abominations. He had a knife in his hand, and I got really scared. He kept rambling on and on, and with every sentence he came closer to me."

"Ben. Don't. This is all going to be over soon. We just need to—"

"I was angry. I'll admit it. Maybe not even at him, but at Johanna, and at you, because I could see it, and I've always known. At myself, too, for thinking that just because I wanted Jo to love me, she was going to someday magically do so. Instead, she found the person she belongs with. I can see that. Any idiot can see that. But I was still hurt. And I was angry. He stumbled and dropped the knife and I took advantage of his weakness. I punched him. As hard as I could. Just once. He fell back and hit his head on the granite of the bar top. I could hear it over the wind, his head hitting that marble. It sounded like his skull had cracked right open. And when he landed, I knew he wasn't going to be okay. Ever. I knew he needed help and I knew he was probably beyond help. But I—I didn't help him. I went inside. I left him there to die. Ruth must have found him after the storm, and maybe she finished the task while we watched. But he was going to die anyway. I know it. And I know it was because I delivered that blow."

A long silence. Grace stared at this man who loved the same woman she did. She thought of what Colin had said, about how none of them should take the fall on account of a monster like Miles. He was wrong, according to the Bible. He was wrong, according to the law. Technically one of them, or all of them, needed to be punished in some way.

But she didn't want to believe in punishment anymore.

She glanced down at Ruth, asleep on the floor. She said, "You are not to tell anyone that story ever. And from this moment on, you are to do everything I say. You are not to ask questions." It surprised her again, this force inside her, as if Miles's death had awakened it. She saw Ben hesitate, but then he nodded and followed her from the room as if there were nothing else he could possibly do. *I'm always certain, Grace.* Those were the last words Miles had said to her. They would stay with her forever. But perhaps one day she would be able to start to see them as the only gift Miles had ever given her: he had made her strong. There was no other choice.

Her: No, it wasn't Ben who killed him. In my dreams
that day, I heard him saying he had done it. But it
wasn't Ben.

Him: Do you have any happy memories, Ruth, from your past,
from your childhood? Sometimes, it helps to remember
something light when it feels like there's only
darkness. I think it helps you, when you get like
this. I think we should talk about something else for
a little while.

Her: [A sob, then a gulp, then silence.] What do you mean,
when I get like this? And *happy* memories? It didn't
last long, but after the suffering, the way he would
hurt me—it just felt so good to have a break from it.
I think those few days were the best days of my life.
Sad, isn't it?

Him: I do feel sad for you, yes. Sad that all this
happened to you.

Her: [Looking up.] Oh, but I'm not a victim. You have to
know that. I'm trying to confess. I was so, so sick
in my mind. [Another sob.]

Him: Try to calm down.

Her: I loved Miles. I let him ruin me. But I shouldn't
have killed him for that. In the end, I murdered the
only man I have ever loved.

Him: Ruth, you know that's not true. You took sleeping
pills because the storm scared you, and when you
woke up, Miles was already gone. Everyone at the
resort corroborates the story that he was drunk or
high, and behaving erratically—and both you and Grace
Markell have confirmed that he often drank alcohol
and sometimes took the prescription drugs he got his
hands on at the resort. It also came to light that
he didn't know how to swim. There were extensive

investigations, and his body was searched for. But the case is firmly closed. Accidental drowning.

Her: No. I wasn't asleep.

Him: Ruth, you *were*. There are many, many people, an entire resort full of them, who say you were. And when you awoke, you had a psychotic break. You couldn't deal with what it did to you, the fact that Miles couldn't be found, the fact that he might be dead.

Her: It's all a lie. All of it. They were all lying.

Him: [A sigh.] Who are they protecting? They all lied to protect you?

Her: Yes. Because I killed him. It was me. If his body is ever found, they'll know. I *stabbed* him. He was saying such horrible things. There was blood all over the restaurant.

Him: There was no blood at all in the restaurant.

Her: Do you know what he said to me? He was talking about what a silly girl *Ruth* was, as though I wasn't even there, how he had no intention of running away with her. I made him repeat it. I said, "You don't love Ruth?" And he laughed. I think he was almost half-dead at that point, and he still *laughed*. And I saw the knife in his waistband, and took it out. And then they were all standing there—

Him: Who?

Her: Them! All of them! They all saw me. I stabbed him. I stabbed him so many times. [Loud sobbing.]

Him: There was no evidence of any of that, Ruth. I believe that you're suffering from a delusion.

Her: No. That's not true. They did something with his body. They hid it. I know it.

*J*ohanna saw Grace and Ben coming up the stairs. Ben had the hockey bag in his hands that he used for all their vacations. It was empty now. Grace was carrying a bottle of bleach and several rags.

Johanna knew that whatever Grace was about to ask her to do, she would do it. No matter what.

"We have to go back," Grace said. "Back to where it all began."

Johanna knew exactly what she meant. The jungle. The cenote. The desolate pool. And those signs that warned of danger, of a crocodile in the water. She could already see his body sinking, could imagine exactly what would happen. It would take so long to find him that he'd probably be unrecognizable by then.

"Whatever you want," she said to Grace. She took the bottle of bleach from her and started pouring it over the blood on the tiles. She wanted to do as much as she could. She didn't want Grace to be the only one to carry this with her, weighted down for the rest of her life by the heft of secrets—the dead body hidden in a hockey bag, moved from the resort in a grounds crew pickup truck, dragged through a jungle by five people, and pushed over a ledge.

Him: You need to start taking your medications again.

Her: *Please*.

Him: Miles's death was not your fault. The only person who got hurt unjustly was you, and the other women Miles abused. He is not the victim here. You are. And you need to forget about him and get on with your life.

Her: What life? Don't you see? He was my life. I am nothing without him.

THE MOST PERFECT COUPLE IN THE WORLD WASN'T SO PERFECT AFTER ALL

In the wake of Hurricane Christine, celebrity marriage counselor Miles Markell is still missing. But while there is still no sign of him, that hasn't stopped more and more women from coming forward online to say that he abused them, assaulted them and drugged them. The most recent accuser was a maid who worked at the Harmony Resort. After she released a statement, Grace Markell released a statement of her own, announcing she was giving up her psychotherapy license, and apologizing on behalf of her husband. "I stood by and I let it happen, and for that I will be forever sorry," the statement read. You can read the rest of it here.

Mexican and US police have been searching the resort grounds, and have reported finding evidence of surveillance devices in all of the intact rooms—and in Grace Markell's office.

Meanwhile, as the investigation into Miles's whereabouts continues, his name has been linked to an all-female cult-like group in Texas—the group that had been offering a cash reward if he or his body were found. Two of the women associated with the group have been arrested on fraud charges.

And just when we think this story can't get any more strange, the news has just broken that Ruth Abrams, Miles and Grace's plucky assistant, has been hospitalized due to a "complete mental breakdown." So much for paradise. It sounds like the Harmony Resort was never anything but pure hell.

Epilogue

Two months after the storm
Red Lake, Ontario

Shell walked to the window and looked out at the lake and the forest. The last box was finished. She had just rolled the packing tape along it, ripped it off, and put the roller down. Colin came into the room. "Hey," he said. "You're done. Thank you. Sorry, I was on the phone with the board—"

"It's okay. Really, Colin. What did the board say?" He had asked for compassionate leave from the Red Lake mine after they returned from Mexico but then, a month in, he came to Shell with news from a friend about a solar energy business, just outside of Winnipeg. "We could invest in it, if you want, and we could move out there," he had said to her, hope in his eyes and voice. "I know it's outside of our comfort zone, but we could learn the industry, I know we could. And we could feel good about what we do." The sun. It reminded her of Zoey, and she knew it reminded him, too. "A new life," he said.

"I don't want a new life. Our life will never be new. But it will always be ours." Shell was going to AA meetings every day. She'd have to find a new place in Winnipeg. There was a time she wouldn't have been ready to do that. She was ready now.

"I love you," he had said then, perhaps knowing what she was thinking.

"I love you, too," she had replied. It was new and old at the same time, this love of theirs. It was precious, and it was hard work and sometimes it made them very sad to look at one another. But they were learning it was also enduring, as great loves always are—loves that have had to withstand tragedy and pain, as many loves do, eventually.

Sometimes, late at night, they talked about the storm. They didn't say his name, but they talked about what had happened—they had to, or it would grow too big inside them. Shell would wake up in a cold sweat and turn to Colin and he would know where she'd gone, and he'd say, "It's all right, it's okay, he's gone. And we did the right thing. We *did*." She would do the same for him, when he woke up afraid. It wove them together, the events at the resort and the choices they all made the next morning. For better, for worse, it had bound them. She knew she would never leave him, and that he would stay by her side always. But she also knew it had always been thus. Even in their darkest moments, they had been beside one another. It was just that they had stopped believing in each other. And it had taken descending into hell to make them understand that they could turn back.

It was enough for Shell. It had to be. Sadness and happiness, sometimes all at once. Life broke your heart—but it didn't have to end it. You wanted to live. Johanna had taught her that. Just when it looked like all was lost was when you often realized how desperately you wanted to live. And you would have done anything, absolutely anything, to save yourself and the people you loved.

Wherever she was, Shell hoped Johanna was happy. And Grace, too. They deserved it.

One year after the storm
Tepoztlán Village, Mexico

"These are for you," Johanna said, tapping on Grace's office door, where she sat in front of her laptop, which was on a desk facing a window that looked out over the mountain range that was now part of their home. "Am I interrupting your writing?"

Grace turned and smiled. She closed her laptop, hid away the words that were the truth, that were her story, and that she knew she would never share with a soul but she still had to get out. She found such comfort in the writing. Some days, she wrote for hours and then deleted it all. It was like therapy, and she knew she needed it, or else she would become wrapped up in the past.

Now she returned Johanna's gentle and familiar kiss. "It was today," she said. "One year ago, exactly."

"I didn't know if you wanted to remember." Johanna put the flowers down beside the computer.

The small green vase was packed with dahlias, red and yellow and white. "My favorite," Grace said, reaching up and touching one. "And it's okay to remember. It's our story."

"Do you ever wish our story was different?"

"Yes, I do. I wish it had all been easier. That we'd met long ago. That I'd never made mistakes. That no one ever got hurt. But now, you're my happy ending. Now, we don't have to be afraid."

Johanna reached for Grace, and pulled her up and into her arms. As she did, Grace thought of all the times they still woke up scared. They still slept with their limbs tangled, holding each other the way they had the night of the storm. She still heard Miles's voice in her nightmares. Ruth's, too. Maybe she always would. But they were safe here, they had to be, in this tiny *pueblo* Grace could never imagine leaving, a hidden place with steep cobblestone streets and pyramid ruins hidden in the mountains, with villagers who seemed to understand they didn't want to be known. Miles's body was never going to be found. And Ruth— no one was ever going to believe her. No one was going to come for them. There was only a very small part of herself that ever doubted those truths.

Grace reached up and touched her now-short hair for a moment. *You're not hiding*, she told herself. *It's not a disguise.* One year ago, still at the resort, she had answered all the police's questions. It had taken days to sift through the debris of the storm. *No, I hadn't seen him after about midnight. Yes, he had seemed to be under the influence of something. Yes, he had been violent with me. Violent with Ruth. Yes, what those women were saying was all true. No, he could not swim. No, he never learned how.*

It had been the police who had found her laptop, hidden in an office, safe in the main villa, and had cracked the encrypted file that hid her Swiss bank account info. It had been frozen for a while, but they had given her access in the end—because while she was no angel, she was no criminal either, as far as they knew. She told herself that every day.

"I called Ben," Johanna said quietly, and Grace chased the thoughts away by looking into Johanna's ocean-green eyes. "I wanted to see how he is. Today."

"And?"

"He's moving on. He's back to work. He visits Ruth. He says she still wants to stay there, at that institution. That she's very unstable, some days. That it's hard."

"I can pay more money for her care," Grace said quickly. "Whatever it costs for however long it takes. Tell Ben, the next time you speak."

"Okay," Johanna whispered. A pause. Then: "Grace, it's not your fault. You're helping her."

"I try to believe that."

"We need to try to forget."

One day, maybe they would. Maybe, they'd stop reliving that

moment when they, all five of them, had colluded in dragging Miles's body over the edge of the cenote. Maybe they'd forget the way the debris-strewn water had begun to turn red with the blood from his wounds.

And maybe one day, Grace would forget that, in that moment, she had started to pray—and not for forgiveness, not anymore. Not even to be saved. What she had wanted was very simple. And it had come. In the light of the sunrise through the trees, she had seen what nobody else had because they weren't looking anymore: the lithe body of the crocodile, attracted by the blood and moving toward the corpse with purpose. She had stopped praying then because she had her answer. They had walked back through the jungle.

But no matter what she wanted to forget, she would always remember how silent they had all been, traveling back to the resort. Creeping across the property and back into the main villa. How Ben and Colin had gone out to the beach and lit a bonfire. Then the bag was gone, and Ruth's coat, and all the rags and cloths they had used to clean up the blood. Then there was no more evidence. They had made promises to one another with all that silence. They would probably never see each other again, but they were tied together for life.

Grace held Johanna tighter. She buried her face in her hair and succeeded in pushing those memories away. "Do you want to go out? Let's."

Johanna smiled. "I was hoping," she said. "I need air. I need sun. I need to walk. And I know I could go without you—but I want to be near you. Today."

"Always," Grace said, and she felt so safe. She clung to it, reveled in it, breathed it in.

Later, they packed a lunch—papaya and cheese and the coarse bread they both loved—and went out into the back courtyard of the house they had bought at the edge of the town with some of Grace's money. It had a swimming pool that overlooked the mountains. Grace was getting used to rocky vistas instead of water. "I have something to tell you," Grace said when they were outside by the pool, intending to swim before they walked out to the ruins with their picnic. "I got a letter from my brother's son. He replied. Maybe I'll write again and ask him to come. If that's all right with you. I'll talk to him first, I'll see how it feels. But I wanted to tell you."

"I know how much you've wanted this."

Grace nodded. She hoped so much that she would see Garrett in his son. That with him, she would feel she still had family. One person could not be your everything. You had to work hard to make your world bigger. She wanted to do that for Johanna.

Johanna stood and walked to the edge of the pool, which took up most of the yard. It was deep, aqua-bottomed. Grace watched Johanna dive in, watched her body slice through the crystal clear water. She stood and stripped off her dress in one fast movement. She dove in and felt perfect and clean. They swam back and forth. Their voices rose and fell.

They didn't talk as they dried off and dressed again and locked the house. They didn't have to. They walked out toward the ruins, carrying their picnic. The sun shone down and dried their hair. Johanna's hand in hers, Grace climbed the ruins, wondering, as she always did, which one of them had reached out first or if they had simply always been holding each other.

There was that same silence between them as they climbed the crumbling pyramid, a silence that hid nothing as, hands still linked, they looked out at their world together and saw more than just ruins.

Acknowledgments

Thank you to my agent, Samantha Haywood, the brightest star in my sky. And her excellent team at Transatlantic agency, including Stephanie Sinclair, Léonicka Valcius, Ana Balmazovic, Megan Philipp and Barbara Miller.

Simon & Schuster Canada, for being my North Star, and especially my queen of an editor Nita Pronovost, my publicists Rita Silva and Jillian Levick, Siobhan Doody, Rebecca Snoddon, Alexandra Boelsterli, Felicia Quon, Adria Iwasutiak, Sherry Lee, Shara Alexa, David Millar and Kevin Hanson.

The team at Graydon House, for giving me a home away from home. And, in particular, my editor Brittany Lavery, who is very smart and very kind (and very into hearing about my cat), my publicist Gloria Bairos; Kathleen Oudit, for the beautiful cover; Lisa Wray, Amy Jones, Pamela Osti, Diane Moggy and Susan Swinwood.

My wicked (in a good way) coven of author friends, who make the hard days bearable and the good days better: Karma Brown, Kerry Clare, Channie Bobannie (Chantel Guertin), Kate Hilton, Elizabeth Renzetti, Jennifer Robson and Kathleen Tucker.

My writing retreat team: Sophie Chouinard, Alison Gadsby, Kate

Henderson, Sherri Vanderveen. Long may we run. Hopefully not on a patch of ice.

The kind authors who read this book first and offered endorsements: Karen Brown, Lucy Clarke, Christina Dalcher, Joanna Goodman, Robyn Harding, Karen Katchur, Hannah Mary McKinnon, Roz Nay and Laurie Petrou.

My friends. If we've made it this far, you're stuck with me now, even if you secretly think you should be on this list of special mentions and I forgot you. For encouragement and communion every step of the way, thank you to: Pauline Bacevicius, Leigh Fenwick, Asha Frost, Jessie Morgan, Michelle Schlag, Amanda Watson, and Nance Williams.

To my readers, as always. When you write or approach to tell me my words meant something to you, it means the world to me.

My wonderful and supportive family: Bruce Stapley, Valerie Clubine, James Clubine (especially for the sermon illustration about secrets! This *Journal of Personality and Social Psychology* study appeared in *The Atlantic* in May 2017.), Shane Stapley, Drew Stapley, Griffin Stapley, Joe and Joyce Ponikowski, Lauren and Mark Matusiak, and Marnie and Greg Webb.

My children, Joseph and Maia. You keep me grounded and give me a reason to write beyond the fact that it's my (dream) job. You remind me that words matter and have the power to change the world. (Change the world, you two. It's not perfect yet—but you are, to me.)

And to my husband, Joe Ponikowski, who read multiple versions of this book while I sat in a chair opposite him saying, "So, what do you think? What do you think now?" I could not ask for a better, more caring partner in this life.

About the Author

© EUGENE CHOI

MARISSA STAPLEY is the author of the bestselling novel *Mating for Life.* Her novel *Things to Do When It's Raining* has been published in nine countries and translated into seven languages. Her journalism has appeared in newspapers and magazines across North America. She lives in Toronto with her family.

www.MarissaStapley.com

 @MarissaStapley

Bookends

When one book ends, another begins...

Bookends is a vibrant new reading community to help you ensure you're never without a good book.

You'll find exclusive previews of the brilliant new books from your favourite authors as well as exciting debuts and past classics. Read our blog, check out our recommendations for your reading group, enter great competitions and much more!

Visit our website to see which great books we're recommending this month.

Join the Bookends community:
www.welcometobookends.co.uk

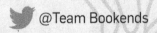 @Team Bookends   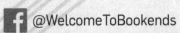 @WelcomeToBookends